Crescendo

Murrells Inlet Miracles, Volume 3

Laurie Larsen

Published by Laurie Larsen, 2018.

CRESCENDO

First edition. September 4, 2018.

Copyright © 2018 Laurie Larsen.

ISBN: 978-0997563047

Written by Laurie Larsen.

Book Description:

Crescendo by Laurie Larsen
2019 Illumination Awards Bronze Medalist!
The ride of a lifetime...

Aspiring country musician Blake Scott will do anything to catapult his band into the big time—even if it means driving Uber to make ends meet. Encountering the beautiful and broken Haley Witherspoon on the worst night of her life, changes everything for him.

The black sheep of a wealthy family, Haley yearns to find passion to add purpose to her life. When Blake offers her the opportunity of a lifetime, she can't refuse. Managing Ace in the Hole is everything she needs—and nothing she ever expected. Despite her family's disapproval and disownment, Haley throws herself into helping the band reach success.

As Blake and Haley grow closer, she realizes that he's hiding something—holding something back. Now it's up to Haley to uncover the truth about Blake's past while battling the rumors that threaten to destroy the band. Putting their trust in God is their only hope. But will the faith they find in each other be enough to overcome the mounting danger, let go of the past, and create a future together?

Chapter One

HALEY WITHERSPOON DROVE her Acura into the parking lot of Winners Lounge. She parked underneath a street light and hoped that it would still be lit at two in the morning. She cut the engine and peered around. Not exactly her kind of place. She'd never frequented Winners Lounge before. She'd never been in this part of Myrtle Beach before. And she'd certainly never walked into a bar alone before.

In fact, she may even go so far as to rename Winners Lounge to *Losers* Lounge.

But, when Blake asked her out on their first date, listening to his band perform, she'd said yes. And, when she'd asked all her girlfriends to join her, so she wasn't sitting there by herself all night, they all had reasons to say no. She thought they were legit. Or, at least she hoped so.

She'd be fine. Blake wouldn't have invited her here if she would be in danger. Would he? Honestly, she didn't know him well enough to know. She'd only met him once.

Just to be safe, she said a quick internal prayer, *Lord, be with me tonight. Keep me safe. Watch over me.*

She took a deep breath, checked her lipstick in the rearview mirror and opened the car door. *Game time.*

She strode purposefully to the front door, a silent mantra running through her mind, directed heavenward, *keep me safe, keep me safe, keep me safe.* Once inside, she scanned the room for a table with a good view of the band. Finding one, she walked straight there and sat down.

She checked her watch. Nine pm. The band should be starting any minute.

A waitress stopped by and she ordered a light beer and left her tab open. Once it came, she took a long, fortifying sip. She definitely didn't want to get drunk tonight, but she needed something to occupy her attention while sitting here all by herself. She picked up her phone. Maybe she could web surf until the band came on. She checked the time again. Nine ten. Where were they?

Two girls about her age approached her. "Haley, right?"

"Why, yes."

"Blake told us to watch for you." They joined her at her table by climbing up into the high bar stools. "I'm Lindsay. Jake the drummer is my boyfriend. And this is Helen. She's with the bass player, Robbie."

"Oh, hi!" Relief flooded through her body and most likely, out through her voice. "So nice to meet you. I'm Haley."

They chuckled. "Yeah, we know."

Haley rolled her eyes good-naturedly. This, she could do. She'd always made friends easily. Her laid-back, friendly personality made her approachable and accepting. A sense of community seeped through her . Three gals watching and cheering on their men. "We're with the band," she imagined them telling onlookers. A sort of sorority. Instant membership because of Blake.

Finally, the band took the small stage in the corner. Haley clapped and cheered, then realized she was the only one at the table doing so. She looked at the girls.

"Look, Helen," Lindsay intoned. "A band groupie virgin."

The comment flustered Haley and she frowned and swiped at her hair. "What do you ...?"

They both laughed. "We're not criticizing. We both went through it too. Everything's so new and fresh and fun when you first start coming to these gigs. You're excited, you clap and cheer. But after a couple hundred of these you start to tarnish."

Haley gave them a grim smile. A couple hundred? They must've been with their boyfriends for years.

The band was all set up now, and Blake took the microphone, his guitar strapped over his shoulder. "Good evening, ladies and gentlemen, and welcome to Winners Lounge. We're Ace in the Hole. Let's let it roll." The music took off, a cover of a favorite Bryan Lucas hit, and Haley immediately settled into the tune. The song wrapped her in a blanket of familiarity and the band sounded great together. Guitars, a keyboard, drums. "Oh my gosh, they sound good!" she yelled to her tablemates over the noise. They nodded.

Then Blake started singing. She didn't know if he was trying to imitate country superstar Bryan Lucas, but he sounded just like him. His voice had a clear, deep tone, with just a little bit of raspy on the corners. She couldn't drag her eyes or ears off him. He closed his eyes as he cradled the mic in his hand, swaying his hips along with the melody. He dipped his head back to hit the higher notes, and then when he opened his eyes, he zoomed in on Haley. Adrenaline rushed down her esophagus and settled deep in her core. She went breathless.

They finished the first song and Haley didn't care what the more seasoned girlfriends thought. She jumped off her barstool and clapped and yipped for Ace in the Hole. They were fantastic. The rest of the bar clapped quietly. Blake smiled and winked at her, then started in on the second song.

Haley got absorbed in the first set, listening to every lyric, every note, every stanza. The band's talent overwhelmed her, especially Blake's singing. This man had talent.

The set ended and while the band was putting their instruments down, she turned to the girls. "Why are they still playing in little tiny dives like this? Have they tried to get a recording contract? They deserve a shot!"

They stared at her, each of them raising one eyebrow, as if in unison. "Gee, Helen, why didn't we ever think of that? You mean they could be playing nicer bars? Stadiums? Recording music? Hmmm. Maybe we need to look into that."

The way she phrased it, and the deadpan monotone of her voice clued Haley in that she was being played. "Oh. So, they have tried? And what, hit roadblocks?"

Just then, the men of the band approached the table, each putting an arm around their woman. Blake stepped in front of Haley and leaned in for a hug. She pulled him in close, squeezed him, and then placed her lips on his neck. She had no idea when she'd met him that he was this talented a musician. After all, he was an *Uber* driver who'd picked her up one night. One very traumatic night.

Blake released her as the waitress came over with beers for the band. He took a long gulp.

"Oh my gosh, you are so good!" Haley said.

"Aww thanks." He looked over at the other girlfriends. "Ladies, I guess you met my date, Haley Witherspoon. I want you to take good care of her tonight while we're up there."

Haley beamed her appreciation at him. From beside her, Lindsay's voice hit her ear, "Witherspoon? Did he say your name was Witherspoon?"

Haley's heart skipped a beat and she took a deep breath in. The joys and curses of a well-known family name.

Blake said, "Yeah, why?"

Lindsay maneuvered so she could look straight into Haley's eyes. "Of the Witherspoon dynasty? The jewelry? The wineries? The clothing lines?"

Blake frowned and scoffed. "Just because she has a famous name doesn't mean she is a descendant of the Witherspoon dynasty. Right, Haley?"

She stared at him and her eyes widened. This certainly wasn't how she wanted to tell him. She wouldn't lie to him. But she also didn't want to spill the beans of her family's wealth and prosperity while sitting at the Winners Lounge with a bunch of near strangers. Instead, she tried to make a joke of it. "Oh yeah, you know, me and Grandpa Emerson, taking over the world."

Blake chuckled but Lindsay wouldn't let it go. "Emerson Witherspoon is your grandpa? Seriously?"

She hesitated, and Blake jumped in. "Can't you tell she's joking, Lindsay?" The conversation moved on to other topics and soon the men finished their beers and headed back toward the stage. Blake leaned over her and placed his lips on hers, a quick kiss for good luck.

Leaving her with the stares of Lindsay and Helen. "Okay," Lindsay said, "if you are a multi-millionaire with the Witherspoon dynasty behind you, I can understand why you wouldn't want to fess up. However, if Blake knows, and just isn't spilling the beans to us, then that sort of explains why you're here."

Haley let the words spill over her. She was usually pretty good at ignoring jabs, especially involving her family's wealth and prestige. After all, she was the black sheep of the family, uneducated and unambitious. She had no desire to take part in the family business, preferring instead to work her own little job, live in her own little place and enjoy her life without pressure. But the truth was, Lindsay was insulting her, intentionally, and she couldn't let this one slide.

"What are you talking about, Lindsay?"

"No offense, but Blake is sort of a lone wolf. He never brings girls to the gigs. Too distracting for him. He wants to hit the country music big time, and he'll do everything he has to, to get there. You won't find a harder working musician than Blake."

Haley shrugged. "What does that have to do with me?" She stared at Lindsay, willing her to say it.

"Knowing your name, maybe he sees you as a fast track. You've got the money to help make it happen. You said yourself they've got the talent to be mainstream. Maybe he thinks you'll payroll them to get there."

Haley's mouth dropped open and then she clenched it shut. When would she ever learn? Her family's wealth was a hindrance, much more than a help, in any situation.

"Blake doesn't know anything about my family. And what's more, he doesn't care."

"Yeah, right." Lindsay drew out the last word, then leaned in to Helen, both laughing like it was the biggest inside joke in the world.

"Hey, look. This is my first date with Blake. We met when he gave me an *Uber* ride. We pulled a dead deer out of a windshield together and bonded in the waiting room of the ER. We talked for hours and my family didn't come up at all. So, I don't like what you're insinuating that he only asked me here because he's interested in my bank account." Her chest heaving with the unaccustomed effort of the forceful words, she locked eyes with enemy Lindsay and wouldn't let go.

Lindsay sat motionless, staring back.

"Thanks for sticking around. We're Ace in the Hole." Blake's magnified voice filled the room, then a few guitar strums.

Lindsay held up her hands. "Okay, okay, I'm sorry. I had no right to say that."

Haley looked away, then her gaze flickered back at Lindsay and she nodded. She'd let it go, but she'd never be friends with Lindsay. Never.

She enjoyed the next two sets of flawless country music from Blake's band and managed to say only a minimal number of words to Lindsay and Helen. She didn't want to believe what they said about Blake, but God knows, they knew him better than she did. She'd have to proceed with this "relationship" with a cautious heart.

It was the bar's closing time of two am when Ace in the Hole wrapped up their performance and everyone started filing out. Blake came right over to the table. "Can you hang out another twenty minutes or so while we break everything down and load up the truck?"

"Sure. Can I help?"

He shook his head. "We sort of have it down to a science now. Won't take long."

She nodded and glanced at Helen and Lindsay. They looked over at her, an awkward silence pounding in their ears. Haley took a shaky breath. She was terrible at handling conflict. She was a people pleaser, always had been, and just wanted everyone to get along.

"Soooo," Lindsay said, drawing out the syllable.

"It was fun," Haley responded.

"They have another gig Thursday night. Are you coming?"

"Oh, I don't know." She had no idea. She'd had one date with a budding country musician. Did that mean she'd come to all his performances now?

Soon, the band had finished their tear-down and approached the table. The other girls slid off their bar stools and waved at Haley and Blake, heading toward the front door with barely a word of farewell. Blake took both her hands in his and she looked into his bright blue eyes. "I'll walk you to your car."

She grinned and nodded as she slid to her feet. They walked the short distance and he accompanied her to the drivers' side, then he walked around to the passenger side and slid in. He turned in the seat and faced her.

"Did you enjoy it?" he asked quietly.

"Enjoy it! Oh my gosh, I loved it. Blake, you are so talented. You all are. You guys sound great together. Seriously. I'm not just saying it. You guys are awesome."

He chuckled.

"But you, especially. Your voice! You have a great singing voice. You ...," she looked down shyly, "you made me melt."

He smiled and leaned in, seeking out her lips, and kissed her slowly. Adrenaline came surging through her chest. His lips had the power to do that to her.

"Well, I'm glad to hear that," he said. He pulled back but stayed in his seat. He appeared to be studying her face and it made her feel just the slightest bit awkward. She felt the flush of heat coming on. "I loved looking out there and seeing you smiling at me. Made me glad you were there."

Remembering the girls' comment at the table, she teased him, "You probably have a different girl there every night." She smiled big to let him know she was joking.

But he seemed serious when he responded, "No I don't. I don't usually have anyone here. I don't really have time to date. My nights are pretty much taken up between driving and performing. What time would I have to give a woman? It's not really right for her."

Haley blinked. What was he telling her? That this was just a one-night thing, and he didn't want to see her again?

"But there's something about you, Haley, that makes me want to try."

Haley was sure her uncertainty flickered across her face. Something about her? What had he seen in her that was so special?

"Would you be willing to go out with me again?"

She had doubts, she had uncertainties about dating a guy with a schedule like his, but when he asked her so nice, and looked so cute asking, the answer was clear. "Sure, I'll go out with you again."

She was rewarded with a happy smile. Without thinking she lifted her hand and brushed her fingers over his stubbled chin, then up through the locks of his dark, curly hair. It was surprisingly soft. "What did you have in mind?"

"How about dinner before a gig? I'll take you out."

She nodded, and he leaned in and kissed her again. She could get used to that.

"I'll call you later with my schedule and we can decide what night works for you."

"So, Lindsay and Helen were nice." She said it tentatively and she wondered if he would pick up on it.

He did. He chuckled. "Helen is nice," he said pointedly. "Lindsay can be a challenge."

"So it wasn't just me."

"No, not at all. She's a little bit on the bossy side, and she is very possessive of Jake, and the band in general, in fact."

Haley sighed, unsure exactly how much of their conversation to share. She barely knew Blake, and Lindsay knew him much better. But she had a hard time believing Blake was only interested in her because of her family's wealth, when they'd talked for hours the other night, and that topic never came up. Wasn't it possible to believe that he asked her out because ... he liked her? "She wasn't particularly friendly, or welcoming. That's for sure."

"Yeah, it's a little uncomfortable right now. Jake, Robbie and I want to take the band to the next level. We want to start playing nicer gigs than local beach bars. But that'll take hiring a professional manager, which we don't have at the moment. Lindsay has been our quasi-manager for the last year, and she does all the bookings on our behalf. But she doesn't have the contacts to take us up a step."

Haley studied his face, her mind taking off. "So you want to fire Lindsay and bring in a professional manager?"

"Well. It's not really firing someone if you never paid them to begin with." He chuckled. "But yeah, we've been saving for a while to hire someone to help us take a major step forward. We feel like we're ready. We just need help."

"And Lindsay would not take kindly to this news, I take it."

"No. Not at all. Jake's worried about what that would do to their relationship."

Haley nodded.

"Well listen, it's three am and I'm thinking it's probably past your bedtime," Blake said.

Haley looked at the car clock. It was, indeed, three o'clock, but she wasn't the least bit tired. Of course, maybe he was. "Okay," she said. "Thanks again for inviting me to listen to you. I really had fun."

"I'll call you with a few nights that we could plan our dinner out. And Haley, my advice to you is to ignore Lindsay. Really."

Haley blinked and thought again about bringing up the other topic about Lindsay that made her uncomfortable, Lindsay's insinuation that Blake only asked her out because he knew she was from a wealthy family and could help them get into bigger venues. With the power of her name behind them, she had no doubt that she could ask her father to make a few phone calls. But that was never her way. She spent her entire life hiding from the Witherspoon moniker, not bragging about it. In fact, Blake had no idea she was a Witherspoon. Did he?

Due to the lateness of the hour, she decided to table that topic. Now was not the time to bring it up. But she would need to bring it up later, if she wanted a chance at an honest relationship with him.

"Good night," she said, and he leaned in for another kiss. Her heart pounded as he placed a tender hand on her cheek and left the car.

Chapter Two

ON MONDAY MORNING, Haley arrived at her desk at the community college where she worked as the receptionist of the Admissions department. She was the first greeter of any students who came into the department looking for help, and she also performed secretarial duties for the Admissions representatives who worked there.

She tossed her purse and her lunch bag into her desk drawer and picked up her ringing phone. A few minutes later she hung up, and saw her friend Carly, an Admissions rep, standing there smiling at her. "Hey, girl," Haley said.

"Hey you, not hey me," Carly giggled. "How was the date with Blake?"

Carly had met Blake the same time Haley did, since they were *Uber* customers together the night of the car accident with the deer. In fact, it was Carly's daughter Grace who was in the car, driven by Grace's grandmother, who suffered the accident. While Haley waited in the hospital for news of both Grace and her grandmother, Blake had generously sat with her instead of going out for more *Uber* fares.

Haley's happy smile couldn't be denied. "He's really nice."

Carly squealed and ran around her desk to pull her into a hug. "I knew it! Any guy who would sit there with you in the hospital when he didn't even know anyone involved, is a keeper."

"Not only is he nice...,"

"And cute," Carly inserted.

"And cute, but he's also a very talented singer. I went and watched his band play, Ace in the Hole. They were awesome. Blake's the lead singer."

"Wow. That's cool."

Haley thought about inviting Carly to come along the next time she went to one of Blake's gigs so she wouldn't have to sit with the nasty girls again. But she hurriedly decided against it. Carly was a newlywed with her dreamboat husband Ryan, and Grace, their toddler, kept them hopping. She was quite certain Carly wouldn't want to give up a night with the family if it meant sitting in a dark bar all night.

"Are you going to see him again?" Carly asked with a wicked grin.

"Yes. He's going to let me know when, but he wants to take me out to dinner before his next gig."

Carly lifted a palm into the air and Haley slapped it. "The only thing is, his schedule is crazy. The nights he's playing gigs, he usually works from eight pm to three am. On the nights he doesn't have a gig, he's driving *Uber* to make money. I work nine to five. When will we ever see each other?" Haley raised an eyebrow at Carly, hoping she'd have a solution.

Carly considered, then shrugged. "If he's worth it, you'll figure it out. You're both youngsters. Start getting by on less sleep." She laughed. A student entered the office and Carly tapped her on the shoulder. "Better get back to work. See you at lunch."

The morning passed quickly. At lunch with Carly, she considered telling her friend about the troubling comment from Lindsay about why Blake had asked her out. But she couldn't. Although she and Carly had been friends for almost a year now, they'd never discussed Haley's family's wealth. Haley always kept it secret because she didn't want it to play a part in her friendships. The wealth that stood behind her father and her grandfather had nothing to do with her. She didn't earn it, and she felt strongly about making her own living without relying on it. Sure, her parents were generous, letting her live in one of their luxurious beachfront condos without charging her rent. Her Christmas and birthday gifts from her parents were much larger and more expensive than her friends'. But the wealth didn't define her. There was no reason to talk about it.

That's why she was caught by surprise when Lindsay figured it out so quickly. That hardly ever happened.

In the mid-afternoon, things around the office slowed down and Haley leaned back in her chair and let out a breath. After taking a quick walk around campus to satisfy the step app on her phone, and filling her cup with iced water, she returned to her desk. Pulling up the internet browser, she tapped on her keyboard. She wanted to get a feel for some of the venues in the Myrtle Beach area that offered live music that were a step above a place like Losers Lounge.

She entered some search criteria, such as "live country music" and soon, her browser presented her with many choices. She researched each one and began a list with links to the venue. She'd share it with Blake and if he gave the go-ahead, she'd call each one to begin negotiations on what they'd pay Ace in the Hole for performing.

She was certain that she could help the band expand to bigger and better paying venues. If they were going to play two or three nights a week anyway, why not play somewhere that paid more money? Then maybe Blake could cut back on *Uber'ing* and play more nights.

Her heart pumped with excitement, but she knew she'd have to put a rein on it. She needed to talk to Blake. He, as well as Jake and Robbie, had to be onboard with her ambitions for the band.

BLAKE SCOTT PULLED into the parking lot of Haley's apartment complex. Walking to the building, he caught a peek of the Atlantic Ocean. Her complex was oceanfront! He didn't realize anyone actually lived in an oceanfront apartment. He thought they were all vacation rentals.

He jogged up the outdoor staircase and followed the numbers till he found hers, then knocked on the door. A moment later, the door swung open and there she was, his Haley, standing in the doorway, grinning at him. Her smile caught him and grabbed hold. It was the one feature that had caught his attention the very first night they met. He'd never known anyone whose pure joy and zest for life was transmitted through her happy smile.

Then he got to know her. And he realized that she was the real deal. She was a happy, joyful, truly loving person. All wrapped up in a beautiful exterior, with long copper hair that shimmered like a swimmer's, full cheeks that popped when she smiled, and a curvaceous body that made him want to stare as she moved. The girl was the full package.

It hadn't been a hardship to spend the evening talking to her in the hospital waiting room. It gave him a chance to get to know her. Coming away from that evening, he knew two things without a doubt: she was a good person, through and through. And, he wanted to get to know her better.

He lucked into the fact that she was a country music fan. It was sort of feeling like it was meant to be.

He put a hand on her back and pulled her closer, resting his lips on hers. Her heart thudded against his chest and he tempered his desires to run his hands over her. He didn't want to rush this one. Something in the back of his mind schooled him on taking it slow, showing her the respect she deserved. He had no idea where that voice came from, because it wasn't the voice of experience. He'd never had a serious romance in his twenty-eight years of life. He'd been too busy with music and his family. But it seemed like good advice.

So, when he'd sampled her lips and caressed her back with his palm, he put a clamp on his desire and pulled himself back. He smiled, his heart and head racing. He took a breath, then noticed what she was wearing. A floral print sundress, covered with a light denim jacket, and red cowboy boots that went mid-calf. "You look cute," he said.

She smiled brighter, if possible, and pulled him inside her apartment. "Thanks. You too."

He was wearing what he always wore when he had a gig – tight, worn blue jeans, boots with a slight heel and either a t-shirt or a flannel shirt, depending on the season. He followed her into the apartment and she strode over to the kitchen counter, where she picked up a sheet of paper. She turned and handed it to him.

"What's this?" he asked, then focused on it. It was a list of names with internet hyperlinks.

"Research I've done. Are you familiar with any of these places?"

Blake looked back at the paper. They all appeared to be names of bars, theaters or amphitheaters. "Yeah, some of these I've been to."

"Have you ever played at any of these?"

He frowned. "Played? Like, with the band?"

"Yeah."

He shook his head. "No, no, these all are out of our range. We've never played places like this."

She grimaced, and his eyes followed the movement of her mouth, while his imagination gave him a pretty clear vision of what he wanted to do with that mouth. He cleared his throat and pulled his eyes up to hers.

"These places are your next step. You've been stuck at Loser's Lounge for way too long. It's time to be promoted."

Blake chuckled and thumbed the page. "Well, yeah, but do you know how hard it is to get into places like this?"

"No, but do you know how good you guys are? Do you realize that you deserve to play in places like this?"

He went speechless then; all his brain could think was how lucky he'd been to meet her. Not only was she a nice person, not only was she gorgeous, but she believed in him. The Triple Crown of girlfriends.

He handed the paper back to her. "What do you want to do? What do you need from me?"

"I'd be willing to do some work. Research these places, contact them, talk to them about terms. You just need to get the band to buy into it."

"Okay."

"I want you guys to move outside of Myrtle Beach too. All up and down the seaboard. Charleston, Hilton Head, Savannah, down into Florida. Do you think you guys are ready for that? Willing to make that next step?"

"I know I am. But you're right, I'll talk to the guys. I'll let you know."

"You do that."

"And Haley? Thank you."

She winked at him. "Don't mention it. Now, what were you saying about dinner? I'm starving."

They went to a pretty nice steak house, if he did say so himself, and he paid more for two steak dinners than he would've ever thought he'd be comfortable doing. But Haley was worth it. When they were finished, and the waiter had cleared the table, he sensed a change in mood. It was so easy to tell with Haley when something wasn't right, because usually she was happy and open.

"There's something I want to talk to you about," Haley began.

He reached over the table and put a hand over hers. "Tell me." Whatever was on her mind, he wanted to hear, especially if it was troubling her.

"It's Lindsay."

Blake rolled his eyes. "Didn't I tell you to ignore Lindsay? It'll be up to Jake to talk to her about your plans for the band. I mean, if you can do it better than her, why wouldn't we want to let you manage the band?"

She looked confused a moment. "Oh, no. Actually, yes, that is something to worry about in the future. How Lindsay reacts to me trying to get the band to the next level. But no, that's not what I was going to say."

He patted her hand. "Go ahead."

"I'm sort of breaking the girl code telling you this ..."

"The girl code?"

She gave her head a quick shake. "I shouldn't be telling tales about what is said when there's no guys around. But. This is about you. And me."

Blake stared. He'd never understand the innerworkings of female minds.

"Lindsay thinks that the only reason you asked me out is because you knew my family was wealthy and you wanted to use that money to help advance the band."

"What?" he exploded. He drew the attention of diners nearby and had to purposely calm himself before continuing. "She said that?"

Haley simply nodded, then studied him to see his reaction.

"I'm really, *really* sorry about that, Haley. That was uncalled for. And mean." He cleared his throat and tried to slow his racing mind.

"But is it true?" she asked in a quiet, little voice.

His eyes darted to hers. "No! Of course not. You can't really think that, can you?"

She sat quietly for a moment, then said, "They said you never bring girls to the band gigs, and they said you really want to try to hit the big time in country music. Then suddenly you show up with me, and I start thinking about how we can get you into bigger venues. I guess it's not out of the realm of possibility ..."

"No."

"I mean, I guess, from Lindsay's viewpoint, I could understand why she'd think ..."

"No. First of all, I didn't know your family was wealthy. Second, we just started getting to know each other. I invited you because ..." What? What would he admit to her without letting too many of his growing feelings for her out of the bag too early on? Was he really going to blow this thing? The first woman in a long time he had feelings for? He cleared his throat and pushed a hand through his hair. "Look. I know we don't know each other well, but I have feelings for you. I can tell you're a really, really good person, and I want to get to know you better. It has nothing to do with what your last name is, or how many dollars are in your bank account. I like *you*, Haley."

She stayed still, her eyes glued to his, and he could tell her mind was churning as she processed what he was saying, but until she opened her mouth and told him, he had no idea what she was thinking. Just when he thought he couldn't wait another second, she said, "I believe you. I believe you, Blake."

A whoosh of relief left his chest. "I'm glad to hear you say that."

"And for the record, I like you, too." She smiled. "And I'd like to get to know you better, too."

The moment seemed monumental, but he carefully guided the conversation back to normal, everyday topics. He didn't want to make mistakes he'd regret later. One thing he made a mental note about: never talk about her family's money, and never let her pay for things just because she could afford them. This relationship was not about money. There was enough about Haley to fall in love with without that.

Chapter Three

BAND PRACTICE NIGHT was the right time to bring up Haley's ideas, Blake decided. The band reserved one night each week when they weren't performing to meet in Robbie's parents' garage in Murrells Inlet. They went over portions of songs that hadn't gone well the previous week, they learned new songs to add to their inventory, and they talked about topics that impacted the band. This week, Blake brought along Haley's sheet of paper.

They played and sang for two hours, and as always, they clicked. These guys were like his substitute brothers. They fought sometimes, they played together a lot, and they always had each other's backs.

They were putting their instruments away when Blake said, "I've got something to show you guys." They gathered around a tall round table that stood in the corner of the garage. "I've got this list of venues that would be a step up for our band. Instead of crowding into the corner of loud beach bars like Winners Lounge, we'd be playing bigger bars, where the music is more the focus. And even theaters that play country music. I really think this is the path we need to take, and I think we're ready to take it."

"Let me see this thing," Robbie said and pulled the list over.

"Here, let's look at it online." Blake pulled up the document on his phone so the hyperlinks were active. He clicked on the first one. "Look at this place."

"Nice," murmured Jake.

They spent fifteen minutes clicking through all the links and Blake was feeling excited that they were on board with the expansion. "I mean, it'll be like a new commitment to the success of this band. We'll be traveling up and down the coast. With the extra money we'll make maybe we can buy a bus or a van for transportation. I don't know. Maybe we'll need to get an accountant to help us figure out how to spend our money wisely. I'm just saying ... if we can pull off these type of places, our lives would change. More gigs, more traveling, more money."

"Yeah, man," said Robbie and he and Jake burst in laughter.

"I mean, I want you guys to really think about this. Are we ready for this step? Do we want to do what it takes to get there? Or do we want to stay in the Myrtle Beach bar scene playing the same bars over and over?"

"For peanuts," Jake added.

Robbie nodded and looked from Jake to Blake.

Blake said, "It'll mean re-prioritizing some things in our lives. The band is number one. You might have to change your day job work hours, take more time off, to make time for the band. Are you guys going to be okay with that?" Excitement welled in his throat. He desperately wanted them to want it as bad as he did, but he really needed them to think about what they were agreeing to. If they were to take off, life was going to change.

"I'm good with it. The band's my priority, and always has been," Robbie said.

"Me too, man," Jake said.

Blake held up both hands and they grasped them, creating a triangle. "Ace in the Hole. Let's let it roll."

They all gave a war cry, raising their joined hands to the air.

"So, where'd this list come from anyway?" Robbie said.

"Haley did the research and pulled it together."

Jake gave him a pointed look. "That was nice of Haley, but she does realize that Lindsay does the bookings, right? Is Haley okay with turning this list over to Lindsay to work?"

Blake's mouth went tight. "Dude, we need to talk about that. I'm not sure Lindsay has the contacts or the skills to get us up to the next level."

"And Haley does? You've known this girl for all of, what, five minutes? Lindsay's been with us for two years."

Blake held his tongue and shook his head. "Yeah, and we really appreciate all of Lindsay's help booking our gigs. But, like we've already said, this is new. This is different. This is our new direction."

Jake huffed out a frustrated breath, but Blake could tell he was thinking about it. "Maybe Lindsay and Haley could work together on this?"

Blake was tempted to agree just to keep the peace. But knowing how unwelcome Lindsay had already made Haley feel, he knew it wouldn't work. "I don't think so. I say we either give Haley a chance to do what she can do, or we hire a professional to take Haley's list and move it forward."

Jake's eyes went wide. "Lindsay's out then regardless?"

Blake paused, looking at his friend. "Yeah, man."

Jake went still. Then, "She's gonna be pissed."

Blake waited. They had to be smart about this. They couldn't keep someone in place, especially someone who wasn't performing up to expectations, just to avoid hurt feelings. He just hoped Jake saw it that way too. "Do you want to talk to her? Or do you want all of us to talk to her together?"

He shook his head. "I don't want her to feel like we're ganging up on her."

Blake nodded. "But can you support this decision to her?" It wouldn't be successful if Jake didn't buy into the decision. He couldn't take the easy way out and just blame Blake or Haley.

Jake stood and walked a few steps away, running a hand through his longish hair. "Yeah. I think so."

Blake watched his friend for a moment but knew not to push it. This would be hard on Lindsay, but it would also be hard on Jake. "Let me know if I can help."

The previous jubilant mood had dampened a bit, but Blake was excited, nonetheless. This was a big step for their little band. They may fail, or they may succeed, but today marked the first step of the journey.

In the quiet of his car on the way home, a seed of doubt invaded his mind. Making the band his top priority, and committing to extending their reach was awesome and all, but it meant more time away from home. Which by itself, was not a bad thing. But it meant less time for his family.

They were a tight-knit little group, him, his brother and his aunt. And they each had their place, their role. He was the supporter, the cheerleader, the eternal optimist who took on the others' fears and took care of them. Wiped them away so they could move on. How would he do that if he were gone more?

On the other hand, he was also one of the breadwinners, helping Aunt Gloria with the costs of caring for a kid with so many financial needs. It was the least he could do, under the circumstances. And he'd taken on that role willingly. From a purely monetary perspective, this change would be a good thing.

He'd have to work through it. Every change had its good and its bad. But fear of the unknown was not the way to go. He couldn't avoid a big exciting move like this just because it meant changes to his daily routine.

He had goals. And it looked like Haley could help him achieve them. *Let's go.*

WHEN BLAKE CALLED TO give Haley the green light to work on her list of venues, she went a little crazy, even she had to admit that. But she was so excited! She had so many ideas, and now she had free rein to try them all.

She quickly realized that she'd need to record the band, sounding their very best, to entice these bigger bars and theaters to book them. Ace in the Hole was entirely unknown to this crowd, and she needed to introduce them the best way she could – by letting the places hear how great they were. She started doing research on how to best record them and quickly her head was spinning with terminology such as pre-amps, convertors, FOH console and microphone placement. She had no idea what she was doing.

But ... she knew who did. She placed a phone call. "Daddy?"

"Hi, sugar plum."

She smiled at his nickname for her. Growing up in the south, her father had a multitude of corny monikers for her, which he rotated at will whenever they spoke. "I have a favor to ask. I want to record a song that a live band will be playing, and I want to create a musical file that I can attach to an email and send it out to people who need to hear it."

"Okay," her father said.

"I realize there's a lot of technology behind that simple request. Would you mind if I work with someone from your audio/visual department to help me with that?"

"Well, they're busy working on a new ad campaign ..." He let the thought hang, but she knew he wouldn't turn her down. Surely he could spare one person to help her with recording one song. "But, yeah,

I think we can probably help you out. Let me send an email with the A/V person's name to introduce the two of you."

"Oh Daddy, thank you so much! I appreciate your help."

They chatted for a few minutes about things that were going on inside the family, and she ended the call. Just as he'd promised, when she pulled up her email account, there was her dad's note with the contact person's name.

A week later, Haley showed up at the band's gig location an hour early. Her dad's employee, Rachel Murphy, joined her in the parking lot and they walked in together.

"How's work going?" asked Haley.

"Busy. But busy is good."

"Sorry to bother you with this."

"No, actually I'm excited. I've never recorded live music, so I'm looking forward to trying it. Of course I'll do your editing and automation too. A new challenge!"

Haley was glad Rachel was enthused. Together they unloaded the trunk of her car. Her equipment was not big and heavy like sound equipment of times past. A compact little sound board, two special microphones, a laptop and several heavy duty cords.

"The miracles of modern technology," said Haley. Rachel laughed and got to work setting everything up. When the band arrived and began preparing the stage, Haley pulled Rachel up for introductions. "This is Rachel. She's a sound expert, and as I told you guys, she's going to help us create a digital file of you guys singing one of your best songs, that I can share with the venues where we're trying to get booked. Once those places hear you, they'll clamor over signing you up."

Jake and Robbie chuckled, and Blake put an arm around her shoulders, grinning and pulling her close. "Did I tell you she's amazing?" he asked the guys. He turned to Rachel. "Thank you for your help. Do we need to know anything, or do anything different?"

"Nope, you just do what you normally do. The only thing I'd suggest is, let's record one practice song, then the second song in your line up will be the one we want to keep for good."

Blake turned to his bandmates. "What song do you think we should use to impress everyone?"

They threw out several suggestions, and then agreed on a Jason Dean number that started slow and soft and crescendoed to an impressive finish.

Minutes passed, and it was time to start. The band took their place on stage, and Haley took her place beside Rachel, who was standing behind the sound board. Haley glanced over at the girlfriends' table, where Helen and Lindsay sat, drinking beer and glowering over at her. Well, maybe she was imagining the glowering part. She hadn't seen or talked to Lindsay since the first time she'd come to see the band. She knew Jake had broken the news to her that Haley would be taking over the managing of the band's schedule, and she fancied that Lindsay wouldn't be happy with that news. She needed to put on her big girl panties and go over and say hello.

But not now. Now, the band was warming up and it would almost be time to start the recording.

"We're Ace in the Hole. Let's let it roll." The music started, a perfect blend of strings, keyboards and percussion. When Blake's sultry voice started, along with harmony by the other guys, Haley got goosebumps on her arms. Rachel had on headphones and she was busy pushing slider buttons on the sound board. She held a thumb up to Haley about halfway through the song, then moved over to the laptop and clicked on a few buttons on the recording software. They were ready for the real song.

The band paused just a couple seconds between songs to alert Rachel, and they were off. The familiar song that graced the country music radio stations started out with Blake picking on his guitar, then Jake joined in with electric guitar and Robbie started tapping the beat with his drumset. When Blake started singing, it was an audio blend that made her heart race and her breath catch. They sounded so good. She held her breath throughout the entire song, and when it ended, she glanced over at Rachel, eyebrows up in question. Rachel gave her a big smile and a vigorous nod. She got it.

Rachel was done with her work, but Haley got her a beer and they hung out together through the rest of the first set. When the band took a break, Rachel and Haley disconnected all the recording equipment and carried it back to her car.

"Thank you so much. I can't tell you how much I appreciate your help and expertise."

Rachel waved a dismissive hand. "My pleasure. These guys are good. I'm glad you're helping them get to where they need to be."

They made quick plans about when Rachel would send her the edited file, and she drove off. Haley went back into the bar and before her nerves could get the better of her, she hiked straight over to Lindsay and Helen's table. "Hi, ladies," she said, as friendly as she could.

Helen glanced at her with a small smile and said, "Hi Haley." Lindsay determinedly looked straight ahead as if she hadn't approached.

"The guys sound great," Haley threw out there, trying to keep the conversation light.

"Yeah," Helen said. After a few minutes of silence, Helen asked, "What were you doing over there during the first set?"

Haley slid into a barstool at their table, although she wasn't invited. "That woman is a sound engineer and she recorded the band singing a couple songs. Once it's edited I'll have a sound file I can send electronically to the venues I'm trying to book the band into."

At that explanation, Lindsay turned her back pointedly toward Haley and rolled her eyes. But Helen responded, "Good idea." Lindsay's attitude was enough to convince Haley that she'd rather sit by herself for the second set than join the two of them, so she gave a friendly wave and left the table.

AT THE END OF A LONG work day, Haley trudged to her car. The late nights and long days were starting to get to her. Maybe she should take a night off of band work. But she couldn't. She had so many ideas, and she was having fun getting them done.

She heard her name on the breeze and turned. "Carly!" she said when she saw her friend.

"Hi. You must've been in a daze. I've been chasing you."

"Sorry. I'm a little braindead."

"What's going on? Are you coming down with something?"

As they walked to their cars, Haley filled Carly in on her latest project. "I have the recording file now and it sounds great. I designed a logo for the band and now I'm working on putting it on all kinds of promo items, you know, t-shirts, coffee mugs, notepads, that we can sell at the shows for additional revenue. I'm working on upgrading all their social media accounts and their website, which has been sadly neglected for way too long."

Carly stared at her, mouth open. "Are you serious? You know how to do all this stuff?"

Haley grinned. "Some I do. Some I'm learning as I go."

"I am totally impressed."

"Want to stop by on your way home and see some of the stuff?"

Carly peeked at her wristwatch and agreed. "I can stop for a few minutes."

Carly followed Haley home. Haley's kitchen table was covered with merchandise featuring the new Ace in the Hole logo. "I love it!"

Haley grinned. "Thanks. They didn't have a logo before. So now it's plastered all over their online presence, look." Haley tugged the laptop over and pulled up newly designed Facebook, Twitter, Instagram accounts, as well as a refreshed band website.

"Wow. Everything looks so good, Haley! Modern and colorful and impressive. Man." She looked up at her. "If I had a band, I'd want you to manage it."

"Thanks, buddy."

"I'm not kidding. You really need to consider doing this full-time. You've found your niche, girl."

Haley playfully stifled a yawn. "I feel like I am doing this full-time, on top of my other full-time job."

Carly planted a look on her. "Take care of yourself. But isn't it fun to find your passion?"

"The hours I put in fly by. I love it. Oh, and listen to this." She clicked a few buttons on the laptop, set the volume to High and soon the band's magic filled the apartment. Carly's eyes went wide, and then she closed her eyes, swaying to the music and soaking it in. When the song ended, she grabbed Haley's hands and squeezed.

"I can see why you're so excited! These guys sound good! They're the real deal, and you're on the ground floor helping them escalate to the top."

She loved Carly. Carly was her girl.

"I'm going to get one of the grandmas to watch Grace and treat my hubby to a night out. I want to see this band in person."

"Oh, Carly, it's so fun. Let me know when you go and I'll meet you there. We can dance and let loose and have a great time."

"Will do." Carly said her good-byes and left. Haley ate a quick sandwich for dinner and got back to her tasks. She had scheduled a photographer from Rachel's department to do a photo shoot of the band. She'd found a rustic barn outside of town a half hour or so and thought that'd make a great backdrop for the shoot. They'd do a variety of shots with instruments, without, and a couple different wardrobe choices. They were building a brand and needed high-quality photos to enhance it.

With all that in place, Haley had an arsenal of justification to entice the nicer venues to hire Ace in the Hole. She couldn't wait to start setting up their schedule.

Chapter Four

"DO YOU HAVE ANY MORE of the pink t-shirt? Size medium?"

They were flying off the merchandise table. Haley squatted and peered into the boxes of extras underneath. "Hold on, I see more pink." She pulled out a stack and started studying the labels. "Here's one! Medium!"

The young woman in front of her did a fist pump in the air and squealed. "Okay, I'll take that, as well as this stuff." She shoved over a can huggie, a band CD and an autographed 8 x 10 glossy of the band. Haley entered them all into the cashier app of the laptop and announced, "Fifty five dollars." The girl handed over her credit card and Haley swiped it. "Want your receipt?"

The girl nodded.

Haley moved the gadget back to her. "Enter your email address. We don't print paper here."

She tap-tap-tapped and finished.

"Thank you for your purchase!"

"I love this band. Especially the lead singer. Blake's a hottie."

Haley hid a grimace in a forced smile. "He sure is."

She took care of the line of rabid fans and when they were all gone, it was two forty-five in the morning. She fell into a chair and closed her eyes for a moment. But only a moment. If she allowed herself longer, she'd likely fall asleep right here at The Loft in Charleston.

It had been a great night. The gig was only ninety minutes from home, much closer than some of their extended reach had taken them over the last four months. Because of that, and because it was a Saturday night, they'd decided not to book hotel rooms. They'd drive home late and sleep in their own beds for a change.

The Loft was on the top floor of a four-story historic brick building in a touristy section of Charleston. The crowd was crazy big, rowdy and supportive. The bar opened onto an outdoor stone patio with sparkly lights and potted plants. The bar staff had opened the doors mid-way through the first set, so Haley knew the skies had filled with Ace in the Hole's beautiful strands of music, and the loud applause and sounds of appreciation from the fans. She could just picture it in her mind – a wave of sound floating up to heaven.

The bar manager stopped by the table as Haley scrambled to fold and replace the remaining merchandise in the box. "Thank you," he said. "They really pulled in a big crowd tonight. We appreciate the business."

Haley beamed a smile at him. "And we appreciate you booking us."

"Happy to do it. In fact, can we talk about another night? I'd love to see this kind of crowd again."

"Sure. Let me look at the calendar and give you a call on Monday. We may have a few free nights in the next month."

"Awesome. I transmitted your payment a few minutes ago so it should've hit your account by now."

"Pleasure doing business with you."

Blake was the next to stop over to the table. He and the guys had finished disconnecting the stage equipment and carrying everything back to the truck downstairs. He looked exhausted, but happy. "You about ready?"

"Yep." She closed the lids of the boxes and he automatically lifted one, then stacked another one on top. She grabbed two, as well as her purse and they headed down the stairs, carefully watching where their feet landed. "Good sales tonight. I'll have to reorder everything."

He pushed the truck hatch closed and pulled her in for a hug. She breathed in his scent, a heady combination of sweat and fresh air. His head dipped and they were in a kiss, her heart rate increasing as it always did when they kissed. This man made her heart race, her head spin, her blood pump. Her thoughts went to a silent prayer of thanksgiving for having met him, and for having partnered together on this business venture. She was having so much fun, and so was he.

"Sorry," he murmured when he pulled back. "I'm sweaty and gross."

Sweaty, yes. Gross, no. They both headed to the truck. Blake swung into the driver's seat. They made their way through the nearly deserted streets of the city and to the highway. Sleep was calling her hard, but he was probably more tired than she was. Conversation would help them stay awake.

"Great night. The manager came over and wants to book you guys again."

Blake did a slow shake of his head. He took a hand off the wheel and put it on hers, squeezing it. "You're a miracle worker. None of this good stuff would be happening for us if it weren't for you. Do you know how grateful we are?"

"I think I do."

"For years we were stuck in a rut, playing beach bars, making a couple hundreds bucks a pop. Now look at us. You show up with all these ideas for making us look good. And suddenly we're in demand."

She chuckled. "It's called marketing, baby. Building a buzz. Making people aware of what you have to offer and making them want it. You did your part all those years. You mastered your craft. You worked hard. You know what you're doing, so when success found you, you were ready for it."

"And you are great at marketing."

"Thanks. I love it. I'm having so much fun."

"So are we."

"I wish we had a crystal ball and could read the future."

He nodded sleepily while he watched the road.

"For example, we need to hire help. We can't keep doing all this ourselves."

"What do you mean?"

"Well, to start, you guys shouldn't be doing your own set up and tear down at every gig. We need a roadie crew to do that. You should be focused on performing."

He looked over, eyebrows up.

"And the merchandise sales. I need a sales crew to take care of that. I'll do all the behind the scenes orders and creative stuff. But I need people to work the sales table at the gigs." She wanted to dream big. She just didn't know where her dreams and reality would collide. "And ... me."

He looked over at her again.

"I'm spending so much time working for the band ..."

"For no money ..."

"Right. That I don't really have time to work at the community college anymore. Between doing all the manager responsibilities for the band, and attending as many performances as I can, I'm exhausted when I go in there."

He drove in silence for a few moments. "Well, you handle our money too. Can we afford to pay you?"

That was the big question. Would this success continue? Or was it a short-term thing? What would their payroll look like? They'd need to pay the musicians a living wage, of course, and if she quit her job, she'd need a living wage too. The other employees she'd mentioned could be part-time.

"Let me work on finding out. I'm going to call in an accountant to look at our books and our future planned income. We have the goal of paying at least the four of us full-time salaries, but I need help with that before I decide if I can quit my job."

"You're amazing."

"Stay tuned." With that, she leaned back in her seat, closed her eyes and let slumber overtake her.

THE NEXT WEEK, THE band was booked in Hilton Head Island for multiple performances all weekend. The venue was an outdoor amphitheater that sported a covered bandstand in the middle of a big waterfront park. Rows and rows of wooden benches stretched out facing the stage, providing seating for nearly a thousand people. It was the biggest venue they'd played yet, and Haley was thrilled that they'd managed to get included in Hilton Head's Battle of the Bands festival. A dozen bands graced the stage throughout the festival. Ace in the Hole was scheduled for an hour on Friday evening, another hour on Saturday afternoon and a half hour finale on Saturday night. Spectators were encouraged to vote for their favorite bands, and a judging panel weighed in too, to come up with the Battle of the Band winner on Sunday. The winner walked away with a trophy and a cash prize.

Late afternoon on Friday, the band had arrived, Haley had checked in with the festival organizers, and received their instructions regarding performance times, lengths, and set up instructions. They were all set.

Blake wrapped an arm around Haley's waist and smiled down at her. "How about we grab something to eat?"

The whole crew was there ... Jake and Lindsay, Robbie and Helen, so they headed toward one of the waterfront crab shacks and waited twenty minutes for a table. They ordered pounds of crabs, which the waitress shoveled onto their table covered with newsprint. No plates, no silverware other than the tools necessary to crack open the crabs and get the luscious meat out. Dipping trays filled with melted butter made it even better, as well as pitchers of iced cold beer. It was messy but it was fun.

Haley was happy that the mood at the table was lighthearted and festive, especially since she had spent little to no time with the girls lately. First, she'd been busy. Second, whenever she had the choice, she avoided them. She knew how they felt about her, well, Lindsay at least. Maybe she wasn't being fair to Helen. But she had no room in her life for negativity.

"This festival is awesome. I wonder how many other country bands there are," Jake commented.

Haley looked up, about to respond when Lindsay's voice came, pinched with anger. "Why don't you ask your favorite band manager? I'm sure she has a spreadsheet and a website and could look that right up for you."

Haley's mouth was open, and she closed it, quiet. Lindsay's comment came from a place of anger, but she'd let it go if it meant they could keep the peace. "About half, Jake, are modern country bands. There's also some classic rock, some hillbilly and even a couple gospel bands."

"It's a really fun environment," said Blake. "I'm happy we got in here. Fun too, being in Hilton Head Island."

Haley winked at him, grateful for his kind comment. But the kindness at the table didn't last long. Lindsay dropped a crab cracker onto the table with a heavy clunk. Jake looked over. "Babe?" he said cautiously.

"Let's all take another moment to worship at the altar of Haley Witherspoon. Let's all sing praises that if Blake hadn't met Haley we'd still be singing at bars like Winners Lounge and The Crazy Crab in Myrtle Beach. Oh hail, almighty Haley."

The air pushed out of Haley's lungs at the magnitude of her sarcasm and obvious hatred. Jake addressed Lindsay first. "Hey, that's not necessary." Jake looked up at Blake.

Blake placed his own utensils on the table and started unrolling from the paper towel roll, wiping the grease off his hands. "Come on now. No need to be mean, Lindsay. Look, we all appreciate the work you did for the band. But yes, Haley is doing the band management now and she's doing a great job. She's booking us at really nice places and getting us seen by a lot more people. Don't take it personally."

Lindsay stood, tugging her legs out from the picnic-style table. She appeared undecided whether she'd storm off or stick around for one more retort. Unfortunately for all of them, she decided the latter.

"I'm getting sick and tired of this new pace. Some of us have to work everyday. I don't have the flexibility to take off work to drive two, three hours to a gig. I'm exhausted from all this. I don't see what was so wrong with the way things were before." She pulled her gaze away from Haley and swept a look at the rest of them. "Why couldn't you leave well enough alone?"

She ran off, while everyone at the table sat, frozen. Haley eyed over at Jake. He stood, watching her go. Slowly, he turned back to the table and sat.

"I'll let her cool down. She's making no sense. She'll be fine."

Haley didn't know Jake that well, but he sounded like he was hoping that would be true but wasn't certain. She glanced over at Helen, who Haley assumed was Lindsay's best friend. Helen raised her head and met gazes with Haley. She shrugged one shoulder. "She's been worked up about this for quite a while. I'm actually glad she let it out."

So, no one was going after her. Interesting. Maybe, as in the way of bullies, no one actually agreed with her. Maybe they just went along with her because it was easier that way.

Soon the table returned to lighthearted conversation and the sound of cracking crabs. Showtime was two hours away and they were just thankful to be here.

Chapter Five

HALEY KEPT BUSY DURING Friday night's performance, and enlisted Helen's help with the merchandise table. With two people, they were busy enough to make a bunch of sales, but still watch their guys doing what they did best. Blake played to the crowd while he sang, leaning down to brush hands with the front-row concertgoers, pausing for an occasional selfie with a fan, making eye contact with as many people as he could. His voice was spot on, and the instrumentals were flawless. Maybe she was biased, but she fell in love with Blake over and over again each time she watched him perform.

One of the festival organizers came over to the merch table and asked, "Do you have a minute?" She gestured to Helen, who nodded. Haley walked off with the organizer.

"They sound great."

"Thanks," Haley said with a beaming smile. Funny how she felt like a proud mom.

"I just wanted to show you two places where you can keep track of their rankings." He led her into a small tent where an electronic tally board listed all the bands in the competition, and two columns of numbers. One was the popular fan vote, the second was the judging panel scores. Both numbers were mathematically blended together throughout the weekend and the bands were displayed in order, the current winner on top.

"Wow. This is nice," Haley exclaimed. Ace in the Hole was in the second-place spot, but the judges' column was blank.

"The judges post their scores within a half hour of every performance."

"So, my guys are doing well."

"They sure are. And, if you can't get over here physically, I'll text you a hyperlink to this same information on the internet." He tapped on his phone and Haley's phone buzzed with receipt.

"Awesome."

"Good luck." He patted her shoulder and left the tent. Haley looked around and sent a quick prayer skyward, *Thank you, God. Thank you for this new excitement in my life. Thank you for hooking me up with Ace in the Hole. Watch over us during this competition.*

She'd grown up in the church, but she was by no means an expert in spirituality. She remembered enough of her early religious training, that when things were going well, she needed to express her thankfulness to God.

Haley returned to the merch table. Helen was holding her own, but the crowd was enthused by the items, so she jumped in and helped. It really was a perfect night. The setting was gorgeous, the temperature was warm with a nice breeze, and the beautiful sounds of the band's music filled the amphitheater. She couldn't think of anywhere she'd rather be.

ON SATURDAY, ACE IN the Hole had two performances. Blake and Haley walked the white sand beach while discussing their performance strategy.

"I know cover songs of popular bands are best received. But we've been working hard on original music and we really want to float some of that out there. I have two new songs, and Jake and Robbie each have an original."

Haley thought about it as the surf ran up over her bare feet. "I think it's great that you guys are writing music. For any band to advance, they need to move away from playing other people's music, to branding their own music."

Blake gave a hearty shake of his head, excited that she agreed with him. It hurt her heart to continue, "But." He turned toward her. "Now's not the time to float some originals. Not for this festival. We're in a competition and every minute you're playing, people are voting for you. Fans and judges. What they want to hear is music they know."

He let out a frustrated breath.

"I'm not saying, never. I'm just saying for today's performances, when the voting is on the line, stick to the familiar. Stick to the favorite songs that everyone knows and loves, and you guys do so well. It might just win you the Battle of the Bands."

Blake nodded. "I see your point. You've never led us wrong so far, and I'll trust you with this too. But we really do want to start introducing our own music into our sets. Starting next week."

"Agreed." She sealed the deal with a kiss on his lips, then they continued walking with her fingers resting in his back pocket.

"Do you really think we have a chance of winning this thing?" Blake asked, and the way he looked over at her, with hopefulness in his eyes, melted her heart. She knew they had a strong chance of winning this thing, because she'd been obsessively monitoring the scoring tent every half hour or so all last evening. When Ace in the Hole's performance last night was done, and the judge's scores had rolled in, they were strongly in the first-place position.

But standing there, watching the numbers change in real time, Haley had made the decision not to tell the others about it. She wouldn't tell the band members, and she wouldn't tell the girlfriends either. It would just make them nervous and possibly throw them off their game. They'd perform better without all that hanging over their heads. She was the band's manager. She would take that pressure on herself. They would find out the official results Sunday morning. Until then, she would be the only one to know how they were doing.

"Yeah, of course I think you have a strong chance of winning this thing."

Her answer pleased him because he stopped walking, pulled her in close. "Have I ever told you ... I love ..." His eyes flickered between both of hers, and his cheeks colored.

She stared up into his face and her breath caught in her throat. Although they hadn't been together that long, maybe he was ready to tell her he loved her. Suddenly, even though she hadn't given it much thought, hearing him say he loved her was what she wanted most in the world.

"I love ... the faith you have in me."

His face wavered a little in her gaze as tears threatened. She couldn't help feeling a little disappointed. Loving the faith she had in him, wasn't exactly the profession of love she was hoping for. On the other hand, she didn't know if she loved him either. But she sure loved what they were creating together, and she loved being with him. That was enough for now. She sniffed and put a smile on her face. "You've earned the faith I have in you."

He pulled her in for an embrace. She felt safe and content in his arms, and she laid her cheek on his chest. A million moments of bliss passed by, or maybe it was only a few, but it was time to head back to the festival grounds and prepare for their afternoon set. On the way back, they discussed their song order.

"Throw all the great country artists in there that you can: Radley Ray, Keith Olson, Chris Parker. Those guys are all gold."

"Yeah. And how about Frontier Fire? We've prepared a set of their oldies and those are ready tonight."

Haley considered it. Frontier Fire was one of those iconic country bands from a decade ago, almost two. After a stellar career lasting fifteen years and multiple hit singles and Country Music Awards, they retired, only to miss the magic. They came out of retirement last year with a new album, new singles that stayed true to their old sound while modernizing to fit into the current country music scene. There had to be some Frontier Fire fans out there today, and their older songs had that sing-alongability that they were looking for.

"Good idea. How many? Three? Four? Then move on to the more modern stuff."

"Sounds good, boss."

Haley punched his shoulder and they headed back to the bandstand.

BLAKE GATHERED WITH Jake and Robbie behind the bandstand, putting their heads together. The current band had five minutes left, then a festival crew would prepare the stage for Ace in the Hole. They would be up there in less than fifteen minutes.

"So, you guys clear on the set order? Or do you want to go over it again?" He peered at his bandmates and tried to ignore the racing of his heart. Nerves routinely hit him while he was waiting to go on, but once they started playing, it all clicked, and he calmed down immediately.

"We got it, we got it," Robbie droned. Blake let out a nervous chuckle. "Seriously, man," Robbie continued, "we're ready. You wrote the set list down and we can all see it. We got this, bud. We won't mess this up."

Blake ran his fingers over the chords of the first song silently without plucking the strings. "I know. I didn't mean to imply that we'd mess this up."

"Hey," said Jake. "We're in this together. Whatever happens, we all do it together. We want to win as bad as you do."

Blake took in a deep breath. "Is that why I'm so nervous? Because I know we're being judged and a big prize purse is on the line?"

Jake shrugged. "That's why I'm nervous."

They all laughed, and Blake felt his nerves start to calm. These guys were his brothers. His crew. One for all and all for one. They'd been together a long time, and that familiarity was comfortable. No need to worry. They'd do the best they could, and if they won, they won. If they didn't, so what? They still had a whole summer of great gigs scheduled, thanks to Haley. Life was good.

His cell phone rang, which was a good reminder to put it on mute. He lifted it to read the screen. "Oh, I better get this."

Robbie gave him an eyebrows-up look of disbelief and tapped on a pretend watch on his left wrist.

"I know, I'll keep it quick." He turned his back. "Hey, Brent, what's up?"

"Taking a study break. I've got a Calculus test on Monday."

"Well, God gave you the brains of the family, so I have every confidence in you. You'll ace it."

His brother laughed. "No pressure, huh?"

Blake turned and glanced at his bandmates. It was time to go. "Bud, I gotta go, but is everything okay? Do you need anything?"

"Oh, no, man, I was just calling to take my mind off absolute maximums and bounded functions."

Blake chuckled. "Well, remember I'm in Hilton Head competing with the band. We're about to go on stage."

"Oh shoot! I'm sorry Blake! I'm totally wrapped up in my own world. Go, and uh, break a leg. You can do it."

Blake laughed again at the encouragement. "You sure you're okay? Don't need anything?"

"Just a new brain. But I guess I'll have to make do with the one I got."

"Love you, bro," Blake said, and closed his eyes as a rush of sibling love and protectiveness surged through him. On a day a dozen years ago, he'd become his little brother's protector and provider, along with Aunt Gloria. A day that changed life forever for all three of them.

Disconnecting the call, he stepped back to his band. He made eye connect with them, one by one. He thrust a fist out, and both his buddies joined. "Ace in the Hole," he said. Followed by all three, "Let's let it roll."

They took the stage and Blake strode over to the fans, slapping hands with them, smiling and greeting them. When the guys' instruments were miked up, they launched into their first song and immediately got wrapped up in the melody, the lyrics, the harmony, the rhythm. Music was his place to lose himself, and it never failed.

They moved seamlessly into their second song in the same key, by a different artist, and the crowd came with them. Girls in short shorts and tight shirts danced and sang along in the crowd, and guys wearing jeans and cowboy hats drank beer and got rowdy. Their applause rose to the sky.

"We're Ace in the Hole from Myrtle Beach. We're happy to be here and we hope you vote for us to win Battle of the Bands." The enthusiastic crowd screamed. Blake went on, "We want to play a few songs in homage to one of our favorite classic country bands who is making a comeback. You know them. You love them. Frontier Fire!"

They moved into the opening strands of their first cover. The crowd knew the words and sang along with him and Blake let his concentration waver for just a moment as he imagined someday, in the future, when he stood in front of a big crowd like this, singing his own songs, knowing that the crowd knew every single word. What an amazing experience that would be.

They ended up doing four Frontier Fire songs in all, then moved back into this decade with another half hour of popular country music covers. When they finished their set, Blake tapped his chest and raised his hands to the air, letting the crowd know that he not only appreciated their support, but thanked the Lord for the experience as well. "We're Ace in the Hole. Thank you, Hilton Head! We'll be back on tonight."

They rushed off the stage and practically collapsed from the high. The crowd was crazy happy with them and it felt so good.

They started the trek back to the truck to store their instruments until the next set later tonight. Haley joined them. "Great job, guys! Awesome work."

He put his arm around her and pulled her in for a kiss while the guys continued on. He owed so much to her. This shift in success and popularity was all due to her. "Thank you," he whispered and kissed her again.

"Excuse me," came a voice from behind him. Blake finished his leisurely kiss with Haley and then turned. A man in clean-cut clothes stood there, a canvas messenger bag strapped over his chest. He wasn't the age of the typical audience member here, and he wasn't dressed like one either.

"Can I help you?"

"Yes. My name is Randall Brown." He reached in his shirt pocket and pulled out a couple business cards, handing one to Blake and one to Haley. "You guys sounded really good out there today."

"Thank you very much," Blake said. He took a peek at the card, but it didn't give him too much of a clue as to who this guy was. "We'd appreciate your vote." He smiled and looked at Haley.

"I especially was impressed with your Frontier Fire set."

"Oh, yeah, we just added that. We'd been working on them the last few weeks and decided to debut them here."

"I'm the manager of Frontier Fire."

Blake went still and stared at the man. Had he heard right? This guy managed Frontier Fire? What was he doing in South Carolina? Blake shook his head, and regained enough awareness to say, "This is Haley Witherspoon. She's Ace in the Hole's manager. And my girlfriend."

Randall laughed and held out a hand. "Nice to meet you, Haley. Look, I'm finalizing the plans for the reunion tour of the band. It will feature our new album on a five-month tour."

Blake nodded, hoping he looked like he was following but all that rolled through his head was, 'What does this have to do with me?' Fortunately, Haley was on the same page as him, and wasn't too intimidated to ask.

"Mr. Brown is there something we can help you with?"

"Yes. There definitely is. I'm here ... at this festival and scheduled to attend a couple more in the south, looking for someone who can sing Frontier Fire songs as well as you can."

Blake blinked. "Why?"

"I don't know if you heard this in the news or not, but Josh Lakely suffered a serious car accident and is injured. He won't be able to tour."

Blake gasped and so did Haley. She looked as shocked as he did. The lead singer of the band injured right before a five-month tour, and unable to perform. It was a disaster.

"Our choices were to cancel the tour, or to find a replacement lead singer. Our investors prefer the latter. But only if we can find a good fit. Someone who knows the songs, can represent them well, and sounds like Josh when he sings. I think I found him. You."

Blake's heart flipped and started beating so fast he felt the pounding in his head. Dizziness came over him and he ardently tried not to faint from the shock.

Haley said, "You want Blake to be the lead singer of Frontier Fire during your five-month reunion tour across the country."

Blake was glad she'd summarized because he wasn't sure his brain was working properly.

"That's right, and I'd be happy to discuss contract terms with you."

"Yes, we need to do that, and I might bring in our band attorney to review the terms as well."

"No problem at all, but we need to move this thing forward. The tour starts in a month, and if you decline the offer, I need to keep looking."

Blake emerged from his fog. "No!" Haley and Randall both stared at him. "No, we don't want to decline. Ace in the Hole will be glad to go on tour with you."

Haley looked at him, her mouth open, no words coming out. Randall said, "Hold on. What? We don't want your whole band. We just want you. The rest of Frontier Fire is on board."

Haley turned to face him, resting her hands on his shirt. "They just want you to sing, Blake. They don't need Robbie or Jake."

He glanced from Haley to Randall and back to Haley. "Well, then that's not going to work. We're a band. We either do it together, or we don't do it."

Chapter Six

HALEY'S WORLD WAS SPINNING. She stood on solid ground and yet she felt like she would fall.

Blake had received a big-time, once-in-a-lifetime offer to front a bigtime band with thousands of followers and he turned it down? Did he know how many small-time singers got an opportunity like this one? Not many! Hardly any! For him to turn it down without a reasonable consideration period, was crazy. He'd regret it later if he let Randall Brown walk away, she was positive.

"Okay," she said, striving to be the voice of reason, "let's hold on here a minute. Blake, why don't you go get some water and sit in the air conditioning for a while. Let me talk contract terms with Mr. Brown and see what they're even talking about with this offer. Then you and I can talk later."

She hoped the glare she was pointing in his direction would supplement her message. It must have, because he agreed. "Okay. I'll leave this to you then. But no decisions till we talk again."

"You got it." She managed a hopeful smile. She reached for his hand and squeezed it, hoping her pride in him was transmitted through. Regardless of what they decided about the Frontier Fire offer, they still had a final set to perform before knowing if they would win Battle of the Bands.

Blake walked away, and Haley watched him, then turned to Mr. Brown. "Please don't take that personally. Blake would be an awesome fit for your tour. And I think he'd be really interested in doing it. It's just that he doesn't see himself as a solo artist. He's very loyal to their threesome. They've been together a long time."

"I understand. He's the best fit I've found in almost a week of searching. I'd hate to leave him behind and have to keep looking, but I will do that if we can't come to an agreement." He pulled a contract out of his bag. They found a picnic table nearby, and they both sat to review it. Randall took out a pen and used it to point out the key contract points.

It pretty much covered everything. Rehearsal timing and location, transportation of the tour, accommodations, payment. The compensation terms were split down by earnings for the tour, the album and residuals from merchandise sold. Haley tried to hold back a gasp and keep her tongue from lolling. These people meant business. These numbers were high.

"Please keep in mind that when Josh recovers, he will return as lead singer of the band, and Blake will move on. But we don't see Josh doing that in time to complete this tour."

Haley nodded, and her mind raced with opportunities for Blake to move on from this tour. This was going to be so good for his future career. This was a dream come true for any musician. He just happened to be in the right place at the right time.

She just had to convince him to take advantage of it.

"Are there any questions I can answer for you?" Randall asked.

"It's very straightforward and I don't think I have any questions."

Randall turned his wrist and looked at his shiny gold wristwatch. "It is now five pm on Saturday. This offer is good until five pm on Sunday. I need your answer before then."

Haley wished she could give her answer right now, "Yes! Yes! Heck yes!" But it didn't work that way. She wasn't the one with the talent to stand up there on stage and lead the band in vocals. She wasn't the one who'd have to walk away from Ace in the Hole when they had a summer full of great gigs scheduled, that *she'd* scheduled for them. She needed to talk to Blake.

But man, she would be completely heartbroken if he turned this down.

"Let's exchange cell phone numbers. I'll be back in touch with you before five tomorrow."

BLAKE FOUND HIMSELF wandering to the beach. He sat to pull his boots off, then rolled up the legs of his jeans. He let the cool, soft sand envelop his feet and he made his way down to the rolling surf. Hilton Head had one of the most beautiful beaches he'd seen. The beach had always been his place to soak in God's beauty and run things through his mind. Maybe the beach would work its magic now.

Sing lead for Frontier Fire? Him? On their national tour? How on earth was this his life now? He had moved so quickly from *Uber* driver doing a few local gigs every week, to potentially headlining with a major country band. He had Haley to thank for that. Her hard work had transformed the band.

But this opportunity didn't include the band. It was just for him. It didn't seem right, to abandon Ace in the Hole just when they were hitting their stride and finding success. He wanted to be a part of that. He didn't want to leave them alone and go hang out with someone else's band. Ace in the Hole was his band. Robbie and Jake were his guys, his brothers, his best friends. He couldn't do this to them.

On the other hand, it was temporary. Would Robbie and Jake want to take some time off from the schedule while he was gone? Cancel the gigs and try to reschedule them when he returned? Knowing them, the answer to that question would be a flat ... no.

And what about his family responsibilities? He knew Aunt Gloria was capable of managing the household chores alone, but what about when Brent needed something? Transportation, money, advice or just an open ear? To his very core, Blake hated leaving her with all the work, all the tasks. His brother was *his* number one priority, and had been for a long time. He would go to the ends of the earth to protect his brother. How would he do that if he was gone?

He needed some guidance. He needed Haley's guidance, but also God's. He tried to let God help him with the major decisions in his life, and this one was the biggest decision he'd ever been faced with. So while he continued walking, he closed his eyes and thought silently, *Help me. Guide me. Let me know your will for me.* He put the sentiments on repeat, letting them run over and over again in his head. No big voice came bombarding out of the sky. No decision became the clear choice for him. He didn't think God had answered him, but he felt confident that He would, eventually.

He turned and walked back. He needed to find Haley.

He found her at the beach entrance near the festival. She smiled her beautiful, happy smile when she saw him and he suddenly felt better, calmer. Her smile always made him feel that way. They would handle this together. No reason to feel distressed about it.

He went right to her, clutched her arm and put his face beside hers. His nose rested against her hair and he breathed in her scent.

"We need to talk," she said.

"Yep."

They walked together, and Haley led him back to the hotel. "I don't want Jake and Robbie to know about this yet. Can we keep this confidential from them?"

Blake considered. "Yep." If he decided to pass, there was no need to even tell the guys.

She led him to a small conference room inside the Business Center of the hotel. They sat at a table, and she laid out a multi-page contract in front of him. "I want to go over these terms with you, and I want you to keep an open mind before you decide. But Blake, whatever you decide to do, I want you to know ... I support you."

He gazed at her. It meant a lot. She talked through each and every contract point, explaining what was being asked of him, what time commitment it would require, and finally what compensation he would receive.

"What?" he blurted, reached for the contract and pulled it closer. "Seriously?"

"Yes." She couldn't say it without bursting into a big smile. "Seriously."

He blinked but the number didn't change. It was the largest amount of compensation he'd ever seen, and even in his wildest dreams he never thought he'd see. He pushed back moisture that had formed in his eyes and focused on the number.

This was big. This was huge. This was monumental for his music career.

"How can I turn this down?"

Haley beamed but didn't respond. She was letting him work through it in his own mind.

"I can't imagine." He turned the paper over so that big number wasn't staring at him, rattling his brain. He closed his eyes, then opened them again. "It's a great opportunity, no doubt. But what about Ace in the Hole?"

"I want you to consider this as two different things. The first thing is, is this a good opportunity for you? Is this something that you want to do? Is this something that will help you in your music career? Make a decision just based on that. Then, if you decide to do it, the second thing is, what about Ace in the Hole?"

He shook his head. "I don't know if I can separate the two. Ace in the Hole is my band. We are Ace in the Hole. If I leave them to pursue this on my own, I'd be abandoning them. And that doesn't feel right to me. Especially when you've got us on a pinnacle of our own." He reached out and grabbed her hand. "Maybe if I stuck with Ace in the Hole, we'd have our own successful ride soon."

Haley said, "Not like this. Not this soon. Frontier Fire is an established band. They've got hundreds of thousands of fans who will be coming to the concerts. Ace in the Hole might get there someday. But not this summer."

Blake flung back in his chair and ran his hands through his hair.

"Think about it this way. What if every single one of those Frontier Fire fans finds out about Ace in the Hole? What if they like you so much that when this gig is over, they seek out Ace in the Hole performances? What if half of them do? What if a quarter of them do? It's still a ton of people."

Blake let that thought run through his mind. "So, you're saying, me doing this could be a good way to drive fans to Ace in the Hole."

"Could be. I could talk to Randall about allowing a wee bit of Ace in the Hole promotion during the Frontier Fire tour. Maybe sell your CD at the merch table?"

"That might help sell the idea to Jake and Robbie." He looked up at Haley. She'd said she'd support him whatever he decided to do. But it seemed clear to him that she wanted him to do this. Who knows, maybe he was crazy for even considering turning it down. Who did he think he was, walking away from such a great opportunity? Maybe Robbie and Jake would want him to do it, would encourage him to do it. He just didn't know.

"Haley, do you pray?" He felt comfortable with Haley. Comfortable enough to ask this question which he had never asked of anyone in his life. When she said, "Sure I do," he relaxed and held his hands out to her. They gripped hands, bowed heads and closed eyes. "Lord, please guide us in this important decision. Help us to know your will and make it clear to us. Amen."

They sat in silence for a moment, then Haley said, "I think it's good to pray about big decisions and this is about as big as they come." She leaned forward and planted a kiss on his cheek. "But regardless of what you decide, I'm proud of you for drawing Randall's interest. He obviously is very impressed by you."

"Haley, this is all you, babe. You got us to this festival, where he happened to be looking for a lead singer. If it weren't for you, we'd never have this opportunity."

"We make a good team." She gathered up the papers. "I'm going to keep these safe in my room until we're ready to make our decision. But our deadline is tomorrow at five."

"Got it."

ACE IN THE HOLE'S FINAL performance of the festival was Saturday night for a half hour. Blake and the guys had agreed on their set order and they came through with some of the best popular music in their inventory. Haley had checked the tally room prior to the performance. They were strongly in the lead. As she made her way over to the tent following the final performance, Haley sported a glad feeling in her heart. They were the frontrunners to win this thing. Not only would the prize purse be a welcome infusion of cash into the band's account, but the win would be a great credential on their musical resume.

The breeze caught her hair as she dipped her head and walked into the tally tent. The numbers were fluid because the judges had not finalized their scores yet. But it was clear that their band was the fan favorite. In fact, they were currently in the first-place position, even without the latest judges' scores. Losing now was almost an impossibility. She stood and watched the board.

"What the heck is this?"

The voice came from behind her, dripping with anger. Haley turned. It was Lindsay, creases in her forehead, frown on her face as she looked at the electronic board, trying to make sense of it. Before Haley could formulate an answer, she figured it out. "These are the judging results?"

Haley nodded.

"How long has it been here?"

Haley froze, then mustered up an answer. "All weekend."

Lindsay strode closer, her mouth dropped open. "And you've known about this. And you never bothered to tell any of us." Lindsay turned on her then, her face so close that the spittle created by Lindsay's angry words splattered on her skin. "How dare you. You are so self-centered."

"Lindsay, hold on."

"No. You hold on. You've known all weekend that Ace in the Hole was winning and you didn't think anyone else would want to know that? You just held onto that knowledge all by yourself, the queen of everything."

"It wasn't like that. I didn't want them to have the pressure of knowing they were in the lead. I just wanted them to play with no pressure and enjoy the festival."

Lindsay sputtered and tried a few words, stopped, before trying again. "And who died and left you Queen of the Universe? They're big boys. You should've told them. You should've told *us*."

Haley considered her accusation. Was she right? Was Haley holding onto that knowledge with clear intentions, or was she somehow being selfish? It didn't take long until she came to her decision: of course she wasn't being selfish. She had the band's best interest at heart. Lindsay could disagree with her approach, but she couldn't question her commitment.

"Lindsay, you may not agree with my decision to keep that to myself. But it was my call and I thought it would be best for the band to not know. So they could play their very best."

"Well, I call bull. They have the right to know. And I'm going to tell them."

She swung around and raced out of the tent. Haley was right on her heels. "Wait. Let's talk about this. Wouldn't it be more exciting for the band to find out when the judges announce their name? What's the point of breaking the news now?"

Lindsay stopped and turned to look at Haley with a look of pure derision. "You are such a child. You want them to be surprised because it's fun? They're adults, Haley. They have the right to know."

Lindsay raced off and Haley started to chase her. Then she changed her mind. She let her go. She had to learn to let go. She wasn't the only one with an opinion. She wasn't, as Lindsay so awfully accused her of, Queen of the Whole Universe. She was a receptionist who had helped a small-time band achieve a little more success. Would it be fun to go to the awards ceremony tomorrow and have the guys be surprised that they'd won first place? Sure it would. But if Lindsay felt strongly that they should know now and be forewarned, then maybe that was the way to go. As much as she despised Lindsay's attitude, and the way Lindsay treated her, she couldn't argue the fact that Lindsay had been around these guys a lot longer than she had. She knew them way better. As much as it pained her to admit it, maybe Lindsay knew better.

That thought made her choke out loud, but she walked back to the hotel and called it a night. She needed a little chill time, and she'd catch up with Blake in the morning.

Chapter Seven

IN THE MORNING, EARLIER than she would've cared to awaken, a knock sounded on the door. Haley ran her hands through her hair, grabbed a robe from the empty bed where she'd left it last night, and flung it on. She stalked to the door and pulled it open.

It was Blake. And all the rest. Robbie, Helen, Jake and Lindsay.

"Hi, babe," said Blake and for a moment, her heart rested at the words he chose and the resulting peace that flowed through her veins.

Then they all crowded to the door, trying to get in. She stepped back and let them. There's no way she could've stopped them at this point.

A few of them were talking at once, creating a crescendo of indecipherable sound. Blake, God bless him, made a T with his hands, a "Timeout" to his friends. "Hey y'all. Let's keep this civil."

So. Lindsay had told them that she'd kept the tally tent from them, and they had all gone to Blake to pound on him for a while. Well, they'd only just begun, and she had enough.

"Listen to me. I think I know what this is about, and I just want to give you my side of this." She looked over at Lindsay and fought the temptation to give her the stink-eye. She looked back at Jake and Robbie. "When we first got here I found out about the Tally Tent. It gave a running tally of the fans' popular votes and the judges' ratings, and the total. At any given time, I could see where we were in the rankings of the battle. You guys have been frontrunners all weekend." She took a step closer to Robbie and Jake, who stood with arms clenched over their chests, chins tucked down, eyes glued to the floor. "The fans love you. You know that. You can feel that each time you step up onto that stage. But, just as importantly, the judges love you too. They've consistently scored you the highest scores of any band in the competition."

Jake looked up. "Why didn't you tell us?"

"I made a judgement call. And maybe it was wrong. But I didn't tell you because I didn't want that pressure hanging on your back. I wanted you to go into each performance, focused on performing the best set you could. I didn't want all this other stuff worrying you, stressing you out or bringing you down." She shrugged and with a half-smile said, "It seems to have worked, right?"

Robbie said, "You could've been honest with us."

His words plunged a knife into her chest. She recovered enough to have the thought, were those his words, or had Lindsay planted them there? "If you see this as me being dishonest with you, then I apologize. But I didn't see it that way. As band manager, it's my job to enable you to play your very best. That's all I was doing. If you don't approve of my methods, then, like I said, I apologize. But you have to know that I did it with the very best intentions. I did it so you guys could concentrate on playing music, and I could worry about the background stuff." She glanced over at Blake and his face said that he agreed with her. He gave her a pointed wink.

"So, what do you say, guys? Haley has been an awesome band manager. She's gotten us some great new gigs, and it looks like we're winning the Battle of the Bands today. She's earned our respect. Can we get past this and move forward? She didn't do anything behind our backs." He pulled her into a hug and she came, awkwardly. "We owe a lot to Haley."

As Blake hugged her, the other guys took a few steps towards them. Haley wondered if they were in for a group hug and her heart lightened.

Then Lindsay's voice rose above the crowd, "What else has she hidden from us?"

Haley's gaze frantically sought out Blake's. Had he told them about the Frontier Fire opportunity? If they knew about that, this would become a completely different conversation. And it wouldn't be an easy one.

Blake caught her look and understood it. He shook his head tightly, his eyebrows creased.

Okay. They didn't know about the big news that would tear the band apart, at least temporarily. But she'd need to be careful with how she responded now, because chances are, they would need to know about it before too long. Maybe it was time for a little tough love.

"Do you guys want me to manage you or not? To do my job, I need to have information that you don't have. I need to use my judgement to make decisions on my own, or know when to come to you for input. This isn't hiding stuff from you. This is managing the band. But if you don't want me to work with you, *for* you, then just tell me."

She waited for a response. She knew what Blake's response would be, but she wanted to hear from Jake and Robbie. Not Lindsay. She wanted them to think for themselves and give her an honest answer.

Robbie put an arm on her shoulder. "You're the best manager we've ever had. All this is because of you. I trust you."

Haley smiled at him. "Thank you, Robbie," she whispered and put her head on his shoulder.

Jake needed to be heard from. But he was standing over in the corner with Lindsay. If he took her side, it would be an affront to Lindsay. And who knew what punishment he would pay in their relationship if he took Haley's side over his girlfriend's?

Still, he needed to say something.

"You're a good manager, Haley. I'm sure you had your reasons for not telling us. I can't argue with your results." He left Lindsay's side and joined the rest of them in the center of the room. He didn't join the group hug because Lindsay's leash probably didn't allow him to go that far. But he came close, reached his hand out and she took it. "Let's go win this thing."

She was so happy that she avoided meeting eyes with Lindsay, who probably had steam coming out her ears. "Great, guys. I appreciate your support. The winners are announced at noon. Let's gather down at the bandstand at 11:30, okay?"

The guys mumbled their good-byes, met up with their girlfriends, then left the room. Blake pulled her into his arms.

"I don't even want to know about the lynching that preceded that," Haley said.

"Lindsay was worked up to a lather and wanted everyone else to be furious too. The guys were pretty neutral about it until Lindsay insisted that we come and confront you." He pulled back to look in her eyes. "I'm sorry about that. You shouldn't have to deal with a jealous wench like Lindsay."

"I've dealt with jealous wenches my whole life. I can handle her."

A curious smile formed on Blake's face. "Oh really? Were you the girl in high school to steal other girls' boyfriends?"

Haley chuckled. "No." She allowed her mind to wander back to those odd and traumatic days of high school. "At least, not on purpose."

Blake fist-pumped the air. "I got the vixen. I got the girl every guy wanted."

"Not exactly. But I know a thing or two about girls who love to make problems for other girls. And I'm unhappy to say after being around Lindsay, that kind of behavior didn't stop after high school."

"Let's grab some breakfast before the awards ceremony," Blake suggested.

"Give me fifteen minutes. I'll meet you down at the restaurant."

BLAKE AND HALEY MADE their way to the bandstand, ready for the awards ceremony. All the bands grouped together in the seats that were filled all weekend with appreciative fans. He let his eyes run over all the bands who had played their hearts out. The music community was a close-knit group. Although he didn't know these individual musicians very well, he knew what they wanted, what they strived for. Because it was the same thing he strove for. They all wanted to improve their craft. They all wanted to reach more listeners. They all wanted to gain more fans.

And yes, they all probably wanted to make more money, if they were being completely honest.

How did a band from a small town do all that? How did his band compete with all the rest of them in the race to the top?

A realization crashed into his brain. The opportunity with Frontier Fire would give him all of that. It would help him reach all his goals. It would give him temporary fans and fame and money while on tour, and if he utilized that exposure properly, it could lead him on a road to permanence.

It all seemed so clear to him as he sat here now. Was this a message from God in his brain, encouraging him to take the gig? Or was it his ego telling him to snatch the gig for himself and leave his bandmates behind?

He turned to Haley, sitting beside him. "I think I got to take it."

She knew exactly what he was talking about, and a happy smile covered her face. "Really?"

He wanted to say more, but the Battle of the Bands organizer had taken on the stage, shouting into the microphone, "It's time to announce the winners of Battle of the Bands!"

He shook his head, content to wait to discuss it with her after the awards ceremony.

"We want to thank you all for coming here, competing, sharing your talent, and making this the best Battle of the Bands in our history! And now in third place ..."

The third-place band was announced and they all climbed on stage to receive applause and their trophy, and an envelope containing their winnings. They raised all their winnings above their heads and soaked in the excitement from the crowd.

The second-place band was announced, and it wasn't Ace in the Hole, so that clenched it for Blake. They'd won. He looked around and made eye contact with his bandmates. This was huge, and they all knew it.

"And now, I'm pleased to announce, the winners of Battle of the Bands, from Myrtle Beach, Ace in the Hole!"

Blake jumped to his feet, and so did Jake and Robbie, and they rushed to the base of the stage. In their excitement they practically tripped over each other's feet. But then he turned back and reached a hand out to Haley. Surprise was evident on her face, but he gestured to her and said, "Come on. You're coming with us."

She laughed and got to her feet, joining him as they climbed up on the stage.

"Ace in the Hole, you are awarded the winner of this year's Hilton Head Battle of the Bands." A huge trophy was hoisted over to Blake, who grabbed it, sharing it with Jake and Robbie, lifting it high above their heads. A check was handed over. "And the monetary award for coming in first."

Blake pointed a thumb at Haley. "Give it to her. She's the reason we're here."

The man with the microphone laughed and handed the check to Haley. She gripped it in her hands and leaned into a microphone. "We thank you very much for this honor." As Blake did a quick scan of the crowd, he caught the angry scowl of one particular bandmate's girlfriend. Lindsay would never be happy about Haley taking over as manager, even with all the success they'd had as a result. *You can't fix stupid.*

The award ceremony ended with all the contestants applauding them. Blake and Haley shook hands with the organizers and thanked them again for running such a great event. On their way off the stage, Blake made a decision.

He'd never been one to take a ton of time to make decisions. Once he'd made up his mind, he usually went with it. Obviously Haley thought it was a good idea to take the Frontier Fire gig. Whatever the fall-out with Ace in the Hole, they'd figure it out. He was ready to make an announcement.

As the other bands cleared out of the bandstand, he gave Haley a look that he hoped forewarned her what he was about to do. "Hey guys, could we gather around here? I have some news."

Robbie chuckled. "More news besides winning the contest?"

Blake took a deep breath. This was going to be harder than he'd thought. Maybe he should wait and give them all a chance to enjoy their win before announcing his decision. But no. The Frontier Fire manager had set 5 PM today as his deadline, and now that the festival was over, they would all head off in different directions.

He had to tell them now.

He gathered them in a circle. Even though Lindsay and Helen were there, he tried to focus on Robbie and Jake. "Guys, remember yesterday when we sang the Frontier Fire set?"

They nodded.

"Well, none of us knew it, but the manager of Frontier Fire was in the audience. He was listening. Did you hear in the news that Josh

Lakely was in a car accident and can't go on their reunion tour that's kicking off soon?"

The small circle went motionless. He supposed they'd already guessed, but he continued. "Their manager was looking for a lead singer to take over for Josh on the Frontier Fire tour. He, uh ..." Blake paused and looked at his friends, "he offered me the job."

Chapter Eight

HALEY HELD HER BREATH as she waited for Blake's news to sink in. She watched the faces of his bandmates. So far, they were still and silent.

Then, a smile broke out on Jake's face. "What? You're kidding me, man!"

Then, Robbie. "That's quite an honor, dude."

Blake's face flooded with relief. "Yeah, I couldn't believe it. We just happened to be at the right place at the right time. Unbelievable."

"What'd you tell him?" Jake asked.

"Nothing, yet." Blake's discomfort was obvious in his gaze flickering uncertainly from one bandmate to the other.

Lindsay was the next to be heard from, her tone crusted with unmistakable loathing. "What are you going to tell him?"

Blake's glance rested on Lindsay's face. A pause ensued, then he looked over at Haley for help. But she wasn't about to speak for him. After the Tally Tent faux pas, Blake needed to stand on his own two feet.

"I keep weighing it in my mind, going back and forth." He cleared his throat. "But I'm thinking that ... I'm gonna do it."

Lindsay let loose a curse word, turned away from the group, then returned. "I can guess who told you to do that."

Fire traveled down Haley's esophagus. She'd had enough with Lindsay and her unbearable attitude. "You know, Lindsay, I think you need to be reminded of your place. *You* are not in the band. *You* are not the manager of the band. You date a member of the band. It's none of your business if Blake takes this opportunity or not. And I'll thank you to quit being so nasty to me."

Haley knew enough about mean girls to stand up to one. For a split second everyone was silent. The next thing she heard was a gasp of breath, and an outburst of nervous laughter. Turning her head, she realized it came from Helen. "Wow. I guess she told you, Lindsay."

Then, Lindsay started swinging. She swung a fist and punched Helen in the stomach. Helen bent over at the waist, and Lindsay climbed over her to get to Haley.

"Hold on to her!" Blake yelled, presumably to Jake, who was in a daze. He shook the cobwebs out of his head and dove to grab Lindsay by the waist, but he'd waited too long. In a split second, she reached Haley and landed an open-handed slap on her face. The *smack* of skin on skin and the instant pain in Haley's cheekbone tore a groan out of her mouth.

Jake dashed and caught up to Lindsay, grabbed her and dragged her away. Blake swung Haley around to face him. "Are you okay?" he asked, deep concern etched into his expression. She didn't know what to say. She couldn't remember a time she'd been slapped in the face, not to mention with such force. It hurt like the dickens. She was mainly concentrating on controlling the flow of tears that wanted to burst from her eyes, because no way would she give Lindsay the satisfaction of seeing her cry. She sniffed and nodded.

Fearing a second attack, she located Lindsay and Jake a few steps away. He had his hands on her shoulders, leaning in close, speaking to her with a raised voice. "I'm sick of this, Lindsay. You're a basket case. You can't treat people like this. You've got such a negative energy."

She was shaking her head back and forth like on a swivel, but she wasn't saying anything.

"I've been thinking a lot about this lately, Lindsay, and you've just made up my mind. It's over between us. I can't live with your brand of crazy anymore. We're done."

She reached up to grab his face and he flinched. "No, you don't mean that. Don't let *her* tear us apart. Can't you see? That's what she wants. Don't fall for it. Don't let her win!"

Jake took hold of her hands and removed them from his cheeks. "That girl had nothing to do with this. I'm tired of it all. We're done, Lindsay."

Nausea pushed through Haley's stomach. "Are they talking about me?" she asked Blake softly.

He was watching them too, and he shrugged. "No idea."

Lindsay backed away from Jake, shaking with anger. "You're going to regret this. And you ..." she turned toward Haley and raised her voice a couple decibels, "you are going to regret this too." She flung herself a few feet away, then turned and yelled to Jake, "Get yourself home."

Jake lowered his head and stared at the ground. Robbie took a few awkward steps toward him and patted his arm. Jake looked up and took in the scene, everyone turned his way. "Sorry about that. It was overdue. She's been unbearable lately and ... I don't want to be a part of it anymore."

The threat of tears stabbed at Haley's eyes. No one was saying it, but it was Lindsay's hatred of her that had brought on the violent outbursts, which had led to the break up. "This is all my fault. I'm so sorry, Jake."

Jake looked up at her, shook his head. He walked closer to her, holding out a hand while she stood with Blake's supporting arm around her. Haley reached out and gripped it. "It's never easy to break up with someone you've been with for a while. But please believe me, Haley, this is not your fault. Her nastiness came to a boil because of you. If you want to get honest, you did me a favor. You opened my eyes."

The fivesome stood quietly, the reality of the last few moments sinking in. Finally, Blake said, "So, we need to talk about this Frontier Fire thing and figure out what's going to happen."

Jake shrugged. "They don't want all of us, right?"

"Right. It's a lead singer gig."

Haley said, "But even if Blake does the tour, that doesn't mean the end for Ace in the Hole. We can discuss options. See what you guys want to do. I'd be willing to help in any way I can." She glanced around and spotted a picnic table a short distance away. She pointed to it. "Would you want to go sit over there and talk about it?"

The guys agreed and they all made their way over to the table. Once they were settled in, Blake said, "I'm torn because although I really want to take the opportunity with Frontier Fire, I don't want to let you guys down. I don't want to abandon the band just when our future is looking bright. We're a team and you're my brothers. You guys know that, right?"

Robbie said, "I have to say that if Frontier Fire or Radley Ray or any of the superstars offered me a drummer job, I'd drop you two like a hot potato." He delivered the line with a straight face and after a moment of silence, the men all started laughing. Haley glanced over at Helen who was chuckling as well.

"No, seriously," said Jake, "we understand, Blake. You're a talented singer. You can't turn this down. You'd be crazy if you did."

Blake looked at the table. "I appreciate you guys saying that. I really want to do it. I think it'll be a blast. But more importantly, it might lead to something in our future. More opportunities."

"Yep. Because the fans are going to love you."

"And it's short-term. Five months or less. It's not a permanent job," Haley explained.

Jake and Robbie looked interested. "Really?"

"Yep, just till Josh Lakely recovers enough to take over as lead singer of the band. In fact, Blake and I had discussed the possibility of selling

Ace in the Hole CDs on the Frontier Fire merchandise table. If they want him bad enough, we can make it a contract point."

"Wow. That's great," Robbie said.

"I guess my main question for you guys is, do you want to give Ace in the Hole a break while Blake's gone, or do you want to find a replacement singer?"

Their responses were almost in unison. "No break." "Replacement."

Blake reached out and put a hand on each of his friends' necks. "I can't tell you what your support means to me. I really can't."

"Make us proud, buddy," said Jake.

"Just make sure you come back," said Robbie.

THE MONDAY MORNING following the Battle of the Bands, Haley went back to work at the community college. She'd cursed when her alarm went off this morning, and she snoozed one too many times. Dragging herself out of bed and into the shower, she hoped for a miracle wake-up cure. Unfortunately, it didn't happen, and she ended up rushing to her desk twenty minutes late.

She tried to immerse herself in her responsibilities, but her mind was on all the work she had to do to get a new temporary lead singer for Ace in the Hole, as well as get Blake ready for his big-time tour. She'd always enjoyed helping new students at the community college. She'd always enjoyed helping the Admissions reps. But her heart wasn't in it anymore.

The middle of the afternoon lag hit, and she leaned back in her chair and took just a moment to close her eyes and rest her mind.

"Haley? Are you all right?"

Her friend Carly's voice wormed into her consciousness and she jumped. She opened her eyes and glanced at the time on her computer. "Oh my gosh Carly. I've been sleeping at least twenty minutes."

"Sleeping? You poor thing, are you sick?"

Haley stood and shook one leg, then the other to get the blood flowing again. "No, not sick. Just exhausted. I'm working so many hours with the band, I'm not getting good rest anymore." She hadn't even filled her best friend in on the developments of the weekend. She'd decided to work through lunch since she'd shown up so late this morning. "You just won't believe all that's going on with the band. It's so exciting. But exhausting too."

"You're worrying me. Why don't you go home and rest?"

Haley shook her head, then stretched her arms out and shook them too. "Because I'll be tired tomorrow too. I can't go home and sleep every time I'm tired. I have to just push through it."

Carly frowned. "Don't make yourself sick."

That's when an idea came crashing into her brain like a fireworks display. "It's time to quit this job."

"This job? As in your full-time career job? Or quit the band side job that doesn't pay you anything?"

Haley sat and motioned for Carly to sit in her side chair. "Look, I know you're building a future here while you get your degree. This job will be a stepping stone to your career in education and administration. I'm happy for you. But that's not me." She gestured to her domain, her receptionist desk, her phone. "It's never been like that for me. I'm not interested in getting my degree. I don't want to build a career here. I'm here because I need something productive to do and this place is as good as any."

As soon as the words came out of her mouth Haley knew Carly wouldn't understand. Although Carly was a dear friend, Haley had never confided in her about her reality, her family's reality. Her parents' low expectations of her. Her parents knew she would never get a degree and run the family business. She was the black sheep of the Wither-spoon legacy. Her brothers had all done what their parents expected; the business was well taken care of. Her parents were happy that she was simply living her own life and taking care of herself. They didn't expect success or achievement from Haley.

Having grown up with that view of herself, Haley lived up to those low expectations her high-achieving parents had set for her. Just barely, no more.

Why bother to kill herself working hard in a career that meant nothing to her? When she lost interest, which she always did, she'd quit and do something else. Her parents' payroll would help her pay the bills and live the life of comfort that she always had. It was a nice arrange-ment she had with her parents, as long as she didn't become lazy and didn't cause them any trouble.

But Carly didn't have that luxury. Carly was a hard-working young woman who had goals in life. No one had handed her anything. Every-thing she'd achieved in life, she earned because of her own sweat and effort.

She tried to explain without telling Carly her entire life story. "I feel like after being mediocre at everything my entire life, I've finally found something I'm good at. I'm good at managing this country band."

Carly grinned. "Yes, you are. You've done so much to help them succeed."

"This weekend we won the Battle of the Bands in Hilton Head against a dozen other bands."

"Congratulations!"

"But even bigger than that, Blake was asked to sing lead on the con-cert tour for Frontier Fire."

Carly's hands shot to her mouth, her eyes wide. "Oh my gosh Ha-ley! That's huge! That sounds like his big break."

Haley nodded, tears forming in her eyes. "And he wants me to be his manager. He wants me there alongside him at every stop, taking care of the details, while simultaneously managing Ace in the Hole as they perform their schedule without him."

Carly paused. "Sounds like a big job."

"Yeah. Not a job that I can do while working here every day."

"Wow. You've got a monumental decision to make."

"I think I've made it."

Carly stood and pulled Haley in her arms. "I'm going to miss you, girl. You're such a bright spot in my days here. But you need to follow your passion. And I think you're right. I think you've found your niche."

As she hung on to Carly, Haley vowed to never forget what this felt like. This was that feeling that others had described, when they knew what it was they were meant to do in this life. When they quit treading water and discovered their purpose. She'd found it. She just needed to believe in herself.

BLAKE HEADED SOUTH on Ocean Highway, his car windows rolled down and the hot summer breeze of Myrtle Beach lifting the locks from his forehead. Excitement filled his heart, brought on by all the life changes that had bombarded him lately, and he could barely wipe the grin off his face.

Life had changed, big time, and all the changes were good. His relationship with Haley. Not only did he manage to find a beautiful, sweet, wonderful girl that he enjoyed spending time with, she had been the instigator of all this professional change. Almost overnight, she'd taken Ace in the Hole, a small-town cover band who only played in Myrtle Beach, to a mid-level band drawing crowds up and down the seaboard.

Not only were they an "award-winning band," he was now going to get a taste of the big time. He couldn't think of his upcoming opportunity without adrenaline and excitement shooting through all his limbs. He knew they'd earned it, they'd worked hard and deserved it. But it was Haley who'd gotten them here. He owed her so much.

He pulled into the driveway of his aunt's house in Murrells Inlet, jumped out of his car and ran up to the front door, holding the Hilton Head trophy in both his hands. He knocked quickly and opened the door. "Anyone home?"

He heard a rustling in the kitchen towards the rear of the bungalow, then, "Back here! Come on back!"

He walked through the tiny house and found Aunt Gloria making sandwiches, and his brother Brent sitting in his wheelchair. "Hey, guys," he greeted.

"What is that?" Aunt Gloria exclaimed, rushed over and grabbed the trophy out of his hands. She read the engraved plaque, "Winner of the Hilton Head Battle of the Bands, Ace in the Hole! Congratulations!" She put the hulking trophy on the kitchen table, then pulled him in for a hug.

"Nice job, man," said Brent.

"Thanks, yeah, it was a lot of fun."

"Want a sandwich?" Aunt Gloria held up one that she'd just made for Brent. The stacks of lunch meat and cheese sat on the counter.

"Sure." He reached for the plate she was handing over the counter. He placed it on the table, then gripped the handles of the wheelchair, pushing Brent into place. "That about right?"

"Yep." Brent leaned forward and picked up the sandwich. "Aunt Gloria's specialty." He put the thick stack in his mouth.

Soon Blake had one of similar size in front of him, and Aunt Gloria joined them at the table with her own plate. Blake filled them in on the Battle of the Bands and they shared his thrill for the win.

"Oh, before I forget." Blake pulled a check out of his side pocket and handed it over to Aunt Gloria. "My portion of the winnings, I want to donate to Brent's college tuition."

"Aren't you sweet?" Aunt Gloria accepted the check casually, then unfolded it and took a look. "Blake! What? No. This is too much."

Blake gestured for her to keep it. "No, it isn't. The band's doing really well right now and I want to help out as best I can."

Brent pressed a closed fist against Blake's shoulder. "You always help out. I can't thank you enough, bro."

"No need. When you're a computer programmer making lots of IT dollars, you can support both Aunt Gloria and I."

Brent laughed.

"This'll be enough for all of next semester," Aunt Gloria said, wiping a stray tear from her eye. "You're a good boy. Thank you."

Blake dismissed her thanks with a wave of his hand. "In fact, something else big happened in Hilton Head."

Aunt Gloria looked interested. "Something else besides winning the contest?"

"Yeah. I got discovered. You know, like you hear about in those crazy once-in-a-lifetime stories."

"What do you mean?" Brent asked, a smile forming on his face.

Blake shared the news about being asked to sing in the Frontier Fire concert tour, amidst the cheers, back slaps and hugs from his family.

"I am so happy for you, Blake," Aunt Gloria said. She pulled him into a tight hug and whispered in her ear. "Your parents would be over the moon proud of you."

A stab of tears threatening his eyes surprised Blake. But today was not a day for tears. It was a day of celebration. A day of blessings.

Overcome with emotion, Aunt Gloria released him and went to the kitchen. "Drinks, anyone?" she croaked, trying to control her voice. Blake looked over at Brent and winked. His brother watched her, amusement etching his expression.

"Yeah, I'll take a Coke if you have it," Blake called.

"Coming right up."

While she bustled about pouring his drink, Blake focused his gaze on Brent. He'd stopped eating and was beaming his pride for Blake on his face.

"You deserve every bit of this success. You're hardworking and a great musician. Congratulations."

Blake took a seat near Brent and pulled him close so that their arms touched. "Thanks. I'm really excited. It's hard to believe."

They sat quietly until a few moments later, Blake looked over at Brent. He was surprised to see his brother struggling with emotion. He leaned closer. "You okay, bro?"

Brent shook his head. "I'm just grateful to both of you for all the help. I feel so guilty sometimes. Aunt Gloria's life would've been so different if, you know."

"I know. But she loves you, and me, and I doubt if she would want it any other way."

Brent shook his head. "It's not fair."

Life's not fair, Blake thought, but it was a cliché Brent had heard a million times, so he didn't say it out loud. Families weren't always dealt a fair hand, but it was best to bond together and make it work.

Aunt Gloria returned with the drinks and they all dug into their lunch together. Blake regaled them with his story about the Battle of the Bands and the little house was filled with love and laughter.

Chapter Nine

WITH HER MIND MADE up about quitting her job at the college, Haley knew she'd have to go talk to her parents. In person, better than on the phone. She braced herself for a confrontation. No, they wouldn't be angry at her for quitting yet another job. They expected that from her. But they would assume the worst, that she was quitting the job because she had no ambition, no goal in life.

What she'd have to make them see is that she'd finally found one, and it was managing Blake's music career. They wouldn't make it easy, they wouldn't be happy for her, they wouldn't believe this was a career worth pursuing. And yet, she'd need to try to make them understand.

She placed a call on her cell phone as she drove home for the day. Celeste, her parents' home assistant, answered.

"Hi, Celeste, it's Haley. Is my mom around?"

"Hi, Haley. Yes, she's out on the patio. Let me get her for you."

Haley waited while Celeste crossed the massive main floor on her way out back. The patio was also large, and housed the outdoor kitchen, lounging circle, firepit, and further down a couple stone steps, a swimming pool.

"Hello, dear!" Her mother's voice came on the line, along with some splashing sounds. She imagined her mother was floating around while reclined on a raft.

"Hi Mom. How's it going?"

"Just fine. It's so warm today I needed a cool down. I'm in the pool with a cold drink."

Haley smiled. Her mother sure knew how to live. She admired her zest for the good things in life. "Are you guys free tonight? I wanted to stop by."

"Absolutely! Come on by and we can get caught up. I'll have Celeste add another dinner plate."

Haley wasn't sure if she'd feel like eating after the bombshell she was about to drop. Maybe she'd wait till after she'd digested a good meal to break the news. "Okay, Mom, see you soon."

She went home first to change into fresh clothes, re-do her makeup, run a brush through her hair, then she got back into the car to drive to her parents'. At the secured gate, she leaned out to the keypad and entered her private security code, then continued to the circle drive in front of the estate. She hadn't lived in this mansion since she was eighteen when she moved out in favor of her own, smaller place.

She parked and walked to the front door. A huge bouquet of freesias in the foyer made her bend and place her nose amidst the blooms, breathing in the delicious aroma. She headed past the kitchen and out the back. Her mother was no longer in the pool. She must've gone upstairs to change. Haley walked back inside, helped herself to a bottle of water from the fridge, and settled into a sitting room couch.

When her mother bustled into the room, the entire air space altered. Mom's signature scent, which she'd squirted from a bottle with her own name on it, filled the air, along with a crackling energy that her extrovert mother always exuded. She glided over to where Haley was sitting, and as Haley came to her feet, her mom enveloped her in a warm embrace. She ended with a peck on Haley's cheek before she moved on.

"Daddy was thrilled to hear you were coming for dinner. How long's it been?"

"A while. I've been really busy," Haley said.

The man himself entered the room, having changed from his work clothes, which Haley was quite certain was a dark suit, white shirt and red tie. He now wore a respectable golfing outfit – khaki knee-length shorts and a tucked in golf shirt made from a fabric that gobbled up sweat without ever leaving a wet mark, and an insignia on the breast pocket from some prestigious golf course or another. It didn't really matter which one – she was sure her dad had played at all of them.

"Hi Daddy." She was still standing from her mother's greeting, so she spread her arms to her dad's hug before sitting again.

"Hi cupcake. Great to see you. You look wonderful." He placed a strategic kiss on her forehead.

Her appearance was something her parents always complimented her on. She looked good, in their opinions; that never wavered. But give them something more meaningful, such as her brains or her ambition or her accomplishments. Evidently, nothing worth complimenting there.

"Did you bring your suit?" her dad asked, jabbing a thumb in the direction of the pool.

"No, I didn't."

He circled to a wet bar on the far side of the sitting room and made himself a hard liquor refreshment. "Would you like anything?"

"No thanks, Daddy."

Dad sat next to Mom on the couch and Haley couldn't help but think for probably the one hundredth time what a lovely couple they made. They had both aged well, exercised, and they still looked healthy and young as ever. Her mother put effort into her looks, even extending so far as facial cosmetic surgery to maintain her good looks. Dad didn't, but his frequent golf and tennis outings kept his naturally slim body fit and strong. She wasn't sure how close their marriage was where it counted, but a couple things were evident. They were still together. And they looked good by the other's side.

A quiet pause ensued, and suddenly Haley knew she couldn't postpone her news until after dinner. No time like the present. "I have some news to share."

"Oh!" Her mother's excitement escaped through a rounded mouth. Whatever her mother was expecting, it surely wasn't this. "I have a new job that I'm really excited about."

"Oh?" her dad intoned.

"You know how I've been working part-time as a manager for the band? Well, the lead singer, Blake was just offered a fantastic new opportunity. He's going on summer tour for a much bigger and well-known band. And I negotiated the contract."

"Wow." Dad's one syllable was more than Mom offered, and his tone didn't sound particularly derogatory, so she went on.

"I need to not only find a replacement singer for Ace in the Hole while Blake is away, but Blake has asked me to manage him on tour. So, I really need to quit my job at the community college and concentrate on this."

Haley's mom tried to prevent an eyeroll and ended up with what Haley would describe as half an eye roll. "Honey, really? A band? What do you know about music?"

Suppressing a grimace, Haley took a moment to think about the question. Her mother didn't even comment on the fact that she was quitting her job with a regular paycheck and benefits. As a Witherspoon, Haley was insured by the family business, and received a supplemental stipend that outsized her salary at the college, so that she could live a life free of penny-pinching and scarcity. So, money and insurance weren't an issue.

No, her mother's concern wasn't the loss of a stable job. Her mother's concern was with what Haley had decided to do next. Haley was following a passion, even though the passion itself was fairly new.

"I don't know much about music, Mom, but my job as the band manager is more about marketing, advertising, scheduling, communicating and organizing. And I'm finding that I'm pretty good at that stuff."

Her mother lifted her shoulders in a shrug and painted a doubtful expression on her face. Dad spoke up, "Well, that's fine, honey, but I'm sure we could find you plenty of opportunities within the enterprise to use your new skills. You've always turned those opportunities down in the past."

Haley pulled her bottom lip in and chewed on it. She sighed. "Daddy, I don't have any interest in working within Witherspoon Enterprises, but I am having fun working with the band. And I'm doing well. I've made a lot of improvements and the band is making more money, getting more gigs, more visibility. The guys in the band are impressed with my skills."

Dad placed his glass on the table with a clunk. "Sweetheart, this is just another in a long line of examples. You have the tendency to follow your heart on every whim that presents itself without having a solid plan for your life. Let's see, you did nails for a while, you schooled to do hair until you realized you'd be on your feet all day. You worked in a clothes store for a while to get the retail discount. You worked at the college to see if you wanted to take classes yourself. Now you're a band manager. And you're twenty-five years old!" He let out an exasperated breath. "You have no direction, sweetheart."

"Maybe by all this trial and error, I'm finding my direction," Haley suggested. Had he ever thought of that? "You say I'm twenty-five years old, like that's old. That's young! I have lots of time to figure out my life and my career."

"You're not a kid anymore, Haley. Even with the flexibility that being a Witherspoon provides you, you can't keep drifting through life."

Is that what she was doing? Drifting from one job to another without having any real ambition for any of them? Well, if she thought about it without emotion, she could see why her parents thought so.

But that was only because she hadn't found her one true spot yet. But now. Now she'd found it.

At least she hoped she had.

"Look, I know I haven't followed the normal Witherspoon path. I didn't get a college degree and take over a division of the family business. Big business doesn't excite me. I don't want to get stuck in a career that I don't enjoy my whole life. But I've been experimenting. Will I be a band manager forever? I have no idea. But I really want to do this now. I finally found something that I'm not only good at, but I love it! I get such a kick out of coming up with a new idea, working on it, and seeing it through. I'm helping. Ace in the Hole has grown so much under my leadership. It's exciting." She gave her dad the smile that had served her well throughout her entire childhood, the smile she knew he couldn't resist. The convincing smile from his youngest daughter that always made him say yes.

"Well, sweetheart, I can tell that you're enthused about this."

He was about to give her his blessing. She knew him so well, and they'd been here so many times. Then, her mouth went into Autodrive and she had no idea why she said what came next.

"Besides, I think I'm in love with Blake and I know I can help him achieve his dreams."

Dad went speechless and his face shut down. "Who? What?"

Mom demanded, "This is about a boy?"

Haley blinked, recognizing her fatal error. She needed to turn this around, and quick. "Well, he's hardly a boy, Mom. He's a man. And yes, it's about the lead singer of the band, and how I feel about him. And I think he feels about me, too." Oh great, now she was babbling. She cursed herself internally. Why had she brought up love? Her parents had always been extremely protective of their fortune and was hesitant to allow any of their children to add to the family without intense vetting of the person involved. Where was her head?

"Look," she said, trying to get this back on track, "I shouldn't have mentioned being in love with Blake. Even though I think I am. But regardless, I have found a job that makes me happy, makes me feel accomplished and satisfied. And I'm doing a good job. I'd like your support, but I don't require it. I'm still going to follow it through. If it ends, or goes south, I can always find another job then. But for now, I'm doing this. With or without your blessing."

Dad cleared his throat and put his empty glass down heavily on the table. "In that case, you do it."

A whoosh of relief flowed through Haley. Until she looked back at her father. He was frowning, a crease marring his forehead. "You do it all by yourself. You want to make this work, make it work. Without Witherspoon Enterprises subsidy. It's time you grew up, little girl, and that means supporting yourself with your own labor and earnings." He strode to the door, then turned back to face her. "Go live your dreams. I wish you the best of luck."

The echo of his footsteps in the hall made her shudder.

Chapter Ten

BLAKE STOOD IN ROBBIE'S parents' garage, the band's normal rehearsal spot, but this time he was in there without his guitarist or his drummer. He held in front of him the inventory of songs he'd need to know for the Frontier Fire summer tour. He knew enough keyboard to be able to pound out the melody, but fortunately, he already knew almost all these classic songs. He'd listened to them over and over when he was a kid. Frontier Fire was one of the most well-known and beloved bands in the US, regardless of musical style. Everyone knew their songs by heart. Which is why he was faced with a challenge. He didn't want to perform them just like Josh Lakely would, a robo-tron copy of Josh up on stage. He wanted to make them his own. But he didn't want to drift too far from Josh's interpretation, either. These fans weren't here to see him, Blake Scott. They were there to hear the familiar, perfect songs from their favorite band.

Quite a dilemma to find a balance.

Haley sat in the corner of the garage on a barstool with her laptop. She was tapping away, doing something, working her magic like she always did, while also supporting him and listening. He was so happy she'd agreed to come with him on the tour. She'd keep him sane in an ocean of uncertainty. She'd help his confidence and ensure that he performed well.

He pressed a palm down on the electronic keyboard, letting loose a jarring combination of notes. Haley looked up with a gasp. He laughed, soaking in those gorgeous green eyes that in some lights, reminded him of emeralds. "I'm done for the night."

"Are you ready for the rehearsal with the band tomorrow?"

"Yep. I know the songs. It'll be interesting to perform them with the instrumentals and back-up singers. Hear the whole thing come together." He pushed himself to his feet and reached a hand out to her. "Are you busy? Or do you have time to go somewhere with me?"

She gave him that sideways mouth curl that got his heart racing. "I'm all yours."

A shot of adrenaline ran through his body. He wished that was true, in every sense of the words. But for now, he'd be satisfied that her time and devotion, at least, were his.

"I'd like to introduce you to my family."

Her expression shifted to surprise. Neither had so much as spoken about their families. She recognized that this was big, and he was glad that she did. "I'd love to."

They jumped into his truck and while he drove, Blake figured a bit of an explanation was in order. "I want you to meet my Aunt Gloria and my brother, Brent. They're my family." He let that settle in while she nodded, then he added, "They're who's left of my family."

Haley darted a quick look in his direction. Her expression asked for more.

He cleared his throat. "I grew up in a pretty normal family, in a house with my mom and dad and little brother. Until I was sixteen and Brent was twelve. I was spending the night with a couple of buddies across town. It was the night after the final football game and we were celebrating a solid season." He paused and took a deep breath, because even though this was now a dozen years ago, it wasn't easy to talk about. "My parents' house caught on fire. No one ever figured out why."

Her hand on his arm was warm and welcome. "Oh, Blake!"

"It was a fast fire and for some reason, the alarm didn't sound. My dad was trapped and couldn't get out at all. He died upstairs. My mom and brother climbed out a window and jumped."

He paused for a moment. Funny how this story still had the power to bring him to his knees. He trapped a sob in his throat and stopped it before it escaped. He concentrated on the road. When he felt sure his voice wouldn't betray him, he went on. "Brent was paralyzed from his fall. He's now a paraplegic, from that day on."

"And your mom?" Haley whispered.

Blake blinked a few times, demanding control over the tears that threatened to erupt. "Mom survived the jump but died two days later of smoke inhalation."

"Oh my gosh, Blake," Haley cried and leaned her whole body across her seat into his right arm, trying to be close to him in their closed quarters. He pulled the truck to the side of the road. She wrapped her arms around him and pulled him into a tight hug. Seconds turned into minutes and they stayed silent, the chirps and calls of insects creating a symphony out the window. "I'm so sorry," Haley whispered into his chest. "I had no idea."

"It's okay. It was a terrible fire, and we paid a terrible price. But life goes on, doesn't it?" He savored the feel of her pressed against him. He caressed a hand through her hair. "My Aunt Gloria took us in. She raised us as best she could. Almost like a mother. She's awesome."

Haley pulled back to look into his face. He missed their contact immediately. "Did she have her own family?"

"No. She was my mom's sister. She was single."

"What a saint."

"You better believe it. An instant family with a teenager and a newly paralyzed kid, suddenly orphans due to a crazy accident. She didn't hesitate. She opened her heart and her home and took us in. It was incredible. Even when I was sixteen I fully recognized her sacrifice."

"She loved you."

"She sure did and does still. She and I have worked together to pay Brent's college tuition. He wants to be a computer programmer. That's a great job to do even with his paralysis. He's got full use of his hands, and of course, his brain." He smiled. "I'm proud of him for how he's handled this."

"Almost done?"

"Yeah, I think he has three semesters left. He's doing well."

Haley nodded.

Blake let a moment of silence go by and then he looked at her, a deep, intense gaze into her eyes. "Brent and I are very close. Like really, *really* close. I'd do anything for that kid. Not just to protect him from harm. I mean, I'd put my own safety on the line if I had to, to make sure he was safe. But I feel like it's my job to set him up for all the success and happiness he can have in life. He hasn't had an easy road."

Haley nodded. "Sounds like none of you have."

"But he lost so much. His parents and his mobility all in one night. I don't know," Blake shook his head. "He deserves as much help as I can possibly give him." He knew there was more he wanted to say, but he let it go there. "So," Blake said as he straightened in his seat and put the truck in drive again, "you know our story now."

"Thanks for sharing that with me. And for introducing me to them." She leaned over as he pulled onto the road and placed a gentle kiss on his cheek. "It means a lot."

Blake drove, trying to remember how many girls he'd ever introduced over the years to Aunt Gloria. With a smirk he realized the answer was none. Haley would be the first. He wondered what Aunt Gloria would make of that.

THE TINY LITTLE BUNGALOW Blake pulled his truck up to was adorable, a little shabby and Haley decided, right out of a fairy tale. She could imagine Snow White bounding out the front door, followed by her seven adoring dwarves. Blake honked his horn, then they both dropped out of the truck and headed for the front door, by way of the wooden ramp. Haley gave him a grin when he reached for her hand. Despite knowing their story, and knowing how much Blake loved his Aunt Gloria, she still felt a shimmer of nerves at the thought of meeting her.

A woman met them at the front door and opened it. Focused on Blake, she gave him a hug and welcomed him with warm words. Then she noticed Haley walking in behind him. "Oh, hello."

"Aunt Glo, this is Haley. She's the band manager I've been telling you about."

"Oh yes," Aunt Gloria said enthusiastically. "You've done wonders with Blake's band. Thank you so much." Aunt Gloria reached out a hand and they shook.

"But," Blake continued as they stopped in the front room, "she's not just our band manager." He shifted his head in her direction, blasted her the most heart-racing smile and wrapped an arm around her waist. "She's something special. To me."

Haley grinned. It was a little awkward as introductions went, but Aunt Gloria got his meaning.

"Oh! I see. Well, in that case, it's doubly nice to meet you, Haley." She stuck both arms out. "Would a hug be appropriate now that I know you're something special to my nephew?"

Haley nodded quickly, and they joined in a hug. "So nice to meet you." The words were inadequate since she now knew she was hugging a true angel on earth after what Aunt Gloria had done for her nephews, but there you go.

"Well, let's sit down and get to know each other a little bit." She raised her voice. "Brent! Come out front."

Moments later, the sound of wheels against the floor came to Haley's ears, followed by the sight of a young man in a wheelchair. He used his arms to operate the chair into the small room. Despite the tight space and the lack of electronic controls, he maneuvered to an open space beside the couch.

"Bro, this is Haley. Haley, this is Brent, my younger and much more immature brother. He idolizes me, so don't say anything derogatory about me. It could crush him."

Haley laughed. She knew about brothers, and the humor between them, considering she had three of them herself. "Hi Brent, so nice to meet you." She leaned from her spot on the couch and shook his hand.

"Hi Haley. And don't believe a word he says. It's actually the opposite. He wishes he could be like me, but the most he can hope for is a sad and disappointing, him." Brent had the same dark wavy hair as his brother, but instead of Blake's stunning blue eyes, Brent's were brown. He sat comfortably in his chair and his upper body was chiseled with lean muscle. The Scott good looks ran in the family, most definitely.

Blake said, "So, I think I've learned all my Frontier Fire songs and tomorrow, we go rehearse with the band."

Brent looked over at Haley. "Oh, *this* Haley! Sorry, I'm catching up. You're the one who's made all the magic happen for Blake's band over the last few months."

Haley felt the warmth of a blush take over her face, but she bathed in the praise. "I can't take credit for how good Ace in the Hole is. Blake and the guys took care of that themselves. But I just had a few ideas of how we could get them more visible, and sure enough, it took off like wildfire."

"You're too modest," Aunt Gloria said. "Ace in the Hole is one of many local Myrtle Beach bands who were all competing for space in the local bar scene. You actually got them up and out of that market. Blake's been traveling and performing and being seen."

"And now," Brent continued, "he's hitting the big time with Frontier Fire. Lead singer, man! We're so proud of him."

Haley saw how they both beamed at Blake, their pride for him evident in their expressions. A sage thought seeped into her mind. She was the one with the solid, traditional family; two parents who'd raised her, loved her. And they weren't proud of her accomplishments at all. She'd go so far to say she was an embarrassment to them, since she was living a life outside the mainstream, opposite of what they'd planned for her. Yet, despite whatever success she'd managed to achieve in her life, they'd shunned her. Cut her off from the family fortune, to teach her a lesson.

But look at this little family unit. Untraditional in every way. They'd faced many challenges. Unspeakable difficulties, with few resources to help them. Yet, they'd come to this point of their lives intact. Happy, loving, supportive.

And now, with their praise and thanks for her skills and efforts, they were including her in their inner circle. It felt good here. She'd never really known what it was like to soak in praise and confidence. She didn't want to give it up.

She tuned in to the happy conversation going on around her. Aunt Gloria rose and left the room, coming back with a tray of iced soft drinks, a bowl of chips and a jar of opened dip. The men dug in, and Haley lifted her drink and took a long sip.

Families. They came in all different sizes, shapes and combinations. But this was one she was glad she'd met. She could learn a lot from these people.

An hour later, after laughter, sharing the tour schedule, and a little bit about Haley's future plans for the band, the glasses and chip bowl were empty. Aunt Gloria stood and looked at Haley, gesturing. "Would you like to help me carry this stuff to the kitchen?"

"Of course!" Haley popped up and caught a wink from Blake beside her. Haley grabbed the glasses while Aunt Gloria took the tray with the food remnants. They walked only a few steps to the little kitchen, and Aunt Gloria opened the dishwasher.

"So nice to meet you, Haley. Thanks for coming over."

"I'm happy to be here. I have to admit it was a total surprise that Blake dropped on me earlier tonight. But after he told me your story, I am so honored to meet you. I hope I don't bother you by saying this, but you are a top rate human being."

"Oh gosh," Gloria said, dipping her head while loading the dishwasher. "Stop. Anyone would've done what I did."

"No, not anyone. Just someone generous and loving as you would've taken in two boys who'd just lost their parents, and one with a terrible medical battle to face."

"It did make life interesting, I'll say that. It wasn't easy. But we loved each other, and we worked through the hardships together. I'm happy to say that we are on the other side now. Life is pretty darn great." She stopped moving and reached out and held both Haley's hands. "But what I wanted to tell you is I appreciate all the help you've given to Blake. He's worked so hard to get to where he is, and you seemed like an answer to prayer to take him to the next level."

Haley stared. She was an answer to prayer? She'd never thought of herself that way. Especially not coming from this living angel on earth, Aunt Gloria. "You give me way too much credit."

"Nope. You may not realize it, but you've given Ace in the Hole a huge jumpstart."

Haley shrugged. "I'm so new to this band manager gig. I just went by instinct. I noticed gaps and tried to fill them. That's all."

"And you've done a great job. Thank you, on behalf of the band."

Haley giggled. "They've thanked me too. They're very appreciative."

Blake wandered into the kitchen. "Ready to get going?"

"Sure." She turned to Aunt Gloria. "So, *so* nice to meet you."

"Well, hopefully it won't be long till our next visit. Right, Blake?" She gave him an exaggerated stare and he chuckled.

"Yes, ma'am."

"Atta boy. Have fun, you two, and be safe."

On the way out of the house, Haley stopped at Brent's chair and put a hand on his shoulder. "It was a pleasure to meet you, Brent. How soon till school starts?"

His handsome face beamed a smile. "Summer session starts next week."

"Good luck."

He nodded and gestured a salute. "Hope we see you before Blake leaves on his tour."

They left, the door closing on the homey comfort inside. They walked to the truck. Settled in, Blake started the engine, then turned to face her, his right arm over the back of her seat. "You definitely won them over. They love you, I can tell."

Her heart filled with emotion. "I love them too. What an awesome family."

He nodded. "It's not your typical family, and we went through some really hard times. But I think God uses hard times to pull people closer together, and closer to Him, too. Brent and I often talk about how our faiths in God are stronger after the fire, than before."

It was a topic she wanted to hear more about, but not right now. She'd never really faced hardship in her life at all. Why would God save her from hard times, and load them on to Blake and Brent? It was a part of life she'd never really thought about. The thought was quickly brushed from her mind when Blake leaned close and laid his lips on hers, a soft, warm kiss, full of emotion. They kissed again, her heart picking up its pace. He smelled so good, and his lips against hers felt perfect.

He pulled back and she gazed into his expressive blue eyes. What was happening to her? Was she falling in love with this man who had launched a brand-new career opportunity for her? The man she'd given up her family fortune for? And was that a good idea?

It didn't matter. She was following her heart and doing what she felt was right. If it was wrong, she'd learn from it and adjust. But oh, what if it was right?

Chapter Eleven

"THANK YOU FOR YOUR time. We'll let you know," Haley said. The scruffy singer nodded, shook out his lean arms and legs and left without a word. His look was all wrong for a country band, with his classic rock tattoos covering his arms and neck, and his long hair and patchy beard. But his voice was the worst of the problems. She could imagine it singing Aerosmith or Led Zeppelin, but not modern country.

They sat on tall barstools in a row in Robbie's parents' garage; Haley, Blake, Jake and Robbie. The judging panel. Haley had advertised the auditions and scheduled them all over a few days' time. Today was the third day and their options were getting scarcer. How hard could it be to find a male singer in the Myrtle Beach area who had a strong, clear voice, a clean-cut look and charisma enough to front a band? There must be hundreds of them.

As they were finding out, it was hard. Way too hard.

Robbie let out a deep sigh after the singer had exited the garage and threw the scoresheet Haley had created up in the air. She watched as it drifted to the floor.

"Do you even want to share scores on this one?" she ventured.

"No."

"Nope."

Blake shook his head.

Haley slouched on her seat.

"How many are left?"

She glanced at the schedule. "Two more." They groaned. "But don't worry. We can find more. In fact, we could go to some local colleges and post the audition notice in their music departments. We haven't tried that yet."

"We're running out of time, Haley." Jake's bleak statement put all their fears into words. Blake's rehearsals with Frontier Fire were about wrapped up. He was leaving in less than a week. If they didn't find a new singer soon, they'd surely have to cancel some of their performances. And none of them wanted to do that. In addition to the lost revenue, it would most likely result in lost opportunity. Backing out at the last minute on a bar that schedules their entertainment months in advance would leave them with a black eye, at least with that particular venue.

"Well, maybe there will be a gem in the next two," Haley said with as much cheerfulness she could force. As if on cue, the three musicians glanced over at her with doubtful expressions but held back their comments.

About twenty minutes later, another singer arrived. At the sight of his cowboy boots, jeans and tight t-shirt, Haley was heartened. But the cowboy hat gave her true hope. As did the guitar case he held in his right hand. At least this guy was country. Now, could he sing?

"Howdy," he said as he strode into the garage. "This the right place for the audition?"

Haley slid to her feet and held out her hand to greet him. "Yes, it sure is. This is where Ace in the Hole does their rehearsing."

The singer looked around, eyebrows up, nodding. "Very nice."

"I'm Haley, the band manager." She made quick introductions of the band members. "We're looking for a temporary lead singer to replace Blake." She turned and pointed to him. "Blake's coming back, but he's got an exciting gig as lead singer for Frontier Fire for their summer tour."

"Really? Way to go, man." The singer pounded Blake on the shoulder. "I read about Josh Lakely getting injured. Pretty cool that a local talent gets to replace him. That's big time. I'm Sam Newton, by the way."

The guys murmured their greetings to Sam.

"So how long is this gig for?"

"Roughly five months. The band is Ace in the Hole, which is a modern country cover band. We have scheduled gigs, about three to four every week."

"Sweet."

"So, tell us about your experience singing country music, Sam," Haley said, emphasizing the word country.

"Sure. I started playing guitar in the sixth grade. As I was learning that, I realized I could sing. Surprise! By the time I was in high school I was doing some acoustic solo gigs at church, at parties, open mic nights."

Haley took notes on her scoresheet.

"I got my big break when I auditioned for a talent show in Nashville. Not a huge one, but big enough that they flew me there, all expenses paid for a month. It was sort of like American Idol, but it was local TV, not national. But for country artists, you can't do any better than Nashville. Anyway, I won the competition."

"Wow!" Haley exclaimed.

"That was about five years ago. It's opened up some opportunities for me. I even got a record deal. But nothing is a silver bullet. Right now, I'm married with a toddler and my wife got transferred to Charleston with her job. Since she pays most of the bills and provides our healthcare, I came too." He laughed. "This gig would be great timing for me because I have some solo bookings in Charleston starting in November."

Haley beamed at Blake. Now they were talking. This guy was a big step up from all the other singers they'd auditioned. He was a professional. He'd be good for the band. Of course, she was getting ahead of herself. They hadn't even heard him sing. But she had a good feeling about him.

"Well, we're glad you're here and we can't wait to hear you sing. Any time you're ready."

Sam pulled his guitar out, tuned it quickly and strummed a few chords. Then he launched into a popular Radley Ray song. Shivers went down Haley's arms at the sound of his voice. It had depth, it had personality and it had perfect pitch. Not to mention, with the guitar in his hands and his mouth held close to the mic, Sam was in his element. He embodied the part of a country singer.

Blake leaned close to her ear and murmured, "I'm glad the Frontier Fire guys didn't audition him. He'd have gotten it ahead of me."

Haley smiled and smacked his arm.

Sam modulated straight into a Jason Dean tune and they heard a new side of him, a slow ballad crooning about broken hearts and dreams. Sam nailed it.

They'd found their temporary singer. Now, Haley just needed to secure him.

When Sam finished the song, Haley turned her head to look at each of the band members, eyebrows up in question. "Would you like to hear anything else?"

"I'm good."

"Me, too."

"Sam, we like you. We need to make a decision pretty quickly here. If we come to an agreement on terms, would you be able to start next week?"

"Yep." He dug into his jeans pocket and handed her a business card. "This is my agent. He'll handle all the communications about the terms. I stay out of that." He gave her a 'good ole boy' smile.

"I'll call him right away," said Haley as she took the card. "Thank you for coming, and I think we're all hoping we can work this out. I don't mind telling you, you're our top candidate."

Sam tipped his hat brim. "Glad to hear it. Nice to meet y'all." He offered handshakes to the line. "And congratulations to you, man." He nodded at Blake. "Good night and hope to hear from you soon."

They all watched him stride out into the night.

TWO NIGHTS LATER, BLAKE got a call from Haley, requesting that he gather the band and meet her at the practice garage. She didn't sound happy. His stomach clenched.

Forty minutes later, the four of them met. They moved their barstools in a circle and sat facing each other.

Haley began, "I've reached out to Sam's agent and I've been talking with him for two days." She paused and sighed. "It's not great news."

The guys looked at each other and back at her. "He's not available?"

"No, he's available. But he's expensive."

"Tell us," Blake said, and took her hand. He appreciated her work in trying to get a replacement for him. He wanted her to know he supported her efforts, no matter what.

"When I first quoted a payment per gig to his agent, he laughed at me." She lifted her shoulders and let them fall. "Like, literally laughed. Then he gave me a number, except that number was double what I'd offered. We negotiated, and we finally got to somewhere in the middle." She sniffed and looked at all of them, one by one. "Not equally in the middle. Closer to where he started than where I started."

"But still lower than his original price," Robbie clarified.

Haley nodded. "I guess price negotiation is not one of my talents. I'm sorry, guys."

Blake rubbed her hand in both of his. "Don't be ridiculous. We know you did your best and we know it's 100% better than any of us could've done. Right, guys?"

They all murmured their agreement.

"So where did we end up?"

Haley shook her head. "We can't afford him."

Jake asked, "Even with the new rates we're getting?"

She shrugged. "The new rates are getting us closer. But my plan was to pay you and Robbie more than him, since he's new. And a stand-in for Blake."

Robbie said, "That's nice of you, but not necessary. We're already getting a raise due to the new venues on our schedule and more gigs. What if we split the pay equally among the musicians?"

Haley stared at him a moment, then slid to her feet, got her folder out of her bag and studied it. She pulled up her phone calculator and tapped into it. Then she shook her head. "No. I mean, by the time we pay for band expenses – gas, rooms on occasion – then I've still written in payment for me and Blake ..."

"Take me out of it," Blake said. "I'll be getting money from Frontier Fire. I don't need Ace in the Hole's money."

She looked at him, then looked back at the calculations and tapped a little bit more. "Me neither. Since I'll be accompanying you on tour, Blake, I'm on Frontier Fire's payroll, too." She used her pen to circle a number. She looked up. "Closer. But not quite there."

Robbie swore and came to his feet. He walked around the garage. "He'd do a great job. And he was by far the best one we auditioned. No one else came close."

Jake added, "And we have a gig in nine days. And he's available."

Blake said, "I'd hate money to be the stopping point if we're close." He glanced at her scribblings. "How close are we?"

Haley ran a palm over her forehead.

Blake had an idea. "Hey, I'll contribute part of my summer earnings back to Ace in the Hole."

Haley stared at him, motionless. "Seriously?"

"Of course. I'm still a band member and I want Ace in the Hole to succeed while I'm gone. I'm willing to pay to make that happen." He smiled and patted her on the back. "Work it up."

Haley went back to her figures and worked another half hour. At the end, everyone gave up a little. Blake and Haley gave up their portion of the band's profits. Blake donated a chunk of his Frontier Fire earnings. And Jake and Robbie agreed to earn less than one third of the band's earnings. Making Sam the highest paid member of Ace in the Hole, at least for the next five months.

It was a lesson in compromise and sacrifice, but they got to where Sam's agent wanted them to be.

When she realized she could make it work, Haley's eyes went wide. "You guys are amazing. I can't believe you're willing to pay Sam more than you're going to make."

"Hey Haley," Jake said, "we're used to being broke. It's only because of you that we're where we are today."

Blake added, "Who knows? Maybe with Sam in the lead, and me coming back with my Frontier Fire experience, Ace in the Hole will shoot to the big time later this year. Then, the sacrifice will be worth it."

Haley wrapped an arm around his neck and pulled him in for a kiss, while his bandmates whooped and hollered. "I'll call him and offer him the deal," Haley said with a beautiful smile, and marched out of the garage.

They watched her leave. "I have a good feeling about this," said Robbie. Blake nodded. He had a good feeling about all of it, and not just the band.

Chapter Twelve

THE LIMO PULLED TO the curb outside the airport and Randall, Frontier Fire's manager, turned to face the ten bodies inside.

"Okay team, just a reminder. I'll gather your ID's and get us all checked in, then I'll come back and get you and we'll go to the private room TSA has provided. We've gotten approved to go through Security as a group, separate from the masses."

The crowd murmured their approval, and Haley made a mental note. She was going to learn a lot about managing a band tour by observing Randall in action. Everyone handed over their drivers' licenses, and Randall paired them up with boarding passes, then he jumped out of the limo. Haley glanced back at the band members. Excited voices filled the enclosed space inside the limo, along with the occasional outburst of laughter. She turned to Blake, sitting beside her.

He squeezed her hand in his lap. "This is it."

She beamed a smile at him. "The day we've been working toward. You're going to be awesome."

He leaned close and rang his tongue over her ear. She gasped at the unexpected sensation.

"Hey now, you lovebirds. None of that since our significant others aren't here." One of the back-up singers, the one named Sophie, piped up. Haley saw that she sported a smile. She was being funny. The last thing Haley wanted to do was misstep on this big tour and do something to annoy the band. Blake, sure, he had some leeway to do whatever he wanted since he played an important role on this tour. But her; she was feeling a little inadequate and didn't want to make waves.

"Sorry!" she giggled.

Blake pulled her into his arms, so she was practically sitting on his lap. She resisted by pushing against his chest, but he retorted, "Just because your partners aren't here doesn't mean I can't love on mine."

Sophie laughed and pointed playfully at them and then turned her attention back to her conversation with her co-back-up singer, Max. Haley found her way back to her own seat.

"You okay, babe?" Blake's forehead frowned with concern as he studied her face.

Haley looked into those deep blue eyes and found her peace there. "Yeah, sorry. I'm feeling a little insecure here, that's all."

"Why? You belong here as much as I do. You got me the contract!"

She shrugged. "But you're the one with the singing talent. You're the one they want. And Randall is already here to manage the tour. I'm not sure I'm needed here as well."

Blake shook his head. "I need you here. I want you here. You're helping me deal with all this craziness. Got it?"

She lifted her chin so she could look into his eyes again. Lord, she loved the color, reminding her of a Husky dog's light blue. "Okay." She tore her gaze away from him and looked around the interior of the limo as they continued to wait. "I really need your help learning the names of all the band members. There're so many."

Blake chuckled. "Yeah. Way more than Ace in the Hole." He leaned closer and murmured in her ear. "Okay, starting to our right and moving counter-clockwise. That's Moose. He plays electric guitar."

Haley held back a laugh.

"Yeah. I don't know his real name, I assume it's not Moose, but that's what he goes by. He's got fire in his fingers. He's gotta be one of the best electric guitarists in the business. Next is Harry. He plays fiddle on some songs, and mandolin on others. He's not on every song, but he adds some great sounds when the song calls for it." He subtly pointed to the next man in the circle. "That's Ricky, the drummer. Easy enough. Then, Len. He plays bass guitar."

"You guys don't have a bass player in Ace in the Hole, right?"

"Right. We also don't have a full-time keyboard player, and that's the next person, Lola."

"Oh! I didn't realize the band had a female instrumentalist."

"Yep, Lola plays keyboards, then of course that takes us to Sophie and Max, the back-up singers. And there you have it. Frontier Fire."

Haley's head swam. She wondered if she'd ever remember the names, and what faces they belonged to. "You forgot one."

Blake's face showed that he knew her meaning.

"Blake Scott, the lead singer," she murmured. "Have you ever thought about how exciting it is for you to be here? I mean, think about this."

Blake snorted. "I can't think of anything else. I just hope I do the songs justice."

She reached and placed her lips on top of his. "You will. You do. I've heard the rehearsals. You sound fantastic."

He was about to respond when Randall returned.

"Okay, gang. We're all checked in. Let's move as a group to the TSA screening room."

They exited the limo. They were only exposed to the public inside the airport for twenty yards before they were again secluded, and in that short time, a dozen observant fans hooted and hollered with shouts of "Frontier Fire!" The experienced band members waved and smiled as they jogged after Randall. Haley held on to Blake's arm and they followed behind.

The plane ride to their first tour stop, Cincinnati, went smoothly. Fans recognized the more familiar band members, and occasionally engaged them in conversation. Moose or Harry would chat comfortably, most of the conversation centering around Josh Lakely's accident and what they were going to do without him on the tour.

On arrival at Cincinnati Airport, a limo whisked them away to the Downtown Hilton where they each had private suites reserved. Haley wheeled her suitcase into the luxurious room and looked around, flopped on the bed and let out a breath. Closing her eyes, she said a quick prayer, "Dear Lord, thank you. Thank you for all this. Never let me take this for granted. Help me to always remember to thank you for all the blessings in my life."

She let her mind drift to what she was doing prior to this huge shift. Working the nine to five grind at the office. An occasional night out. It was a decent life. But this was so much more exciting. Hard work at the community college meant answering phones and making photocopies. Her work here was so much more energizing, and she saw a direct link from her efforts to where they were today – on the first stop of Frontier Fire's concert tour. It was pretty amazing.

Her mind shifted to her dilemma with her parents. She hadn't dwelled on it since it happened because she'd been so busy with the band and she didn't want to be sad. But her parents had disowned her, was that the right word? She knew they were trying to teach her a lesson, to maybe teach her to appreciate the Witherspoon dynasty more than they evidently felt she had been. But to push her out of the family fortune? Was she still a Witherspoon, in their opinion? She'd always been somewhat of the black sheep in the family. She was the only one of her siblings who didn't go to college and go to work for the enterprise. Did that mean she was dispensable? She was their daughter, for goodness sake. It was that easy to push her out from under the family umbrella?

But she recognized the irony of the timing of their ejection. They were punishing her because she flitted from one interest to another without any true plan or commitment to her work. But look at her now. She was a successful band manager for Ace in the Hole, and she was accompanying her "client" Blake Scott on a top-notch concert tour. In her mind, that was pretty committed. Pretty successful. It was more than she'd ever accomplished before in her life.

Well. She would rise above. She would continue to work her hardest, to achieve results, to do well. And when she no longer needed her parents' assistance, she would prove that she was completely self-sufficient.

The feeling of acceptance in her heart made her optimistic. This was unusual for her. Because as much as her parents' punishment seemed ill-timed and incomprehensible, she was doing okay on her own. She was succeeding. And maybe that's exactly what they had in mind?

A knock on the door brought her out of her deep reverie. "Yeah?" she called while she scrambled to her feet.

"It's me," came Blake's voice.

She went to the door and opened it. He stepped into the room and pulled her into a tight embrace. Closing her eyes, she rested her cheek against his chest. He made a growling sound in his chest and the vibration tickled against her ear. She chuckled and looked up at him.

"Do you believe this?" His smile was like a sunrise lighting his face.

"No, I really don't." She tilted her head back and they joined lips. He caressed her cheek with one finger and she savored the shiver that ran down her spine, generated by his gentle touch.

They broke their kiss and stood silently for a moment. Then Blake said, "Randall wanted to meet us for dinner and go over some information about the first concert."

"Wow. Should we go then?"

He nodded with a smile and gripped her hand.

BLAKE WANDERED OUT from the green room backstage to stand directly behind the thick closed curtain. From here, he could hear the murmuring of the crowd without being visible to them. He stood alone in the dimness and let the crowd's energy revitalize him. He closed his eyes and drew deep breaths while he let their voices, their movements, feed him.

This was a technique he'd often used in his bar gigs, but tonight was taking it to a whole new level. There were ten thousand people out there! Nerves stabbed his system and his hands started to tremor, his breath no longer solid.

No. He couldn't allow his own weaknesses to steal this opportunity from him. He continued to breathe and concentrate on drawing energy from the crowd, and in his mind, he transitioned to saying a prayer to God: *help me, Lord. Give me strength. Don't let me blow this. Help me do well.*

Before long, the rest of the band members wandered out. He was ready. He was at peace. He was in good voice, and his nerves had settled. Moose, the electric guitarist, patted him on the back. "Have a good show, man," he murmured softly. On his way up the pedestal to the drum set, Ricky gave him a thumbs up. Blake hoped his face provided them with a feeling of confidence that he had this. He wasn't going to mess up their first tour gig due to his inexperience.

He was playing in the big leagues now and he was ready.

Once they were all in place, still hidden behind the curtain, the crowd's cheering shifted into overdrive. The energy level catapulted through the roof with loud screams and applause. Blake knew the slideshow featuring pictures of Frontier Fire in concert in their prime was playing on the screen, and then it moved into the current day band. The other band members were a little bit older and maybe a little bit grayer, and there was a short introductory section of Blake as the new lead singer. Nobody knew him, but they were Frontier Fire fans, so they were willing to give him a chance and accept him.

Before he knew it, the curtain started to rise, and the unencumbered wall of sound hit him full force. The lights wouldn't let him see individual faces, but he certainly got a feel for the massive crowd. The band members started playing one of the band's classic fast songs that was certain to whip everyone into a frenzy with its iconic opening bars and lyrics. Blake could probably sing this one in his sleep and he put a smile on his face and started singing on cue.

His amplified voice rose miraculously over not only the din of the crowd, but also over the instrumentals. He expected this – he knew it would be like this, but it amazed him that any little sound out of his mouth could be heard by ten thousand people. He finished the first verse and moved into the chorus. It seemed like all his audience was singing along with him. His heart pounded with the immensity of the moment. He'd asked if he could hold an acoustic guitar and the band agreed to allow him one, but not mic it. It was more of a prop so he'd have something to do with his hands. He strummed along, knowing it was not contributing to the phenomenal sounds they were producing, but doing so increased his comfort zone.

He finished the first song and the band modulated straight into the next. Yes, he knew this one too. Another fast song to keep the audience whipped up, on their feet, screaming and singing along. He flipped the guitar onto his back, grabbed the microphone off the stand and moved to one side of the stage. The fans cheered and reached out their hands, and he realized he could multi-task: sing, walk, bend over and give high fives, which resulted in ripples of pleasure from those he touched. The stage was set up with several walkways into different parts of the crowd – Randall had briefed him on all this last night – and as he gained comfort he moved to all of them. Tomorrow night, maybe he'd leave the guitar behind. He didn't need a prop to make him feel less awkward. He was living a dream and he wanted to make the most of it.

The second song ended, and it was time for him to talk to the crowd. His heartrate increased. Funny that he was more nervous about talking to ten thousand people than singing to them. But he walked back to the mic stand, secured it in and gripped it with both hands. "Hello everyone!" he yelled into the microphone. The crowd's volume increased as everyone responded back. "Thank you for coming tonight." He learned quickly that he needed to pause between each sentence to allow time for the rabid fans to quiet down or else they'd miss his next sentence. Good problem to have. "You guys are our first audience since coming out of hiatus. Thanks for being here!"

The crowd went wild at this news and eventually Blake could continue. "I'm Blake Scott, and no, I'm not the singer you normally see up here. I'm sure you've heard that Josh Lakely had an untimely injury and couldn't join the band on this tour. We're praying for Josh's recovery, so he can join the band just as soon as he's able." The audience cheered their approval. "Meanwhile, I'm honored to be singing all these classic Frontier Fire songs for you." The volume increased. Blake took it as a good sign that they'd heard him sing two songs and they were already cheering for him. Hopefully they were in good hands for a strong concert. "Happy to be here."

With that, the band took off on a favorite ballad, one where Blake could really string out the notes and showcase his voice. He saturated each and every note with his very best effort and lost himself in the song, while still playing to the crowd. Singing for a crowd of this size was an education he never could've anticipated, but he was going to take advantage of it.

After a few more songs it was time to talk to the crowd again, and he said a few words about how great it was to be on tour, and he introduced each of the band members along with where they hailed from. It was a script he'd memorized and he'd repeat on each of the tour sites. Then, back into more fantastic music.

They played for one hundred minutes solid, Blake operating on a rush of adrenaline. He'd prepared, sure, but he knew these songs like the back of his hand, due to being a fan for so long. When they reached the end of the long set list, he held up a hand, yelled, "Thank you, Cincinnati. God bless!" and they all ran off the stage.

They knew they wouldn't be back there for long. It was a game popular bands always played with their audiences. Let the fans yell and cheer for a while, then they'd return to stage for an encore, as if the audience had convinced them to come back. However, sometimes the band had saved one of their recent hits to sing on encore, so obviously, they always intended to come back.

Blake watched the more experienced band members gulp water, pound each other on their backs and celebrate a great show. All Blake had eyes for was Haley. She came running to him and almost knocked him over with her enthusiastic hug. "Great job! You sounded awesome. You were perfect. Just perfect."

He soaked it in, loving her praise, but he knew he wouldn't be completely convinced until Randall and the rest of the band gave him their critique. Meanwhile, he gripped her body against his and reveled in the best moment of his life.

A few minutes later, Ricky the drummer ran back out on stage, and the rest of them followed closely behind. Blake planted a solid kiss on Haley's lips and winked. "Have to go to work," he joked, and ran back on stage to greet the massive sounds of approval from their people.

Chapter Thirteen

THREE WEEKS NOW, THE Frontier Fire tour had been charging along. Every night the crowd was appreciative and enthusiastic, showing their support. Nights in hotels, meals in restaurants, days traveling either on the road or in the air, evenings on stage playing awesome hit songs. It was a dream come true for Blake, and he was working hard and doing well.

Haley made the conscious effort to enjoy every minute, to not take anything for granted. As much as she enjoyed the excitement, on the occasional free night, a sense of relief washed through her. She didn't know how Blake was keeping up the pace.

Thursday, the band had a night off in Savannah, Georgia. Their buses pulled in from Charleston about three in the afternoon and they were awarded with a blissful twenty-four hours of free time till tomorrow's sound check. Blake and Haley got settled into their rooms and then looked blankly at each other. What would they do with all this free time?

"How about we go explore Savannah and find some dinner later?" Blake suggested.

It sounded good to her. They dressed in comfortable clothes and headed out on foot. The hotel was located downtown, making it easy to walk to places of interest. They wandered and ended up in Forsyth Park. Cobblestones covered the walking paths, oak trees covered with Spanish moss shaded their journey.

After spanning the park they walked through the historic section of the city. "Look at that mansion," Blake commented, and they walked over to read a bronze etched plate. "It's antebellum architecture, built in 1850."

"Wow," murmured Haley. Her imagination conjured up women in hoop skirts descending the stairs of the mansion, out into the front yard to climb into horse-drawn carriages, summoned to take them to cotillions and parties. "I wonder if it was any cooler around here back then."

"I doubt it. And just think, no air conditioning."

They moved on and observed more historic homes, then noticed a horse-drawn carriage riding by on the street.

"Want a ride?" Blake asked as he took her arm and tucked it in the crook of his elbow.

"Actually, I'm loving this," Haley said. "Just walking with you, enjoying the scenery, exploring this beautiful city. I can't imagine anything more perfect." She wondered if the love she felt for him was evident on her face as she gazed up at him.

In a few hours they were starving. Blake hailed a cab and told the driver to take them to one of his own favorite restaurants. The cabbie nodded and drove them straight to The Grey, a restaurant housed in a renovated Greyhound bus depot from the 1930s. Inside, Haley gazed up at the skylight casting spots of sun on the floor. The décor was art deco, and the open kitchen was refurbished from an old cinema ticket booth.

"I love this!" Haley said with a smile, her heart light.

They sat and ordered clams as a start, and whole roasted trout as their entrées. They enjoyed a leisurely meal and talked easily about the tour, stories about the concerts they hadn't had a moment to share with each other. Like the concert in Lexington, Kentucky when a woman standing in the mosh pit directly in front of the stage held a baby up in the air as Blake strode by, hoping he'd lift the baby onto the stage.

"What? I don't remember that at all!"

"I know, you didn't see the baby. Good thing you didn't, really. Can you imagine if you accidently dropped or hurt the baby?" Haley said. "Imagine the liability."

Blake's brow furrowed as he thought. "Who would bring an infant to a big concert? Couldn't the baby get jostled? And think how loud it is in there. Couldn't that be damaging to a baby's ears?"

Haley shrugged and smiled. "Like I said. I'm glad you didn't see her. You probably would've felt like you should lift the baby up. At the very least it could've thrown you off, distracted you from your lyrics."

"It takes all kinds, huh?" Blake took a long sip of his lemon water. "But in general, Frontier Fire fans are fantastic. So supportive and positive."

"Oh, that reminds me. Randall has agreed to put out some Ace in the Hole merch on the sales tables at the shows."

"Great. That might give some visibility to us. Drive some traffic to our shows."

Haley directed a fond eye to Blake at his comment. Even though he was in the big time right now, he still referred to Ace in the Hole as "us." He was still a member of the team and had their best interests at heart.

They wrapped up their dinner with a shared slice of apple pie, then decided to walk the calories off. It was mid-evening; the sun had gone down but since this was a tourist district, the streets were well lit as they strolled. Twenty minutes later, something caught Haley's eye. "Oh my gosh. I can't believe this."

"What?"

She grabbed his arm and pulled him across the street to face a bar. "Look," she said, pointing at a banner in the window.

Blake read it, "Tonight: Ace in the Hole, country cover band." He turned to her with a grin.

"It didn't even dawn on me to check Ace's schedule tonight. How cool that our night off puts us in the same city as their gig?"

Blake took her hand and guided her into the bar. It was close to nine, and that was most likely the time they started. Having been in hundreds of bars, Blake located where the band would be hanging out backstage. A quick knock on the green room door and they opened it.

"Dude!" yelled Robbie.

"Blake!" yelled Jake.

Even Sam looked happy to see them both. "What are you guys doing here?"

"Frontier Fire plays here tomorrow night. We have tonight off," Blake explained with a wide smile.

Haley said, "In fact, are you guys still here tomorrow night? I could get you all free tickets to the concert." Being able to offer them free perks made Haley's heart feel good.

"That'd be awesome!"

"You going on soon?" Blake asked.

"Yeah, you want to sing lead?" Sam asked with a chuckle.

"No, man. I want to hear you sing lead."

Sam feigned a stab to his chest. "Aw, no pressure there, huh?"

Haley and Blake pulled the small band into a circle and they formed a group hug, then made their way to the door. "Have a great show, guys. We'll catch up with you afterward." They made their way back out to the bar and found a table in the corner with two open stools. Haley looked around. Now she remembered. She'd found this place online and booked the band here. It was a pretty good-sized bar with a big crowd and a decent stage along one wall. The band equipment was all set up. She glanced around the crowded room and estimated that about five hundred people were here, ready to be entertained.

Ace in the Hole took the stage and launched into the set list, starting with a rowdy favorite by Bentley Dirks. They had strategically placed this song at the start because of its probability of getting the crowd riled up. It worked. Sam sounded great and Haley had to admit, he looked good too. Fronting a band required a great voice, but so much more. Charisma, good looks, charm. All those qualities were necessary to engage the audience, and Sam had it all. She smiled over at Blake. She knew he'd recognized it too. Mixed emotions blended on his face. Euphoria that the band was doing so well. Nerves that Sam was giving Blake a run for his money.

A waitress walked by and they ordered drinks, ready to settle in for a fun night.

AFTER MIDNIGHT, ACE in the Hole wrapped up with their finale, a slow beloved ballad by Brook Garthson. They had kept their big audience engaged through the whole show, and the fans now sang along, their voices blending as the instrumentals quieted. For a few bars, the audience sang *a capella*, no instrumental accompaniment at all. Blake's lips curved into a smile. Effective technique to end the show. The audience enjoyed the solid block of vocal sound of their own creation and started cheering at the serene resonance. Five hundred disparate voices combining as one at this moment to form beautiful music.

It sent chills down Blake's spine.

Being a member of the music community. Combining lyrics and tunes together that spoke to people's hearts, that described their lives, that entertained them. It was a worthy occupation. It was worth all the effort. He let his thoughts transform into a silent prayer of thanksgiving to his Creator.

When the show ended and the crowd slowly cleared out, Blake and Haley approached the stage. Blake held out a hand to Sam. He grabbed it and with his other, pulled his cowboy hat off and used his bent arm to wipe the sweat off his brow.

"What do you think, boss?" Sam asked with a tentative grin.

"I think you're awesome. You sounded great up there." Sam pulled Blake up onto the low stage and into a manly embrace. Robbie and Jake made their way over and pounded Blake on the back.

"Great job, everyone." Haley joined them. "Blake and I had fun listening and obviously so did this big crowd."

"Good. Despite what social media is saying," said Sam with an ironic tone.

Blake frowned. "What do you mean?"

Robbie said, "We seem to have a hater or two who's spreading garbage about us all over the internet."

Blake turned to Haley. She blinked. "After you guys pack up, can we go talk somewhere? I want to hear about this."

They agreed to meet at Blake and Haley's hotel in thirty minutes. They took the time to walk through the now-cool city streets and clear their heads. Settling into the couch on one end of the spacious lobby, they didn't have long to wait before the guys had finished their tear down and driven over.

Robbie pulled a laptop out of his bag and tapped on the keys. "Read the comments," he said and handed it over to Blake. Haley leaned in close. Robbie had pulled up the Ace in the Hole website. The way she'd designed it, fans could leave comments on the bottom of the home page. A dozen or so comments had been written, spanning over the last two weeks. Blake read them silently, and he knew Haley was reading them too from the gasps coming from her mouth.

"Ace in the Hole's new singer sucks. Bring Blake back."

"Ace in the Hole used to be my favorite cover band. What happened to them? They don't entertain me anymore."

"Blake Scott thinks he's a hot shot touring with Frontier Fire. What a loser to leave Ace in the Hole in the lurch. A band manager with the band's best interest at heart would've never allowed him to leave."

There were more, with increasing levels of vitriol. Blake closed his eyes and decided he'd gotten the gist and didn't need to read each and every one. Beside him, Haley's arm was shaking. She was reading to the bitter end. When Haley flopped herself back, he closed the laptop and handed it back to Robbie. All were silent.

"Well, that was uncalled for," Haley said, her voice distraught.

Jake snickered. "You could look at it this way. A band isn't a true band until they start getting criticism." He looked at Robbie. "We're not that worried about it."

Robbie nodded. "It's not affecting our crowds. I mean, look at tonight. Full house, and they were all having a good time. Most of them stayed through the last set."

"But this is outrageous!" Haley spit. Blake looked at her. Her wide eyes and flaring nostrils revealed her outrage. "This is what I hate about the internet. Anyone with a wi-fi connection can go anywhere and post nasty reviews and hide behind anonymity. It's cowardly. How come no one is coming up to any of us and telling us this to our faces?"

Jake shrugged. "Because this is a minority opinion. We play to a couple thousand people every week. How many bad reviews are there, ten? Twelve? It's nothing to worry about."

"Well," Haley said, "I can do something right now." She grabbed the laptop and started tapping on keys. "I designed the webpage to be able to leave comments. Guess what?" She hit a button with a flourish. "Gone."

Blake gave her a questioning look.

"No more comments. It's closed down."

He studied her, and the emotion playing havoc on her features. She was really taking this thing hard. "That was a little impulsive."

She gave an exaggerated shrug. "I'm the webmaster. I decide what goes on the website. And I don't want that garbage on there." She slammed the laptop shut and handed it to Robbie. He winced as he took it. "I promise to stay more in touch with your tour and what's going on. I should've been on top of this. I'm sorry."

Robbie shrugged. "That's not why we showed you. We weren't pointing blame at you at all."

"No, but I'm still your manager. I have time during the day when I'm with Frontier Fire to work on your stuff too."

"I'm not sure there's anything you can do about random internet comments, Haley," said Blake. "Don't stress."

She stood and faced them all. "We worked hard to get where we are today. I refuse to let some internet trolls ruin it for us." She puffed out a pent-up breath. "Now, if you'll excuse me, I'm going back to my room."

They all watched her leave, then after a moment of silence, Sam said, "She's pissed."

Blake nodded. "Yeah. I just hope she doesn't think she can fight a losing battle."

"She's taking it personally," Robbie said.

Blake's heart ached for her. He'd developed somewhat of a thick skin over the years as a performer. It wasn't easy, and it wasn't fun. Every bad review used to peel away at his confidence. But he eventually realized; as much as he tried, he'd never please everyone. Performance was subjective, and criticism was a part of this business. Haley had never really faced that reality before. It killed him that she was dealing with this pain because of him.

"Look guys, I'm going to check on her." Blake stood. "Despite this blip, we really had a great time tonight, and you guys sounded solid."

After saying their good-byes, he made his way to the elevator, then tapped his knuckle on Haley's door. Waiting a moment, he tapped again. "Haley?"

A small voice came from inside the room. "Yeah."

"Let me in."

"I – I just want to be alone right now, Blake."

He rested his forehead on the door and ran his hands over the wood. "I won't bother you for long. I just want to make sure you're okay." Another pause, and he said, "Come on, babe."

A rustling on the other side of the door, and finally it inched open. Mascara-stained cheeks and teary eyes were visible through the strip of light between the door and the frame. Protectiveness flared inside him and he pushed the door open, startling her. He pulled her into his arms. He shushed her, striving for a calming presence. The tension in her shoulders eased gradually.

"I know I'm ridiculous for taking this so hard," she murmured into his chest. She pulled back to look at him. "But I have to make this right." She stepped into the room and he followed her, letting the door close behind him.

She walked to the desk where she had opened her own laptop.

"Those comments are gone from our website, and you blocked all others. It's done."

She looked at him with wide eyes, head shaking. "No, it's not. Look at this."

He stepped behind her and looked. She'd pulled up the website of the bar Ace in the Hole had played at tonight. She jabbed an index finger at the comments there. He read quickly and saw that five negative reviews had come in prior to the concert, urging people not to come see Ace in the Hole perform. Another ten came in after the show, with derogatory comments. He sought her gaze. "What the heck? They had a full house. Hopefully nobody read those."

"They did. Look, each negative comment was marked helpful." She scrolled through them, validating her comment. "I looked at all these email addresses to make sure they weren't the same person posting multiple times. They're all different."

A flush of nausea formed in Blake's stomach.

"And look at this." With a few taps, Haley brought up Ace in the Hole's summer schedule. "Next stop is in Charleston. Here's the venue's website." She clicked on the link and brought it up. She scrolled to the bottom of the page to the comments. She pointed. Several negative comments had already been posted there regarding the band.

Blake stepped backwards toward Haley's bed, flung himself onto it and scrubbed his hands over his face. "This is crazy. What the heck is going on?" Just when life was absolutely perfect and couldn't get any better, this thing came out of left field.

"I do have an idea."

Blake sat. "Tell me."

"It almost seems like someone is trying to sabotage Ace in the Hole. Someone is trying to spread the word that the band sucks and isn't worth seeing. Someone who is not happy about our success and growth. Someone who has an ax to grind."

"Yeah, you're right. But who ...?" He flew to his feet. "Lindsay?"

Haley nodded her agreement so fast he feared a neck injury. "That's what I'm thinking. And I wouldn't put it past her, that crazy witch."

Blake considered, nodding slowly. "It does seem to be her MO. But all those different email addresses."

Haley shrugged. "You can open all the email addresses you want from the free sites, Gmail, Yahoo, as long as they're not previously taken. She could've created a dozen email addresses, used each one to leave a nasty review, then used the others to Like or support the comments. Making it look like they're all legit."

"So, it's feasible that she did it. But ... why? Why would she go to all the trouble?"

"Other than being a vindictive wench who is out of control, I don't know. But you can bet I'm going to find out."

Blake stared. "Promise me you won't go see her by yourself. Do not engage with her. She's a crazy woman." And she could be dangerous, he thought but didn't want to put into words.

She looked at him intently and finally nodded. "I want to shield you from this. You need to concentrate on the tour."

"No way. We're a team. Honestly, I think we need to let this go. It'll blow over when she gets bored or when she realizes it's not making a difference. But I will tell Jake what our theory is and tell him to keep an eye out for her. If she is truly doing this, then she's unhinged."

Haley shrugged and nodded. He gripped her chin gently and positioned her lips for a warm kiss. "Let's count our blessings. We are still on top of the world. Lindsay notwithstanding."

"Yeah, you're right."

"Okay, I'm going to bed. Sleep well."

Walking to his room, he hoped he'd convinced Haley to let this drop.

Chapter Fourteen

HALEY WITHERSPOON WAS a woman with a mission.

She'd studied the negative internet comments about Ace in the Hole over and over till she practically had them memorized. She copied and pasted them into a Word document, and then broke them apart, detailing each comment's sentence structure, word choice and voice. Analyzing them for similarities, she used different colors to highlight and draw lines until her document resembled the map of the world's busiest airport.

After all that work, she was more convinced than ever. These comments were all written by the same person.

She could verify and explain and convince anyone of why she had come to that conclusion. Who knows, maybe someday she would have the chance to, if this thing went further than she hoped it would.

And when her mind led logically to who had done it, she couldn't think of anyone except Lindsay. It had to be Lindsay. No one else harbored a hatred for Haley, or for Ace in the Hole's success, but Lindsay.

Who else would bother to create multiple fake email addresses, search out the band's website, along with the websites of all the venues on their schedule, and leave a trail of negative reviews all over the internet? Who else cared enough to go to all that trouble?

Nobody. And to prove it, Haley had embarked on a separate investigative thread. She made a list of a half dozen other local Myrtle Beach cover bands and visited not only their band websites, but the websites of all the venues on *their* summer schedules. It was an extensive effort,

but the results proved her premise. *None* of the other bands had attract-
ed the type of nasty comments that Ace in the Hole had.

And why would that be?

Because Lindsay wasn't angry at those bands. Because Lindsay
hadn't started a vast sabotage campaign against any of those other
bands. Only with Ace in the Hole.

Haley flopped back in her chair, frustrated. No doubt remained,
not a single one. Now, what could she do about it?

Her phone buzzed. A text had come in. She picked it up and read
it. A note from Blake: *Are you coming? We're on the bus.*

She scrambled to find the time. Wow, six pm. The meeting time for
the band and crew to get on the bus to go to tonight's venue. She'd eat-
en up the whole day with her research and hadn't even had a shower.
Hadn't left the room. Had barely had anything to eat.

She typed back, *I'll take a cab and meet you there later.*

She waited for a response and when it didn't come, she tossed her
phone on the bed and rose to her feet, stretching her arms above her
head to work the kinks out of her spine. She'd been sitting at that desk
all day. She really needed to put this behind her for now.

The phone finally buzzed and she picked it up. *OK*, Blake had written after a significant pause. His delay was telling, and she knew exactly
what he was thinking. He had stopped by twice while she was working
and had asked her to drop it. But she was a dog with a bone. She had
become obsessed with proving that Lindsay was behind all of this.

And ending Lindsay's reign of terror.

Haley rushed through her shower, makeup and hair and ran down
to the lobby of the hotel. She grabbed a fast food hamburger to provide
her body with protein – somewhat dubious protein, but still – and
Ubered to the coliseum where Frontier Fire would play tonight. She approached the security guard at the backstage door and flashed him her
associate badge. He let her in and as she entered the murky, dank space

the strands of the first warm up act soaring over the murmur of the large crowd filled her ears. Wow, she really was late.

She maneuvered to the row of green rooms until she found Blake's. She tapped on the door and opened it, stuck her head in. He sat at his vanity table looking in the mirror while a makeup artist touched up his face. His back to the door, their eyes met via the mirror's reflection. The fact that he didn't speak or smile validated what she'd been nervous about the whole way over here. He was mad at her.

She bit her lip and grimaced at him, her attempt at a peace offering, a silent apology. An important job faced him, fronting one of the biggest comeback bands in the history of country music, in front of a huge crowd of twelve thousand fans. He didn't need to be distracted by his unhappiness over her actions today.

She came up behind him and placed a kiss in the warm crevice where his neck met his shoulder. He shivered. "Sorry," she murmured to the makeup girl, who shook her head and grinned.

"That's okay. We're almost done here. Can't improve on perfection." She laughed, dabbed at Blake's cheeks with a long brush and stepped back to look.

Haley looked, too. Blake looked great. He'd always been a rugged, handsome guy, tall, lean and fit. But he'd grown into his own confidence and sexiness since he'd started with Frontier Fire. The way he moved, the way he held the mic close to his lips as he sang. His hips as they swung to the beat of the song. That unintentional swagger that women found so attractive. There was not an arrogant bone in his body, but maybe that was part of the reason Blake so easily drew women's attention. And maybe that was one reason the Frontier Fire reunion tour was so successful, beyond anyone's wildest expectations, according to Randall. Blake wouldn't be the sole reason for that, but he was certainly part of the equation.

The makeup girl gathered her things, walked to the door and said, "Break a leg," on the way out, closing it and leaving Blake and Haley in a silent room buzzing with tension.

"I'm sorry," she started. She recognized that she needed to get that out there to break the chill of anger he directed towards her. "I'm sorry I was late and missed coming over here with you."

Blake stared into the mirror, connecting gazes with her as she stood behind his right shoulder. "Were you tied up with the Lindsay thing all day?"

Haley started an immediate defense for all her hard work, and then she bit her tongue. He wouldn't understand, he wouldn't buy it, he wouldn't agree with her obsession, no matter how she defended it. "Yeah, and I got a lot done. But now it's time for Frontier Fire. This is my priority right now."

His mouth curled up at one edge. He had words he wanted to say but he was reconsidering putting them out there between the two of them. He was nice that way; she knew he didn't want to hurt her feelings. And words said in anger sometimes ripped deep holes that were impossible to mend.

"Tell me," she urged him. She didn't want secrets between them. Even if she disagreed. They could have disagreements between them. Hidden away, is how they would start to tear holes.

"Last night I asked you to drop this whole Lindsay thing. She'll get tired of it and stop eventually. It's obviously not harming Ace's gigs. Their shows are full."

"Yes, I know." She dropped her gaze and looked at her feet instead.

"I thought you agreed with me. But today you spent all day long working on it. I just don't think it's necessary. And I don't think it's healthy."

"No, you're right. It's probably not necessary or healthy but ..." she let her line of thought drop because she really didn't want to say what she was thinking. *I want to catch Lindsay at her game. I need to show Lindsay that I'm on top of her. That I can make her stop.*

Haley closed her mouth. Is this what she'd become? Vindictive and angry and determined to expose Lindsay's nasty campaign? Haley had to dig deep to figure out ... was she this engaged in stopping Lindsay because of the negative impact it was having on the band she managed? Or was she this engaged because she couldn't stand Lindsay and wanted to best her?

Was this business or personal?

Blake pulled out of his chair, turned and faced her, placing gentle hands on her elbows and nudging her closer. "Don't let her get the best of you. You need to let this drop." He placed a kiss on her lips, then her nose, then her forehead. "Okay?"

She closed her eyes. His gentleness sent a shudder through her torso. She breathed in his clean soapy scent and whispered, "You're such a good person. I wish I could be more like you."

He let out a scoffing laugh and shook his head. "You're a good person too. You're just getting swept away by this Lindsay thing."

"I can't let her win."

He chuckled, and then looked closely at her. "Maybe you need to pray about that?"

She thought for a second, and then nodded. She admired his faith. Although he wasn't in the least bit vocal about it, whenever he made comments like that one, she realized that he had a relationship with their Creator. God was his confidant, his guide, the path Blake wanted to walk. He may not be an evangelist or loudly preach about his faith, but it was there, it was quiet, and it was strong. Much stronger than hers.

She could learn something from Blake about her own faith in God. She could follow his example.

"Good idea," she said, nodding her head emphatically. "I'll do that."

"I gotta go," he said, gave her one last kiss, and made his way to the door.

"Break a leg," she repeated the phrase since it was tradition and why mess with success?

He smiled at her, gave her a playful salute and left, the door swinging shut behind him.

BLAKE FOUND AN EMPTY corner of the massive backstage. Time to start his pre-game warm up. He closed his eyes and concentrated on his breathing. In slowly, hold for the count of ten, release over another count of ten. Breathing. So important for musicians, especially singers. He'd wanted to be a big-time musician his whole life. He'd read all the behind the scenes stories of famous singers and instrumentalists and what they did to warm themselves up. Most of them followed the same routine show after show after show. This was becoming his.

After his breathing exercise, he ran through scales with his voice. Using "mee-moo-maw" he covered both octaves of his vocal range, using vowel sounds. Then he started consonants, "Toe bee doe" to get his words working. A slow, gradual warm up was important, and prevented putting rough edges on his voice. He wanted it to be responsive when he called upon it, and a good warmup did that.

He moved on to warming up his body. He shook out his arms, loosey goosey. Then his neck. Back and forth in a semi-circle on the base of his spine. Then his legs. Shake 'em out, shake 'em out, then his ankles. Circles, get the kinks out. Next, wrists and fingers. A few steps from the wall, he pushed his hands against the surface and stretched, bending first one knee, then the other. Then bend at the waist, fingertips touching the floor. Hold for the count of ten. Standing up again, he lifted his arms straight over his head and joined his fingers, pushing up, up, up.

Done. He was stretched out, relaxed and his breathing was flowing. Ready for the concert.

Well, not quite ready. His body was ready, his voice was ready, but his mind and spirit weren't quite there yet. He closed his eyes and said silently in his head, *Thank you Father. Thank you for putting me right here at this moment. Please be with me as I entertain this crowd. Leave me in good voice and let me sing well for these people. Be with them too. Keep us all safe.*

Eyes open, he clapped his hands and went off in search of his band-mates.

HALEY USUALLY LISTENED to the concert from backstage, but tonight she ventured into the coliseum and found an empty seat in the first level balcony beyond the floor seats. She wanted to observe her man and his band like a fan would. Blake's words about letting Lindsay get the better of her enticed her to fully absorb Blake's tour and love every second.

From the moment the band trotted on stage and took their places, till the instant the huge mountain of sound started from their instruments, the people in the audience screamed, coming to their feet and clapping. Haley laughed and rose as well. Looks like it would be a night of standing or else she'd never see over heads. A few bars in, Blake made his entrance, waving, smiling, moving to the edge of the stage to lean down and make eye contact with people close by. He personally welcomed them. Video cameras shot his image up on the jumbo screens on either side of the stage, giving those further away the same feeling of intimacy in the vast amphitheater.

Blake started singing, and the already-crazy crowd roared louder, crazier. They loved him. He'd been touring with Frontier Fire long enough now that he was comfortable with all the songs, knew them like he knew his own life history. Sure, he wasn't Josh Lakely, and the crowd knew that. But their acceptance of him was complete.

Blake moved easily, covering every square foot of the main stage, and often moving to far corners and walkways to make himself visible to as many fans as possible. He looked up and pointed at the faraway balconies; he leaned down and sang directly to the closer-ups. He owned the stage, and everyone knew it.

His strong voice rose over the instrumentals and even though he was busy moving, his vocals on each song were perfect and poignant. His first priority was to do the song justice.

Young girls in the seats to the right of Haley were *oohing* and *aahing* over Blake's handsome face, his eyes, his hair. He'd become a teenage heart throb, at least in these girls' eyes. She swallowed a grin, along with the urge to tell them that she was his girlfriend. What would they do if she revealed her relationship with Blake? Ask for an autograph? A personal introduction? Free tickets to another concert? Instead, she admired him from afar, and let her heart take in each detail of his performance.

At the end of the concert, but before they returned to the stage for the encore, Haley's phone buzzed. She pulled it out and glanced at it. Frontier Fire's manager, Randall had sent her a text. *Need to talk to you. Backstage? Now?*

She rose to her feet as she wondered what the heck this was about. Randall had never sent her an urgent text, but this one qualified. She climbed over the lovesick girls and into the aisle, taking the steps down at a faster pace than was safe, trying to control her accelerated heartrate.

All she needed was to hook her foot on someone else's to take a tumble down the cement steps.

She slowed down to ensure her own safety but made her way directly backstage.

Chapter Fifteen

FLYING BACKSTAGE, FLASHING her associate badge to Security, searching for Randall, her fingers tingled from her accelerated heartrate. Haley took a moment to calm herself. Maybe this was no big deal. Maybe Randall was just checking in with her, touching base. A normal, routine meeting.

Yeah, right.

Randall arrived backstage a half minute after she did. She spotted him, and he lifted a hand, gesturing for her to join him. "Hey," she said, and he nodded in greeting.

"Let's find a place we can talk," he said loudly in her ear, and they headed for the green rooms, recently vacated by the band members for their encore. Settling into an empty one, Randall sat down and pulled out a laptop. He wordlessly pulled up a website and pushed it over to her to read.

Haley took a moment to orient herself. Randall had pulled up the Frontier Fire website. In the Open Forum section that encouraged fans to interact, he pointed to the top of the list. Haley leaned closer and a sick feeling attacked her stomach.

Lindsay was at it again. She'd infiltrated the Frontier Fire website with negative reviews. Haley recognized the email addresses. They were exactly the ones that had attacked Ace in the Hole.

Haley pulled her eyes away from the comments. She didn't want to read them. She imagined what they'd say, and they evidently were se-vere enough to cause Randall some concern. She looked at Randall. "I can explain this. In a nutshell, when I took over as Ace in the Hole's band manager, I replaced one of the musician's girlfriends who was doing their bookings. I wanted to take the band to a whole new level, and she resented it. We eventually severed her from the band, and her boyfriend broke up with her."

Randall nodded slowly. "So, a sabotage campaign."

"Yes. She's done the same thing with Ace in the Hole, leaving terrible comments about them all over the internet. I didn't even think to look up Frontier Fire sites as well."

Randall tapped at the paging bar on the website. "This one woman wrote all of these?"

"Yes."

"Making it look like a dozen different people are unhappy with Blake as lead singer."

"Yes. It's just one. She's doing her best to sabotage both bands. But she's not successful. Ace in the Hole is playing to full clubs, and obviously, so is Frontier Fire."

Randall put his hands over his eyes, a tired swipe over his face. "I guess that old saying is true. Hell hath no fury like a woman scorned."

A wave of regret washed over Haley. "I'm so sorry about this, Randall. I feel at least partially responsible for this, since she's doing this because she's mad at me. But I had no idea she'd go so far as to involve Frontier Fire."

Randall shrugged. "She sounds like she's crazy."

"She wasn't exactly stable even when she was happy."

Randall chuckled.

"Is there anything we can do to stop her? I've been wracking my brain all day, to be honest."

Randall thought for a moment, then shook his head. "Not really. She's not doing anything criminal, so the police won't be interested. And like you said, these reviews aren't resulting in reduced crowds. Our live audiences seem to love Blake."

Haley blinked, a big idea forming in her brain on the spot. "Maybe we can do a counter-cyber-attack. Enlist a ton of people to go online and rebuke Lindsay's negative comments with something positive. That way, the positive will outweigh the negative and people who don't know any better won't be sucked into believing Lindsay's lies."

Randall thought for a second. "I guess it won't hurt. Could be a lot of work though."

"I have time," Haley responded quickly. "Please let me run with this, Randall. It'll make me feel better at least taking some action."

Randall nodded. "Okay, you do that then. And let's not talk to the band about this. I mean, they may find it on their own if they're looking on our website, but no need to worry them about it. I think the band has bonded really well with Blake and he's doing a great job." He snapped the laptop closed. "Welcome to the age of the internet. A negative review is one click away at any moment."

Haley agreed. She walked away from the meeting with Randall feeling better than she had all day. She had no idea if a counter attack would be effective. But at least she would be doing something.

GIVE ME A CALL WHEN you have a minute.

Blake was lying in a mound of puffy white bedding in his hotel room just after noon, not quite asleep, but not quite awake. He picked up his phone from the bedside table, read the message from Brent and immediately placed the call. His brother answered on the second ring.

"Geez. I didn't expect that fast a response," Brent joked.

"I hear so rarely from my baby brother that I figured I should call before you forget my name," Blake joked back.

Brent laughed. Blake's exaggeration probably made the thought funnier. Despite his busy schedule, he made sure he checked in with Brent twice a week, like clockwork.

"Seriously, between working all night and sleeping in, the best time to reach me is in the afternoons. Good to hear your voice."

"You're living the life, that's for sure. Long way from *Ubering* and singing at the Drunken Parrot in Myrtle Beach."

"Can't argue with that." Blake's lips curled into a smile. "How's school going?"

"Good. In fact, I'm almost done with my summer schedule and I've got three weeks off before fall semester starts."

"Awesome."

"And I figured, what better way to spend my break than to see my bigshot brother making his dream come true?"

Blake grinned. "You want to come see a concert?"

"Absolutely! I can't miss an opportunity like this, man."

"Great. You give me a date and I'll pull up the schedule."

They discussed possible dates and where the band was performing on those nights. They settled on a Saturday night in Pittsburgh, followed by two free nights. Brent would room with Blake, attend Saturday's concert, travel to Philadelphia with the band on Sunday, and fly home on Monday. They'd have time to catch up and do some fun things together.

"I'll book the flights for you," Blake offered.

"No. I got it."

"No need. Save your money for when school starts. I got this," Blake insisted. He hated Brent always being short on cash, and he could easily book the flights for his brother.

Brent relented. "Okay, thanks. I appreciate it."

"No big. I'm just thrilled to spend some time with you and glad you're not going to miss this."

They finalized plans and hung up.

WITH A PLAN IN MIND and Randall's support, Haley dove into her project to combat the negativity on the web with positivity. She started by letting her brain soar. She needed to spread the word, create a Positivity Campaign tagline and logo. Create a compelling communication to send to Frontier Fire's massive fan base and they'd buy in to the cause. They'd want to help, and soon, Lindsay's measly little presence would be quickly overcome. A sea of positivity overcoming a few drops of negativity.

The best people to report honestly about the quality of Blake's performance would be those who had come to a concert. So, how could she reach those concertgoers? How could she ask them directly for their help? Most tickets to Frontier Fire concerts were purchased through online ticket retailers. Would those retailers share the email addresses of the concertgoers with her? As long as she could prove she was working with the band? Or would that be against their privacy policy?

She pulled up the website of the biggest online ticket retailer. She clicked on their Privacy Policy and scanned their Frequently Asked Questions. *Bingo*. This seemed to address exactly what she was hoping for:

"Who We Share Your Data With and Why: **We will share information with our business partners.** This includes third parties such as the artist, promoter or sponsors of an event, or those who operate a venue where we hold events. Our partners use the information we give them as described in their privacy policies, which may include sending you marketing communications."

Haley sat back in her chair. If she could work with the ticket retailer to get the email addresses of those who had attended a Frontier Fire concert, she could prepare a newsletter explaining the Positivity Campaign. Making the internet a more positive place. She didn't have to go into detail about Lindsay the Crazy Woman. She'd keep it generic and high level and ask for their help in spreading positivity.

It could just work. Now she needed to get a contact phone number or address for the ticket site.

She was digging deeper into the website when her cell phone rang, distracting her. She frowned at the screen to see who was calling.

Mom?

Her thoughts abandoned the Positivity Campaign. She hadn't spoken to either of her parents since their blowout a few months ago. She reached for the phone, then pulled her hand back as if it were a snake ready to strike.

It rang again, and Haley knew with one more ring it would go to her voicemail, leaving her with more time to think about this. However, one thought – would she ever want to return her mother's voicemail – made her hastily accept the call. "Hello?" she said, schooling her voice to sound neutral.

"Hi, sweetheart," came her mother's voice. Haley knew her mother well enough to know that her voice was strained. Strained with the effort of sounding kind and casual.

"Hi, Mom." She sat back in her chair and waited.

"How – uh, how's it going?"

"What, the tour?"

"Everything, darling. You. I haven't talked to you in ages."

A scoff emerged from Haley's mouth, but she managed to hold back the words that were at the tip of her tongue. Spiteful words that would assuage Haley's anger over how her parents had treated her but would damage their ongoing relationship in the future. She took a silent moment to decide how to proceed. "The last time I talked to you guys I got the impression that you were angry at me."

"Not angry," her mom said. "Concerned. With your lack of direction. In your professional life."

Haley nodded slowly, pursing her lips in concentration even though her mother couldn't see her.

Her mother hurried to continue, "I miss speaking to you. You're my daughter. I don't think we've ever gone this many weeks not speaking in our lives."

"You'd never disowned me before," Haley said flatly, and then popped a hand over her mouth. Well, there it was, out in the open.

"Sweetheart, we didn't disown you."

"What do you call it?"

Her mother's deep breath was evident over the phone line. "We wanted to give you an incentive to get your professional life moving forward. As long as you knew that you could fall back on Witherspoon Enterprises money to fund your life, you'd have no reason to work hard to be successful on your own."

"It wasn't that at all, Mom. As long as I kept working at jobs I had no passion for, I'd have no reason to work hard to be successful. But all that has changed now."

Mom hesitated. "Yes. Daddy told me he'd been looking at that band that you're traveling with. They seem like they're having a very successful tour."

"Frontier Fire?"

"Is that what it's called?"

Haley counted to five. "Frontier Fire's tour is going extremely well. In fact, they're breaking records in the country music industry."

"That's wonderful, sweetie. I knew you could do it if we gave you the encouragement."

A line of indigestion dripped down her esophagus. "No, Mom. I'm not their manager. I really had nothing to do with the popularity of their tour."

"Oh. Then why are you traveling with them?"

"I'm managing Blake, their interim lead singer," Haley said, speaking slowly to get her message across.

"Each member of the band has their own manager?"

Haley huffed out her frustration. "No. Listen, Mom, I'm the manager of Ace in the Hole, Blake's permanent band. He's only with Frontier Fire temporarily."

"But you're traveling with this other band." Her mother's frustration was obvious in her words. "You're not explaining this very well."

Haley clamped her mouth shut. She supposed it was confusing for an outsider looking in like her mother. Someone who had never paid any attention to her daughter, in favor of her high-achieving sons.

"Is Ace in the Hole breaking records too?" Her mom sounded hopeful.

"No, but they're doing much better than they were before I started working with them." That was safe, and it was true. And maybe it would prove to Mom that she was successful.

"And they're paying your salary?"

Haley balked and let her eyes study the ceiling. "Well, not exactly."

"No? You're a volunteer band manager?"

"Mom, I really have to go." Another conversation with her mother that made her feel worse after than before. Her mother's uncanny knack at making her feel like crap about herself, even when everything was going well in her life.

"But we've barely talked, dear. I wanted to tell you about the grandkids, since I guess you won't see them at all this summer."

Haley closed her eyes and allowed the subtle guilt trip to flow over her. Now she was neglecting her nieces and nephews. What an awful aunt she was. "Go ahead. I'll give you five minutes." She listened to five minutes of conversation about her four nieces and two nephews, how Mom and Dad had them over for swimming in the pool, how they visited an amusement park, how they were getting summer family portraits taken on the beach.

Wait, what? "You're getting family photos taken on the beach without me?" Her parents had excluded her from all family communications, news, finances and activities all summer, but for some reason that one really stung. They did a photographic family portrait on the beach every year, and instead of someone thinking to wait till a time that Haley was in town and could attend, they'd just do it without her. No one thought twice.

"Yes, dear. You're out of town."

Haley shrugged. Well, if she meant so little to them, she'd have to return the favor. They would mean little to her. "Okay, Mom, thanks for the call. I have to get back to work. Bye." She hung up quickly and tossed the phone on the bed.

She sat still as a statue, her eyes wide, mentally fighting the onset of tears that wanted to burst. Then she gave up and let them come, a waterfall of heartbreak. She would mourn the loss of her relationship with her parents once. Then, she would move on.

Chapter Sixteen

BLAKE STEPPED OFF STAGE following the encore in Denver, the crowd's response making his mood fly and the massive wall of sound they'd created all night long making his ears ring.

Moose followed him and hung a palm in the air. Blake slapped it, a high five of pure pleasure, followed by slaps with Ricky and Len. Sophie and Max ran up, *woo hoo*'ing in excitement.

Then, what had become Blake's favorite post-concert tradition: Haley ran toward him, smile radiating across her face, pure happiness and fun. She flung herself at him, arms around his neck, legs around his waist, and he held her in place while their lips joined in a happy, sweaty, celebratory kiss.

"It's so cool that even though this band is in the big time, they celebrate each concert like it was their first one," he said in her ear.

"Yep. This band is awesome."

Randall joined them backstage, shaking hands, congratulating them. The band drifted toward the green rooms and hung out in Lola's room, not wanting their magical camaraderie to end. They opened chilled cans of beer and spent a cherished half hour sharing favorite moments of the concert. Eventually Blake wandered to his own room and showered, changing into fresh clothes before he met Haley in the hallway.

They rode in the limousine back to the hotel and sat together in the lobby. Blake sank into the comfortable couch, his adrenaline now drained, leaving him fatigued. Haley leaned over him and ran soft fingers over his cheeks, his eyelids, his forehead. He closed his eyes and savored the gentle touch. "That feels good."

"I should schedule a massage for you."

He didn't mean his face to display his terror at that thought, but it probably did. "I don't know about that."

"Have you never had a massage?"

"Nope."

"I can't believe that. They're wonderful. Very relaxing."

Blake stayed quiet, imagining a masseuse's hands probing every inch of his back, shoulders, neck. Would he be relaxed, or would he tense up?

A memory hit his mind, something he needed Haley's help with. "Oh, guess what. Brent is joining the tour for a couple days."

"Really?" Haley smiled with pleasure at the idea.

"Yeah, he'll fly in the Saturday that we're in Pittsburgh. He'll go to the concert, stay with me, then ride the bus with us to Philadelphia the next day. He'll fly home on Day 3."

"Great! It'll be so good to see him."

"Yeah. I need your help with logistics."

"No problem. I'll take care of everything."

"Flights?"

"Yep."

"And don't forget his, uh, special accommodation needs."

She leaned in and placed a kiss on his forehead. "Leave it to me."

"You're the best." He wrapped his arms around her and pulled her in for a proper kiss. Despite his physical exhaustion, his heart woke up and pounded due to the tangling of their tongues. He was becoming more and more certain: Haley was his one person. The one he was falling in love with and could see spending his future with. Sharing his life, his thoughts, his earnings. The one to build a life with, build a family with.

He knew she had feelings for him. Obviously. But did her feelings match his? Were they on the same level? And how should he go about sharing his thoughts? When?

He returned his concentration to sharing his unspoken love through his kiss, not wanting to be distracted from this moment.

HALEY TOOK CARE OF Brent's airline tickets, flying into Pittsburgh and flying out of Philadelphia three days later. She also spoke to an airline reservationist about his paraplegia and wheelchair. Aunt Gloria would get him onto the plane in Myrtle Beach, and Haley would get him off. Haley would get him back on the plane and Aunt Gloria would get him back off. It would all work out fine.

Haley also crossed another item off her To Do List by calling Robbie and Jake. She'd vowed to stay in better touch with Ace in the Hole, despite physically accompanying Frontier Fire, and she wanted to carry out that promise. She set up video chats with them once a week and talked about the venues, the crowds, and Sam's performances. If there were any post-gig follow ups needed to the managers of the venues, they would tell her, and she would make the calls.

Of course, she also asked if there were any Lindsay sightings, or any nasty business observed because of Lindsay's reviews. So far, none.

Haley hung up on today's call with the guys feeling satisfied. She was making this strange arrangement work. She was providing support to Ace in the Hole, and she was also providing support to Blake. She was stretching herself in several directions, but it appeared to be working.

Those tasks done, she turned her focus to the Positivity Campaign. In the past ten days, she had successfully acquired a list of email addresses of concertgoers, about twenty thousand strong. She'd designed a logo and tagline for the campaign: "Help Spread Love." She'd created the content of the newsletter describing their pledge to wipe out negativity on the internet. She'd strived to make it a cause everyone could buy into, ending with a call to action to bombard the Frontier Fire website and concert venue sites with positivity.

Next, she'd set up a band account with a major newsletter provider that met all the legal requirements for spam mail and opt-ins. Then, she'd sent it, breath held, and fingers crossed.

Every day now, she scanned the websites for results. And they were monumental. Legions of Frontier Fire fans had responded to her call to action and left positive reviews everywhere they could find. In addition to the Frontier Fire website and the venue websites being flooded with positive reviews, they also appeared on websites that sold Frontier Fire music, both in physical and digital form.

Haley's heart took flight, seeing the results she'd hoped for, but way bigger than she'd expected. Unable to contain her excitement, she jumped up in her hotel room and did a burst of jumping jacks. An ecstatic whoop of excitement escaped her mouth.

A knock came at her door and she flung to face it. She walked to the door. She struggled to make her voice sound calm despite the adrenaline pumping through her. "Yes?"

"Was that you?" Blake's amused voice was filtered through the heavy door. Haley pulled it open and grabbed him. Squeezing his arms, she gave him a hearty hug.

"Yes! Success! Come look." She ran over to her laptop and pulled up the Frontier Fire website. She pointed at the legions of comments. He approached cautiously, gazing at her like he was afraid of what he'd see. "Look! Read some of these. People love Frontier Fire! People love you, Blake. Your reviews are awesome!"

He bent at the waist, squinting in concentration as he scanned the website. "Hmmm," he murmured and read another one.

"All good stuff," Haley verified. She took the mouse and paged through the list. "See? Every single one."

He shook his head, shaking off what he'd seen. "Okay," he said dubiously. "Why? Why are thousands of fans leaving positive reviews this week?" He turned to look at her.

"Because of my Positivity Campaign!" She beamed at him.

Her exuberance did nothing to remove his frown. "What's that?"

"I know I mentioned it to you. Maybe you forgot with all you have going on." His frown deepened, and then Haley wondered if she had, indeed, mentioned it to him at all. "It's something Randall and I have been working on together," she said, stretching the truth a little bit. She needed him to be happy about it, because, darn it, *she* was so happy about it.

She took his hand and led him away from the laptop. She sat on the bed and he sat beside her. "Remember when Lindsay left all those nasty reviews on the internet about Ace in the Hole?"

"Um. Well, someone did. We don't know that Lindsay was behind all those."

Haley paused. Oh gosh, he was so far behind. "Okay, granted. I have theories, but I can't prove it was all Lindsay. But anyway, some of the reviews started infiltrating the Frontier Fire site too."

Blake's eyebrows went up nearly into his hairline. "Bad reviews? Did they mention me?"

Haley blinked, remembering Randall's instruction not to unsettle Blake with news of bad reviews. She needed to re-track here. "Let me start over. You know how the internet is a breeding ground of negativity?"

Blake shrugged, and he looked confused.

"Think about it. Anyone with an internet connection and an electronic device can leave a review on a product and hide behind the curtain of anonymity to say horrible things that they'd never say to someone's face."

"O-o-o-kay," Blake said.

"So Randall and I ... well, I, mostly, and Randall okayed it, came up with a Frontier Fire Positivity Campaign. I created a campaign and sent out a newsletter to a whole bunch of Frontier Fire fans and encouraged them to spread the love."

"How do they do that?" Blake's voice was quiet.

"If they truly liked the concert they recently attended, they could go on the internet and leave a positive review. That's all."

Blake stared at her. His creased forehead and his darting eyes told her that his brain was whirring. "You solicited for positive reviews? That's not ethical, is it?"

Haley's mouth dropped open. "What do you mean? It's not *un*ethical. What's wrong with spreading positivity? It's making the internet a happier place." How could he possibly have a problem with this concept?

"But reviews are supposed to be uncoerced. Someone who liked something enough to leave a review. Asking for a positive review ... I don't know, there's just something sketchy about it. Especially when it's about me."

Haley scanned her brain and couldn't understand his resistance.

"This is back to the Lindsay thing, right?" His gaze was piercing her, and she looked up. "Lindsay left a few negative comments and now you're using an army of Frontier Fire fans to fight her. That's not right, Haley."

She tried to think of a response but couldn't. Was he right? Even though the Positivity Campaign was, on its own, a constructive thing, was she doing it for the wrong reasons? Spreading positivity with no ulterior motive was a good thing. Spreading positivity to get the better of an enemy. Was that so wrong?

Blake went on, "I feel uncomfortable with this. You're putting me in a position that you're leading this big campaign that without you ... and without me ... Frontier Fire wouldn't be doing. Or have the need to do. It just seems ... forced. I don't know." He cleared his throat. "Frontier Fire fans will either like me, or they won't. Don't force them to say they like me. It's ... I don't know ... embarrassing."

Haley put her hands over her eyes and rubbed them down her cheeks. She needed to be a mature professional about his reaction. Just because she thought it was a great idea, and just because she was so happy about the vast positive results, didn't mean that he had to agree with her.

But darn it, he was putting a major damper on her parade!

She shrugged. "I disagree with you."

He studied her face. "And I disagree with you." He paused, then leaned in closer to her, his voice urgent. "Let it go. Let this whole Lindsay thing go. It's not healthy, Haley."

"But the Positivity Campaign ..."

"Is done now, right? You did it. You got a ton of positive reviews. Good for you. Now, it's over."

But she had more plans. What if she could use the power of Frontier Fire fans to support Ace in the Hole? Chances are, if they liked Blake as front man, they'd be interested in seeing Ace if they were at a venue close by. What could possibly be wrong with using their contacts to increase Ace's popularity and audience? This was the way to do it. She had all these Frontier Fire fans in the palm of her hand. What was wrong with that?

But she knew enough to keep that to herself. Blake would blatantly disagree with her, and she didn't want to cause an argument. It was just another of those band manager-behind-the-scenes things that the talent didn't need to know about. The musicians didn't need to see how the sausage was made, but they sure would enjoy the wonderful taste of the finished sausage.

She gave him a sweet smile. "Let's agree to disagree, shall we?"

But his face hardened. "What do you mean? What do you plan to do next?"

"Nothing for you to worry about."

He shook his head. "No secrets between us, Haley. I feel strongly about this Lindsay thing. It'll blow over. Don't enrage her. We're above that."

Haley scoffed. "I'm not scared of her." She reached up to run a finger over Blake's tense features, but he pushed her finger away.

"I want you to drop it."

"I know you do. You've made that very clear. But I disagree."

Blake stared at her, then the light went out of his eyes. His frown creases eased as he got to his feet. "I need some time to think about this, Haley. I'll catch you later." He strode to the door.

Haley got to her feet and raced after him. "Blake ... don't ..." she said as he left through the doorway.

He lifted a hand and disappeared into the hallway.

Chapter Seventeen

BLAKE TRUDGED TO HIS hotel room, but halfway through unlocking the door, he changed his mind. He walked to the stairwell and jogged down it, across the hotel lobby and out the front door, into the streets of ... what town were they in? Geez, it was so easy to lose track when they were in a new town every couple of days.

Omaha. They were in Omaha, Nebraska. They'd arrived yesterday and would do their first gig tonight.

He headed off down the sidewalk. Walking always helped him think and after the argument with Haley he really needed to blow off some steam. As he walked, he concentrated on reducing his irritation level. He was really worked up. Why did Haley continue to hold on to her need to best Lindsay? Her obsession was not healthy, of that he was sure. The woman had been detrimental to their lives, and they had evicted her. End of story. Lindsay was free to move on with her life, and they would do the same. So, why did Haley continue to poke the bear? He knew Lindsay had a vindictive personality. If Haley fought back, Lindsay would escalate. Two strong female personalities butting heads and battering horns. Soon, the fight would be more than either of them could handle.

Blake turned a corner and kept walking. He forced himself to think about the root of his annoyance. Haley's complete dismissal of his instructions to her. He'd told her to drop her obsession with Lindsay, and she'd initially agreed. But she'd obviously lied because she was still pursuing it. She'd kicked off this whole Positivity Campaign, which on its surface, sounded like a good thing. But underneath, it was just a method to use the power of Frontier Fire fans to best Lindsay.

Blake slowed his pace to analyze his intentions. At its basest level, he was angry because he'd given Haley a direct order, and she'd disobeyed him.

When he looked at it like that, he didn't like the way that sounded. Like he was a dictator and expected full obedience. This was Haley he was talking about here. His girlfriend. The woman he was falling in love with. Was he that kind of guy? Did he expect blind obedience from his life partner?

He shook his head. No, of course not. He didn't want Haley to blindly take his orders and obey him. He wanted a full partner, someone with her own mind and talents. And Haley certainly did.

So why was he so upset about this?

Because of their professional relationship. Haley wasn't just his girlfriend. They worked together too. In some ways, she was his boss. The manager of the band, the one who set up everything so they could perform. But in some ways, he was her boss. And in this particular case, his order to her about leaving Lindsay alone was to be obeyed. No questions asked. No arguments.

He returned to the hotel, feeling like he'd made a discovery. The fact that Haley worked for Ace in the Hole, and by extension, *him,* was causing conflict in their personal relationship. Now, how were they going to handle that problem?

Was it possible for a man and a woman in love to work together?

He headed for his room and changed into a pair of shorts and a t-shirt. He took the elevator to the workout room and to work himself into a sweat on the treadmill and the weights.

A FEW DAYS PASSED, and with each interaction she had with Blake, the ice between them had started to thaw. They weren't back to normal yet, but she hoped that they soon would be.

On their last free night before a string of three shows in Kansas City and St. Louis, Blake asked her out on a date. They dressed up and walked to a nice restaurant near their hotel. Haley was pleased, hoping it was Blake's attempt at a reconciliation. She didn't want this Lindsay thing causing a rift between them and she hoped he'd come to the same conclusion as her – that it wasn't worth arguing about.

They walked a few blocks and came upon a brick one-story building. The three-dimensional metallic sign near the front door read, Lidia's, Kansas City, Italy.

"Mmm, I love Italian," she murmured.

He pointed a fond grin at her and led her to the door. Inside, an enormous open room was grouped into separate spaces by tall wooden dividers. The bar was the centerpiece of the entire place, positioned in the dead center. A huge rectangle of light quartz surrounded the busy bartenders working within and sported close to forty bar stools around the perimeter. Up above, dozens of black tube lights hung on metal strands suspended from the ceiling.

Blake gave his name to the maître de, who led them to their table. He helped Haley into her seat, then handed her a cloth napkin. Their small table gave them a close view of a large refrigerated cabinet of bottled wine nearby. Looking straight up, Haley exclaimed, "Look at these chandeliers. They remind me of big honeybee hives."

Blake chuckled, and observed them. Lumps of colored glass with ceramic balls hanging down, all the golden hue of honey.

"This place is beautiful," she said.

"Yeah, I took a chance on it, but I figured how could we go wrong with Italian?"

She beamed her appreciation at him. He'd wanted to plan a nice evening for them. Maybe all the craziness was behind them.

The menu was extensive, and Haley spent an inordinate amount of time studying it before dropping it to the table and ordering the pasta trio. He settled into a wordless quiet after ordering, his eyes flitting around the open room, taking in their surroundings. Haley scanned her brain for conversation topics, nothing that would bother Blake. Nothing about Lindsay, or the Positivity Campaign. Those risky topics were off the table. Best to keep it safe.

"So, have you heard from Brent? Is he excited about his trip?"

"Oh! Yeah, he is. Are the flight reservations all made?"

"Yep, all done. I emailed him and your Aunt Gloria with the details."

"Perfect, thank you."

"That day of the concert when he arrives, I'll need to go pick him up. The flight doesn't get in till late afternoon, so it'll press you a little too close to concert warm up time."

"Oh, I can't pick him up at the airport?"

Haley shook her head. "No. The only flight I could get doesn't arrive till close to five." The disappointment evident on his face caused a little stab in her heart. "But don't sweat it. I'll get him and bring him straight to the venue. You can see him backstage before your show starts. He'll get the whole star treatment."

His expression relaxed and a spark of affection showed in his eyes. "Thanks, Haley."

"Don't mention it." She knew how important it was to him to show his brother a good time, as well as letting him share in the whole magical tour experience.

Blake was quiet again. Maybe he was preoccupied. Haley reached over and put her hand on his. He looked up at her. "Everything okay?"

He nodded. Then he sighed. He met her gaze directly, and his blue eyes pierced into hers. "Haley, there's something I need to tell you."

She figured. Something was on his mind and it was good to get it out on the table. Talk about it, resolve it quickly and move on to a nice evening. That's what good couples did. Right?

"I've been thinking about this a lot. I want to explain exactly what I'm thinking but I'm sure I'll mess something up so bear with me."

His words made her catch her breath, but she gave him a nod of encouragement.

"First of all, I want you to know." He cleared his throat. "I really like you, Haley. I don't know if I've shared with you exactly how I feel about you."

The cautious breath she'd been holding eased out. Anything that started this way couldn't be bad.

"I feel like our personalities go well together. You're beautiful, of course, but not just that." He struggled adorably for words to describe his feelings and her heart filled with love for him for trying. "You're fun and kind. You're smart and accomplished. What I mean to say is, there are so many things that I love about you. I ... I think I'm falling in love with you, Haley."

She grabbed his hand, squeezing it. "Oh my gosh. Blake! Me too! I've never felt this strongly for a guy before. You make me happy and fulfilled."

She glanced around for the waiter. They should order champagne! Surely a toast of bubbly was warranted when a couple navigated their way through the dangerous waters of dating and realized that they were mutually in love.

But the waiter wasn't around, so she rested her gaze back on Blake's blank face. It took a moment for her to realize, something wasn't quite right. Why wasn't he happy? Shouldn't he be sporting a smile? Or, at the very least, not have that concerned frown on his face? "What's the matter?"

"I'm sorry," he said. "I have more on my mind than just this news."

"Okay." She tried to tamp down the excitement level a notch or two, so he could continue.

"I've come to realize that by being in love with a woman you work with, it puts certain strains on the relationship."

Blake paused, and Haley stared.

"I've told you several times that you should drop your counterattack on Lindsay, that it will go away on its own if we just ignore it. But you seem obsessed with fighting back with her. Despite what I'm telling you. And I have no idea how to deal with that."

Haley kept her expression even, but her gaze darted around his face while she thought of a response. She wanted to stay calm. She wanted to bask in the fact that they were newly in love. But this turn of conversation made her want to get defensive. She kept her voice low, despite her desire to get loud. "Maybe I don't know how to deal with you either. I've done nothing but help this band. I've instituted a ton of improvements that have all paid off. The website, the photos, the logo, the improved bookings. Heck, even getting you into the Battle of the Bands, which, let's not forget, is why you're sitting here today, fronting the most successful band in country music history."

"No, I know. You've been awesome, Haley, it's just ..."

"I'm not trying to toot my own horn. I'm not saying you all don't deserve to be where you are. But all my judgement has been good. I don't know why you don't trust me on this one too."

He sighed. "Something inside me is deeply against this."

She sat and stared at him. "Do you feel a protectiveness towards Lindsay? I mean, you've known her a lot longer than you've known me."

"No," he said firmly. "It's not that at all. Lindsay was a negative force in our lives and it's good that she's gone. But by you engaging her and fighting with her, I feel that she can retaliate and give us more of a battle than we want. She's not stable, I think we all know that."

Haley listened, or at least she tried to, despite the anger pounding in her head. How dare he? How dare her boyfriend confess his love for her, and one second later, chastise her about job performance? Way to forever mar the memory of this special moment between the two of them. She took a moment to calm herself, then looked up into his eyes. "Or is it because you want to control me? You want me to give you complete obedience and not use the brain I have in my head."

He looked down at the table and shook his head. "I sure hope it's not that. I hope I don't have that trait inside me." He looked up at her.

Once she'd said it, she regretted putting it out there. Maybe that was her own hang up. Maybe her parents' lack of faith in her had prompted her to go crazy now that she'd actually found a line of work she was good at. She was a workaholic now, and she had developed into someone who couldn't take criticism without turning into a raging lunatic. Even successful businesspeople had to take advice and guidance without attacking their co-workers. Even if they disagreed with the criticism.

It's nothing personal. It's just business. That would become her new mantra when Blake, or anyone else who put up a bit of resistance to one of her work plans. Even if she disagreed.

Man, this "adulting" thing was hard!

She brought in a lungful of cleansing air. "I don't think that either. You're not a bully or a know-it-all. If you were, it would've materialized before now, and you've been nothing but kind and supportive of me."

The waiter interrupted them with their entrees and placed them on the table. The pasta that had looked so delicious on the menu now sat, an unappealing lump on the plate. They picked up their forks.

"Look," Haley said. "We're a good team. I know it's hard to work with someone you love, but I think we can do it. I'm sorry you've been stressed over me. That was definitely not my intent. My job is to remove all the stress from you, so you can perform. I should've been listening better." She took a deep breath and pushed it out, along with her determination to get even with Lindsay. "I don't know why you feel so strongly about this Lindsay thing, but I respect you enough to abide by your wishes."

He looked up, his handsome face transforming into a hopeful expression. "Really? You'll stop fighting with Lindsay? You'll turn your focus away from those negative reviews? You'll leave them alone?"

She nodded, the hint of a smile breaking forth. "Yes. Because *you* feel so strongly about it. Not because I agree with you, but because I love you, and I don't want this to be a bone of contention in our relationship."

His happy smile was a thing of beauty and suddenly all the tension between them was wiped away. "Thank you, Haley. Thank you. I owe you one."

She held up a finger to make a point. "And not because I'm blindly obeying you, and not because you're my boss. Got that?"

He chuckled. "Yes. I understand."

"You can catch more flies with honey than vinegar, isn't that the saying?"

He shrugged, still looking at her with his happy grin. "I have no idea. I'm just happy we're past this. We are past this, right?"

She nodded. "It's all about communication. We'll be open and honest with each other and give each other the benefit of the doubt."

"Sounds good to me." He reached over their steaming plates to squeeze her hands.

"So, I propose a re-do. Do you mind?"

"What do you mean?" The crease in his forehead spoke to his confusion.

"My boyfriend just told me he was in love with me and then went on to reprimand me about a work thing. Not cool, dude."

She knew the moment he realized what he'd done because his eyes focused clearly and an amused grin appeared on his face. He took her hands and pulled them close to rest on his heartbeat. "Haley, I'm falling in love with you."

She beamed her love and pleasure at him. "Blake, I'm falling in love with you too."

Suddenly the pasta aroma in her nose made her stomach growl. Her appetite was back. She dug into the trio with gusto.

HALEY PLACED HER WEEKLY conference call with Robbie and Jake. The normalness in their voices brought her peace. In this corner of her professional world, things were going well.

"We played a really cool place last Friday," Robbie said. "It was in Charlotte and it was called Coyote Joe's. Man, that place rocked."

"Oh yes!" Haley exclaimed. "I remember that place when I was booking it. I was so excited about getting us in there."

"They have a huge dance floor, and a really nice sized stage. They packed the people in."

"I remember. They call themselves the premiere country nightclub of the area. I'm bummed I missed seeing you there."

"We weren't the headliners, but we had a nice hour-long opening gig. What do you think, Jake, how many people were there?"

Jake hummed while he thought. "Lordy, at least a couple thousand."

"Wow. And the gig went well?"

"Yep. Sam put it into hyper drive; he was in his element. Sang great, engaged the crowd."

"Okay, I need to call them for a repeat performance. Great job, guys."

They discussed other shows of the week. Places they'd like to go back to, places to avoid. As they talked, Haley updated her list.

"Anything else I could be doing for you guys? Anything you need?"

They paused. "Not really. Just looking forward to getting Blake back."

Haley smiled. "Yeah, getting close now. About six weeks left?" About to wrap up the call, Haley remembered something she wanted to mention. "Hey, before we hang up, let me run an idea by you. I've obtained a list of about twenty thousand email addresses of people who have come to Frontier Fire concerts since Blake joined. What would you think about me sending them an email with a link to the Ace in the Hole website? Just a friendly mention that you guys are Blake's band and you're keeping the wheels on while Blake's filling in for Josh Lakely?"

"Yeah, that sounds good. Couldn't hurt to spread awareness. Might get us bigger audiences too."

"Okay. I'll run it by Randall, Frontier Fire's manager, to make sure he doesn't object. But I see it as good business." She didn't mention the original reason she'd obtained the email addresses. The Positivity Campaign to combat Lindsay's negative internet attacks was over. Done. Successful. No need to continue it further. This was just marketing. Reaching out and finding new listeners for Ace in the Hole, which was her job. Any good band manager would do it.

"Oh, and one more thing. Any Lindsay sightings?"

"No."

"Okay, good. She's still posting negative reviews, but not at the rate she was before. Maybe she's getting bored."

"Jake, maybe you should just contact her and tell her to cut it out," Robbie said.

"I appreciate the offer, Robbie, but Blake and I have talked about this." *Incessantly.* "He feels strongly to just let it go. Leave her alone and let it run its course."

"Whatever," Robbie said. "Let us know if you change your mind."

She ended the call amidst their well wishes and thanks. Haley pulled up her newsletter program and drafted a simple, cheery newsletter explaining the connection between Frontier Fire and Ace in the Hole, added Ace's new logo and promo photo, and a link to their website. Once she was happy with it, she saved a draft, and sent a link to Randall with a note, "Are you okay with me sending this out to 20,000 Frontier Fire fans?"

Then she left to invite Blake to lunch.

Chapter Eighteen

LIFE WAS GOOD, IN HALEY's humble opinion. She and Blake had gotten over the craziness of the Lindsay drama. They were getting along better than ever, and their new love was growing. He made her heart beat faster from the affection he shared with her daily.

Frontier Fire concerts were mountaintop experiences for both her and Blake every single night, and Ace in the Hole gigs were going extremely well too. In the week since she'd gotten Randall's approval to send out the promo email, Ace in the Hole had seen slightly bigger crowds, even to the point of venues having to turn away fans at the door because they were beyond capacity.

Haley was busy with phone calls to venues for repeat performances, taking Ace in the Hole's schedule well through the end of the year.

In fact, life was going so well, Haley had to remind herself just how far they'd come ... how far *she'd* come in her life. Whenever she stopped to think about it, she made the effort to be grateful, and to verbalize her thankfulness to the One who had made it possible: *thank you, Father. Thank you for your love and blessings, today and every day.*

Today was a big day, the day Brent was arriving. Blake had been looking forward to Brent's visit for weeks. Haley knew the brothers would want to spend every moment they could together, talking, catching up and having fun. She would make herself available to them if they wanted to include her, but she'd also be willing to make herself scarce so they could have time alone.

She'd awakened mid-morning after last night's late concert, wanting to get a jump on some of her booking phone calls. She was on the phone, on hold with a country bar in Hilton Head when another call buzzed through. She glanced at it and saw it was Robbie.

She continued to wait for the bar manager to pick up her call, figuring she'd call Robbie back when she was done. But instead of leaving a voicemail, Robbie sent her a text. She held her phone away from her ear to read it: *Spotted Lindsay in the crowd last night.*

Haley's heart jumped. She hung up on the bar in Hilton Head—she'd call them back later—and immediately phoned Robbie. He picked up right away.

"Hey, sorry to bother you," he said, his voice sporting a tired edge.

"No, it's not a bother. Tell me what happened."

"Nothing, really. We were local last night, playing The Bowery, and we're there again tonight."

Haley nodded. The Bowery was an iconic Myrtle Beach landmark, a bar and grill with a long history of offering live country music for going on fifty years. It was not only a tourist favorite, but it boasted thousands of local fans who stopped by for a burger, beer and music every weekend. It was one of those places that Ace hadn't broken into until recently, and Haley was determined to get them into the regular rotation.

Robbie continued, "We had a two hour gig, and I didn't see her until well into our second set. In fact, I wasn't sure it was her at first. But I kept my eye on her while we were playing, and I watched her push through the crowd to get closer to the stage and then I knew. Definitely Lindsay."

"Did she make eye contact with you?"

"No. She glanced at me, but looked away."

"How about Jake?"

"He didn't notice her."

"Could you tell anything about her demeanor, her mood?"

"Well, she wasn't smiling and dancing like most of the crowd there. I guess she seemed pretty low-key."

"Low-key angry, or low-key calm?"

Robbie let a sound out of his teeth. "I don't know, Haley. I'm not a psychiatrist or a psychic. I don't know what she was thinking or feeling. But you told me to tell you if we ever saw her, so that's what I'm doing."

"No, that's good. Thanks. I appreciate it. Stay safe tonight."

Haley hung up with Robbie. So, Lindsay had made an appearance, finally. She didn't even have to travel to go see her ex-favorite band. They were performing right in her back yard. But Lindsay wasn't stupid. She was well aware that Ace hadn't been playing in The Bowery when Lindsay was in charge of their schedule. She knew what a huge step up this was.

And Haley knew that fact was killing Lindsay.

Jealousy, anger, envy. Haley knew all those things were swirling around in Lindsay's head. Not to mention she was still getting over Jake's breakup. This was a recipe for disaster. Lindsay's negative review campaign was one thing, spreading her anger on the internet. Now she was there in person, in front of the band. Did she choose last night, the first night of a two-night gig to scope out the place, get the lay of the land? Stay quiet and unassuming so she could come back tonight and wreak some havoc?

Was Lindsay that unstable? Or were Blake's fears about Lindsay's potential for danger prompting Haley's imagination to run away with itself? Were they creating drama where it didn't exist?

On the other hand, maybe she was being an intuitive and proactive band manager, preventing a potentially dangerous situation for her guys.

Haley stood and paced the length of the hotel room. She wrenched her hands, squeezing them, shaking them out. She couldn't shake a bad feeling about this. Why had Lindsay shown up?

She walked to her laptop and sat down. It wouldn't hurt to find out about flights to Myrtle Beach today. She knew her mind would be completely wrapped up tonight if she weren't there. She wouldn't be able to concentrate on anything until she got a report from Robbie, and that wouldn't be until late night. She'd be absolutely useless to Frontier Fire, when her heart and soul were telling her that her place tonight was with Ace in the Hole.

She jumped on the airline websites and discovered she could get to Myrtle Beach today, but flights were limited. She'd use the Ace in the Hole credit card to book her flight, and she'd go to The Bowery tonight. Heck, maybe she'd even enlist a few extra security people to provide protection and an extra set of eyes. Who cared if she was going overboard? The safety of her band members made it well worth it.

She navigated through the screens to book a flight, and then glanced at the time. She'd have to hurry. Between catching a ride to the airport, checking in and getting through security, she didn't have much time to waste.

She pulled a small bag out of her closet, threw a handful of clothes into it and zipped it shut. Her heart was racing but she didn't want to speed off half-cocked. She needed to let Blake know what she was doing.

He was normally sleeping at this hour, and would be for at least another hour. She didn't want to wake him with a phone call or even a text. She'd communicate with him the old-fashioned way.

She grabbed the hotel notepad and jotted a note: *Blake, I'm flying to Myrtle Beach today. I'll explain later. Have a great show tonight and I'll most likely see you tomorrow. Haley.* She ripped it off the pad, then after a second thought, she inserted the word, *Love,* in front of her name.

She rushed out the door and wandered down the hallway, trying to remember Blake's hotel room number. 403? 405? "Shoot!" she exclaimed, and then remembered. She slid the note under the door and raced to the elevator.

BLAKE AWOKE, THE ROOM artificially darkened by the light-cancelling shades. He rolled to his side to glance at the digital clock. It was noon. His normal wake up time. He stretched his arms above his head and rotated his hips. He pushed himself out of bed and trudged to the shower.

Then he remembered. Tonight he'd see Brent! Haley would pick him up at the airport and bring him right to the amphitheater tonight and he'd get to show off a little in front of his brother. Elation washed over him as he stepped into the shower.

As he lifted his face to the oncoming spray his thoughts went to Brent. Although it had been a fantastic summer traveling with Frontier Fire, the opportunity of a lifetime, he had really missed his small and dedicated family. Aunt Gloria worked way too hard, and couldn't possibly take a few days off to travel across the country to come see him. And without her, it was difficult for Brent to travel solo. He needed help and accommodation. This mini-vacation for Brent was unique, and the two of them would savor it to the hilt.

Showered, shaved and dressed, he placed a call to Haley to see if she wanted to grab a meal with him. It went straight to voicemail. She either had it powered off or she was on the line. Neither one surprised him. He sent her a text, telling her where he was going and she could meet him there if she wanted.

He left the room with a happy whistle.

HALEY WAS SITTING ON the airplane, 30,000 feet in the air midway between Pittsburgh and Myrtle Beach when a thought assaulted her mind: Brent was arriving today! Brent was quite possibly en route at this moment from Myrtle Beach to Pittsburgh while she was flying in the opposite direction. Or maybe he hadn't boarded his plane yet. Regardless, she needed to contact someone to pick him up.

How could she forget that detail?

Her pulse flitted through her veins and she tried to talk herself down. She had a lot on her mind, and she had completed a million details correctly. She only missed one. Her odds were pretty darn good.

However, the one detail she missed was a huge one. No way could she let Brent arrive at the Pittsburgh Airport and not have anyone to welcome and assist him.

She pulled out her phone which she had placed on Airplane Mode. She typed a text to Randall, knowing it probably wouldn't be sent until they landed. She stuck the phone back in her pocket, and swallowed the lump in her throat.

She'd have time. Once she landed, she'd immediately call Randall and ask him to go to the airport or send someone. No reason to stress. There would be plenty of time.

She *had* to make it happen. If she abandoned Brent, Blake would never forgive her.

BLAKE FINISHED HIS meal. He had developed this weird schedule of sleeping till noon and eating his first meal of the day when most normal people were eating their second meal of the day. He couldn't dive into eating with a hamburger and French fries. His stomach would revolt. So he normally found restaurants that would serve him breakfast for lunch. Today's selection, a ham and cheese omelet with toast hit the spot.

He'd eaten the entire meal alone. He wondered where Haley was, and whether she'd remembered to eat. The girl was a work horse, which was a fact that gave him a mixed reaction. As her boyfriend, he worried that she would throw herself full force into a project, forgetting to stop and do anything secondary, like eat. Or sleep. But because the work she was always doing benefitted him professionally, he reaped all the reward from her efforts. And they were monumental, he couldn't deny that.

She was a delightful blend of smart and forgetful, determined and flexible, confident and insecure.

She was his, and of that, he was most proud. He had no idea what he'd done to deserve her, but he sure was glad she'd fallen in love with him.

He paid for his meal and a tip with his band credit card and left the restaurant. On the walk back, he placed a call to Haley again. Maybe she was done with her previous phone call and he'd reach her.

Nope. The phone went straight to voicemail again.

IT WAS ONLY BECAUSE Haley was sitting by the window directly over the left wing that she was aware of a problem. And it was only because she was staring out the window, obsessing over her communication failure surrounding Brent's pick up that she wasn't calmly reading a magazine and missing the whole thing.

No, she had the best seat in the house to observe a small metal flap on the far end of the airplane's wing suddenly flip up, drawing her attention with a muffled thud. The strong airstream flowing over the wing caught hold of it, and after a few frantic flaps in the blustery breeze, it ripped away from its connection. Now, instead of being held down firmly in two corners as it was designed to work, one nut and one bolt succumbed to the pressure and disengaged, flying never-to-be-seen-again into the air, while leaving the metal flap rapping wildly against the wing like a rock climber in trouble, determined to hold on for dear life with one arm.

Haley gasped as she stared wide-eyed out the window. She tore away her gaze long enough to reach above her head and push the button to summon the flight attendant. A young woman came a few minutes later. "May I help you?"

Haley pointed out the window. "You see that metal flap? Right out there on the wing? Look, it's hanging on by a thread."

The flight attendant leaned closer and her attention followed the direction of Haley's index finger. "I'm sure it'll be ..."

Before she could finish her sentence, the remaining screw, weakened by all the battering, gave up and flew loose, releasing the metal flap into the air, leaving a three by two inch rectangular chasm in the wing.

The flight attendant looked at Haley, her eyes wide with surprise. Haley was certain, based solely on the woman's age that she had never come upon this situation before. It may have been in her flight attendant training class she had a year or so ago, but practical on-the-job experience didn't aid her here.

"Excuse me," she said and headed quickly up the aisle of the plane, her hip bumping every three seats or so on random passengers' arm rests.

Haley darted her attention back to the hole in the wing. Searching for a sign of trouble or despair, she was relieved that she couldn't detect one. The flapping sound of metal against metal was now gone. The wing seemed to be operating as expected, despite the portion now exposed.

In ten minutes, a dinging over the sound system alerted everyone to a message. "Good afternoon, everyone. This is Captain Miller in the cockpit. I have an announcement. We have become aware of a minor maintenance issue regarding the left wing of our aircraft. Although we anticipate absolutely no issues or problems at all, we have been asked to make an unscheduled landing in Charlotte en route to Myrtle Beach. The Charlotte Airport has promised us they will provide maintenance professionals to examine our aircraft promptly and make any repairs needed on a priority basis. We do not expect to be off schedule for long however I must warn you that we will most likely arrive at Myrtle Beach later than originally planned." He turned the microphone off briefly, then his deep, calm voice returned, "Please stay in your seats with your seatbelts on until we land. Again, nothing to worry about. Slight delay. Thank you for choosing to fly with us today."

Haley stretched her hands out in front of her, observing the fingers shaking. Delay, delay, delay. She hated being off the grid, especially with a dire need to use her phone. Helpless, she closed her eyes and concentrated on breathing in and out.

Chapter Nineteen

BLAKE FINISHED DRESSING for tonight's concert, left his hotel room and headed for the front. The limousine that would transport the band to the venue waited outside. He glanced around for Haley and then rolled his eyes, chuckling to himself. Creature of habit. Haley wouldn't be joining them tonight. She was probably at this moment driving over to the airport to pick up Brent. Like he hadn't thought about Brent a thousand times today, a shiver of excitement went through his shoulders.

He still hadn't actually connected with Haley. It was odd, but maybe she was busy with Ace in the Hole stuff. She was usually pretty good about leaving him out of the details so he could go into each performance unencumbered.

He climbed in and settled into a seat. He looked around at his bandmates. "Big show tonight, guys. My baby brother will be in the audience."

"Cool!" Lola, the keyboardist, said. "Can we meet him?"

"Of course. In fact, I'd love to get a photo of him with all of us." He launched into his normal brief explanation. He hated for anyone meeting Brent to be caught off guard and expose Brent to an uncomfortable greeting. "Just so you guys know, my brother is a paraplegic. He's permanently in a wheelchair."

Murmurs of what was probably sympathy, acceptance or surprise filled the limo. "What happened to him?" someone asked.

Blake smiled. No way was he going to transform their carefree ride into an emotional story about the tragic house fire that killed his father and mother and permanently disabled his brother. It was too fun a night for that. So he said, "He jumped out of a window."

They stared at him in surprise, then they all laughed and moved on to a new topic. "Where's Randall tonight?" Blake asked, noticing his absence in the limousine.

"He had to leave, had some personal business to take care of today. He won't be at the concert but he'll be back tomorrow or the next day."

The ride to the venue went smoothly and they all exited the vehicle and entered the huge concert hall through the back doors. Randall had told them it was their biggest venue yet, seating nearly twenty thousand fans. Blake claimed his green room, set out his few belongings, and started his stretches and vocal warmups. About a half hour in, his hair and makeup artist arrived. He was halfway through preparations when his phone rang. It was Aunt Gloria.

"Hey, Aunt Glo. You get Brent off okay?"

"Well, yes I did." Her tentative voice caused him to tense immediately. "He got on his plane fine, but that's why I'm calling. He just called me. He's at the Pittsburgh Airport but Haley isn't there to greet him."

"What?"

"Yeah, the airline associates helped him off the plane and into his wheelchair, but he's not sure where to go next."

Blake frowned. This wasn't like Haley, who was always so reliable and on top of all the details. "Aunt Glo, let me make some calls. I'll let you know what I come up with."

"Okay honey," she said. Blake detected the nerves in her voice. Although Aunt Gloria wasn't the overprotective type, this was a new experience for Brent. He hadn't taken a solo flight since his paralysis, and admittedly, they were both a little nervous about it.

"I'll call you back." He ended the call and called Haley. He felt huge relief when she answered on the first ring.

"Blake! Oh my gosh!"

"What's going on?"

Her elevated stress was evident in her normally calm voice. "We had an unexpected detour. The wing had a mechanical problem and we had to land in Charlotte. I'm delayed."

Blake frowned at his phone. "What are you talking about?"

"My flight to Myrtle Beach. We had to make a landing in Charlotte for mechanical problems."

He huffed his frustration. "Haley, why are you going to Myrtle Beach today? You're supposed to be picking up my brother in Pittsburgh and bringing him to the concert."

"I know, I know. I've been trying to get a hold of Randall to do that but I haven't been able to reach him."

All his triggers were tripped simultaneously and even though he knew he'd regret it later, Blake let his anger take over. He raised his voice and barked into the phone, "Haley! Randall's out of town. Brent's flight landed and he's all alone with no one to help him."

"Oh, my gosh," she started, and he interrupted her.

"You knew how important this was to me. My family is my top priority, and you assured me you'd take care of him." Blake's hair girl went still, eyes widened and tiptoed away, leaving him alone in his green room.

"I'm sorry, I ...,"

"Let me guess, this has something to do with Lindsay. You're abandoning my brother and rushing off to Myrtle Beach half-cocked because of Lindsay."

Her hesitation told him he'd hit the mark. He lowered his voice. "I can't believe this. I can't believe you'd do this, Haley."

"I'm so sorry. Didn't you get my note that I was going to Myrtle today?"

"Note? No note. Where?" He hadn't seen a text, a voicemail, a private message. If she'd left him a note he hadn't seen it. "Never mind. I'm gonna have to go to the airport myself and hope I can get him back before the show starts."

"No, Blake. Just ask someone ..."

"Haley, Brent is my responsibility. I thought you understood that. I trusted you with him. Now, I will pick him up." She started to speak again, but his anger and now the urgency in leaving for the airport got the better of him. "Good bye, Haley." He disconnected the call, rose out of his makeup chair and raced off.

HALEY SOBBED, HER EYES filling with tears that dropped down her cheeks as her shoulders wracked. She struggled to cry soundlessly to attract less attention in the busy airport, but she couldn't. She didn't cry often, but this one had the weight of the world behind it and she let it all out, her despair emitting from her. To discourage attention, she dropped her head and placed her hands over her eyes. *Nothing to see here, just keep moving.* A clean tissue infiltrated the barrier she'd built around herself and she grabbed it, lifting her head to see the back of a kind woman who'd tried to meet her physical needs without interrupting her misery.

Haley allowed herself a solid, unremitting cry for ten minutes and then dragged herself to her feet. She made her way to a public restroom. She took one look at her face in the mirror and wanted to cry again. Every last shred of makeup was either gone, or running a dirty track down her cheeks. She washed her face thoroughly with soap and water, then pulled her makeup kit from her small bag and reapplied. A quick brush of her long hair, and she could almost convince herself that she looked fine.

For it being the worst day of her life.

She'd blown it. She'd never heard Blake's voice infused with so much anger. In all the time she'd known him, he'd never so much as raised his voice. To anyone, let alone her. Even when they'd had the uncomfortable conversation about her job performance, he'd done it kindly. Sharing bad news with a gentle demeanor was so much better than with anger.

But today, she pushed him over the edge. She'd made him so angry that he yelled at her. Worse, she'd let him down and disappointed him in the worst way possible. She'd neglected her commitment to pick up Brent, when she knew what a big deal it was.

She was aware that couples fought at times and recovered. But Blake was so easy going and kind that she doubted that this was reversible. She made her way back to her seat in the terminal, waiting for the plane to be fixed. They were trapped in the Charlotte Airport while the world went about its activities outside of here. They had no control over when they would leave, when they would arrive.

Meanwhile, she had limitless time to think. And worry. And obsess.

Yes, she knew exactly how important Blake's family was to him. She knew exactly how Blake and Aunt Gloria took care of Brent. And this one time when Haley was in charge, Brent paid the price with her forgetfulness. He was stuck, unattended to, in a strange airport. Who had helped him into his wheelchair? Who had guided him to the baggage claim? That had been her job, and she'd dropped the ball.

Would Blake ever forgive her? How about Aunt Gloria? She'd only met the woman once, but Haley's regard for her was very high. She admired Aunt Gloria for the unselfish act she'd demonstrated all those years ago. She had let Aunt Gloria down too.

So Blake was, at this moment, racing to the airport. She wondered if he somehow found a car to drive himself, or did he ask the limo driver to take him? Would he get back to the concert in time? Would they have to extend the warm up acts and delay Frontier Fire's start time?

They'd never had to do that yet. Frontier Fire's concerts were always professional and executed like clockwork. Until today. If Blake's tardiness caused a change to the concert timing, Haley would never forgive herself.

She wondered if Blake would break up with her over this. Could their relationship recover? The threat of renewed tears made her stop going down that line of thought. No more crying. She was done with that. If Blake broke up with her, she'd have to deal with it. It wouldn't be the end of her life.

Despite the fact that she was in love with him.

She closed her eyes to try to stop the flow of thoughts in her head. She tried to doze but her mind was still too active.

If Blake did break up with her, would that be the end of her job with Ace in the Hole? Could they ever work together after this? Would he even trust her with his band's business, or would he fire her over this?

If she lost her job with Ace in the Hole, what would she do? Her parents had already disowned her due to her tendency to flit from job to job with no direction. Getting fired from this job that was supposedly her niche would just cement their accusations. She'd been so sure that she'd found her career, the one thing that she excelled at, that she naturally gravitated to and delivered solid results. But if she could no longer work with Ace in the Hole, would any other band hire her?

She jolted her eyes open. She was driving herself crazy inside her own head. Her thoughts were leading her toward one worst case scenario after another. She needed to put all that aside for now and focus on getting to Myrtle Beach and helping Ace in the Hole deal with the potential Lindsay threat. Maybe it was the last task she'd ever accomplish with Ace, but she was determined to make sure that they were safe tonight. She had no idea how, or what she would do tonight if Lindsay tried something, but she had to be there.

Chapter Twenty

NINE PM.

Nine o'clock in the fricking *night*!

Haley's blood tumbled through her veins so fast that her pulse could be seen pumping under the skin at her wrists. It had been a torturous, never-ending, horrible afternoon and evening of waiting, but finally, the wing of their plane had been fixed, the inspector arrived from a distant airport to look at it, he declared it safe, they re-boarded and flew to Myrtle Beach.

Now, they were deplaning at nine o'clock. Ace in the Hole's gig had just started across town. She needed to get there ASAP. As she raced through the airport to the front door, she summoned the *Uber* app on her phone. Thankfully, she lived in an age where she only had four minutes to wait for a car to pick her up and take her directly to her destination.

As she stood on the sidewalk outside, her mind went to Blake. Had he gotten Brent without incident? Had he arrived safely back at the concert? Did everything go off on time, without a hitch? The absence of any communication from Blake spoke volumes. Normally, they were right in sync on work tasks. If she hadn't made such a huge mistake and left Brent hanging without a ride, Blake would've naturally contacted her, *Got him. Got back safely. Everything's fine.* His silence had to mean either they *hadn't* gotten back safely, or he *had* and specifically chose not to tell her. Which meant that he no longer thought of her as a trusted teammate.

Tears poked her eyes but she wiped them away. Her Uber arrived and she had a job to do. She'd worry about her love life later. Maybe Lindsay had nothing nefarious planned for The Bowery. Maybe this whole unfortunate day was a big flub.

But what if it wasn't?

The Uber driver took her to The Bowery and she tipped him heavily, thanking him for his promptness. She entered the big bar, and immediately the atmosphere sucked her in, the darkened lights, the massive crowd of people, the bodies pushing all around her, but most of all, the festive sound of Ace in the Hole, rocking it. She took a moment to listen. The flawless sound ascended and circulated above the heads of the crowd. They were covering a popular upbeat Radley Ray song and the blended instrumentals filled the room with music while Sam took control of the lyrics. He sure looked the part of a top-rate country singer up there, dressed in tight jeans faded in all the right places, snug cotton shirt, rounded off with cowboy boots and hat. And he knew how to move. Ace was in good hands while waiting for Blake to return.

The crowd thought so too. Many of them were standing still around the perimeter, sipping on a drink and listening, but a good number had taken the dance floor, couples swinging each other around, or groups of girls dancing together while facing the stage, keeping their eyes fastened on Sam.

Back to work. The room was so dark, Haley couldn't scan the crowd for familiar faces. She'd need to move around, inspecting each section for Lindsay. It would be a big job since it was such a large place, and so full with fans. Haley started. She made her way around the perimeter walls first, pushing through the crowd, not disruptively, just trying to cover ground. The dance floor was a little easier. Dancers often pushed between each other trying to claim a better spot on the floor, so she serpentined, putting eyes on each and every one.

After forty minutes of searching, she'd covered every square inch, but hadn't located Lindsay. This was a good thing. No Lindsay, no danger. If Lindsay showed up for the second night of Ace's gig, what other motivation could she have, other than trouble? If she spotted Lindsay, she'd better be prepared to act.

She leaned against the wall, thinking about her next move. How was she prepared to act? Here she was, one woman, no weapons, no defense training. She had to be realistic. If Lindsay was here to cause trouble, what could Haley do about it? She needed help. She pushed to her feet and made her way back through the crowd to reach the bouncer at the front door.

He ignored her at first, and then she leaned in close to his ear and in the loud room, yelled, "I need to talk to you about a security concern. I'm Haley, the band's manager."

He looked into her face, and he must've recognized the seriousness of the situation. He grabbed his cell phone out of his pocket and typed in a text with his big fingers. A moment later, he got a response. He read it and held up one finger to her. *Wait a minute.* She nodded.

A few minutes later, two men made their way to the front door. One took the bouncer's station, freeing up the bouncer and the other man. They motioned for her to follow them. They made their way to the rooms behind the stage, and entered one, closing the door behind them. A muffled quiet provided relief to Haley's ears.

The man turned to her and offered a hand. "I'm Doug, the bar manager tonight."

"Oh hi, Doug. I'm Haley, the band manager."

"You said something about a security concern?"

"Yes, thank you for letting me explain."

Doug nodded. "We take security seriously. Obviously, with a crowd this big and the liquor flowing so freely, things could get out of hand quickly and that's when someone could get hurt. This is Michael, our bouncer."

They nodded at each other, and Haley explained as best she could. "I don't know if we have a concern or not. But we have a potential situation with a disgruntled fan. She was spotted in the crowd last night, and there was no trouble. But I just wonder if she was scoping the place out, ready to make her move tonight."

"What do you think she'll do?"

"I have no idea. But she used to be the guitarist's girlfriend and unofficial band manager. When all that changed, she got mad. She blames me. Lately, she's gone crazy on the internet, leaving bad reviews on websites about Ace in the Hole. It hasn't worked, though. Ace's crowds have been bigger and bigger, despite her comments."

Doug nodded slowly.

"Maybe I'm being paranoid, but I'd hate for her to do something crazy tonight that could end up hurting people. I'm ... I'm so sorry."

Michael shook his head. "We'd rather know and be prepared than go in blind. Thanks for telling us." He turned to his boss. "You and I can talk strategy, but we need to know what this girl looks like so we can keep an eye for her."

Haley nodded. "I've just done an entire sweep of the place and didn't spot her. At least for now. Not to say she can't show up later."

"Do you have a picture?"

Haley was about to shake her head, and then she pulled up the Photo Gallery on her phone. Paging back and back, she hit gold. "Yes!" She had a group shot holding up the Battle of the Bands trophy in Hilton Head. There was Lindsay, standing beside Jake. She enlarged the shot so the screen was filled with only Lindsay and held it out to both men.

Doug took the phone and they glanced at it quickly. "Mind if I screen shot this and forward it to the security staff?"

"Not at all," Haley said, relieved that she had brought in these professionals. She was willing to put herself in a dangerous position to protect The Bowery and Ace in the Hole, but she didn't have the tools or the knowledge to stop Lindsay if she meant business. Now, she had a team.

Doug finished with her phone, returning it to her. "Haley, you continue to scan the crowd and let us know immediately if you see her." Haley nodded in agreement. "Michael, you and I will speak to each of the bouncers tonight to tell them to check the text I sent them and be on the lookout for this girl." He looked back at Haley. "We'll stay in touch tonight."

"Thank you," Haley said, hoping her appreciation was evident on her face.

They disbanded and Haley walked back to the crowded room, continuing her search. Thankfully, after an hour and two more trips around and through the entire bar area, she hadn't spotted Lindsay. She made her way over to where Michael was stationed.

"Nothing to report."

He nodded, his big face looking satisfied. "That's good news."

She needed a break. A moment away from the crowd, a place she could spread her arms and sit down. A rest, to turn her attention away from the intense scan that had taken up her last few hours.

She made her way backstage to the green room. Unlike the venues where Frontier Fire played where each musician had their own private room, Ace in the Hole shared one. Actually, sometimes they didn't have the luxury of a green room. Sometimes they had to change and prep in the men's room or in a store room.

She opened the green room door and noticed The Bowery actually provided a large room with couches and a mini-fridge stocked with water bottles.

"Hey boss!" came Robbie's voice.

"Hi!" Haley greeted them. "Break time, huh?"

"Yeah, we're in between sets. Great crowd out there."

"I know, I've been making the rounds of the place for almost two hours. They're loving you guys." She turned to Sam. He lounged in a recliner in the corner. "You sound great, Sam."

"Thanks. We're having fun here."

Robbie glanced over at Jake. "Man, Haley's here because we're a little worried that Lindsay has something up her sleeve tonight."

Jake frowned, his mouth dropped. "Lindsay. Why?"

"She was here last night. I spotted her."

Jake took that bit of news in, his eyes working the room while he processed it. "Really."

"Yeah. First time since Sam joined us. And you know she's become a little unhinged."

"Yeah." He couldn't deny it after reading the poison spewed over the internet that they had attributed to her. "So what do we do?"

"You guys, absolutely nothing," Haley said firmly. "I've got the professionals working on it. I shared her picture with The Bowery security team, and they're doing it all. You guys, just keeping playing great music."

Jake walked across the room to where Haley stood. He put his hand on her arm. "And you? What are you doing?"

Haley's heart melted at the tender question, and the motive behind it. Jake knew Lindsay's tirade was mostly directed at her. "Keeping my eyes open and my mouth shut."

Jake squeezed her arm and let it go. "Good. You stay safe."

The guys finished their break and returned to the stage. Haley could hear the minute the crowd noticed their return because they went crazy screaming and clapping, welcoming their band back. Haley settled into the couch, ready for that break. It had been a long day.

The music began, muffled by the walls and her distance from the main room. The activity of the day, the draining emotion, the sheer length of the day, all started to take a toll on her. Her eyes drifted shut and the couch was so very comfortable. She started to drift off. She allowed it, since all here in her world was taken care of. Just a short zone-out and she'd be recharged.

BLAKE RAN BACKSTAGE after the encore, his adrenaline high, a beaming smile on his face. Instead of hanging around for the regular high fives with the band before heading to their dressing rooms, he had a higher priority. "Hey guys, hang here for a sec. I'll go get my brother for that photo opp."

He raced off behind the huge curtain to the far stage left ramp. Before he went on tonight he'd arranged with one of the venue's attendants to wheel Brent there, ahead of the crowd, safe from the mass exodus. Brent had actually been located here for the entire encore.

He ran to the designated spot and waved, catching sight of Brent sitting in his chair with the amphitheater attendant close by. Brent was stoked, he could tell. Blake's heart relaxed, happy that he could share this with his brother. He approached Brent and leaned down, pulling him into a hug. His enthusiasm actually pulled the kid's one hundred and sixty pounds out of the chair, and into Blake's embrace. Brent laughed and pounded him on the back.

"Awesome, man. Wow, you were great. I'm so happy to have seen it."

Blake laughed lightheartedly, all the care in the world released. All the stress and strain of the evening, all the worry, all the anger, gone in this instant. This moment made it all worth it.

He turned to the attendant, shook his hand, and tucked a twenty dollar bill into his pocket. "Thank you. Thank you so much."

The attendant nodded and left.

"I want you to meet the band. Come on." Blake knew this would be a huge moment for Brent. He'd grown up on Frontier Fire music, been a huge fan in his adolescence, in Frontier Fire's heyday. He wheeled Brent over to where the band congregated, waiting for them. "Guys, this is Brent."

True celebrities, the band members all exploded with hearty greetings and welcomes. Surrounding Brent's chair, they leaned down to greet him with heartfelt words about how much it meant to them that he'd come. They praised Blake's singing abilities and the great job he was doing. Blake knew they were laying it on thick because of the special bond he shared with Brent. But he loved them for doing it. This moment, right here, was the best of his life, and most likely, Brent's.

Blake handed his phone to one of the stagehands and they all gathered for a picture. They positioned Brent in the middle and everyone gathered around him, kneeling or bending to position themselves at chair level. "One, two, three, cheese!" Big smiles and happy pats on the back, and more thanks to Brent for coming. It was unreal. Larger than life.

They all disbanded, leaving Blake and Brent a little breathless. "Take you to my green room," said Blake and he grabbed the handles of Brent's chair, moving the chair and pushing. Once they got settled in, he retrieved a couple water bottles from the fridge and handed one to Brent. "You hungry?"

"No. Sit down man, before you fall down. You don't have to wait on me, geesh." Brent shook his head in wonder.

Blake chuckled and fell backwards into the couch. It felt good to be off his feet, off his mind. All was good. "So, pour it on. Praise for your big brother. What'd you think?"

Brent shook his head. "I'm sure I can't come up with the right words. It's inadequate to say great. Or awesome. Or even unbelievably monumental. But all those things are true. You are amazing. You did so, *so* good up there. You belonged. You have talent. I mean, I always knew it. But you can perform at this level, Blake. This is just the start. You're on your way. Sky's the limit."

Blake listened, motionless while his brother shoveled it on. What he didn't expect was the stab of tears in his eyes. He sniffed and grabbed a tissue from nearby. Brent wouldn't make fun of him for crying. This was too huge, and both of them knew it.

"How many cover band singers get to do this?" Blake said, and his voice caught. "How many dream about this chance night after night while they're scraping by, singing for small crowds who aren't even paying attention to them while they're talking and drinking and partying? There's no comparison between that kind of gig, and this."

"And you've done both," Brent said with a happy smile.

"Yeah. I still can't quite believe it."

"What comes next?"

Blake shrugged. "Josh Lakely comes back in a few weeks. He'll take his spot and I'll go back to mine with Ace in the Hole."

"Okay. And Ace is doing better now too, right?"

"Yeah, absolutely. They're playing bigger bars and even a few cool venues with stadium seating. We're scrabbling and climbing the ladder. Up, always up."

"With Haley's help. She was a game changer for you guys. You'll get there."

Blake tossed his tissue but didn't respond. Brent noticed. "What? Don't tell me you're mad at Haley for forgetting me at the airport."

Blake avoided his brother's eyes. Brent knew him way too well.

"Bro, come on. Seriously?"

Blake brought his hands up and ran his fingers through his hair, leaving his curls ragged. "Brent, this is not for you to weigh in on."

Brent studied him silently for a moment, and then wheeled his chair so he was facing Blake, inches from his face. "Yeah, I think it is. Because if you have even half a notion to punish Haley for forgetting to give me a ride, then man, your priorities are way off."

Blake exhaled a frustrated breath. "She knew how important it was to me to pick you up without a hitch. And she raced off on a wild hare.

And she left you stranded." He looked away. "I can forgive a lot, but I have my limits. And I don't think I can forgive her for that. Maybe it's time to end it."

"Hold on. *Stranded*, is a bit of a stretch. I wasn't in the desert in the middle of nowhere without any food or water. I was in an airport. If I had to, I could've used my little brain to get myself to the venue, bro."

"No, that's not the point. It's not that you couldn't ..."

"Bro, stop it. Okay? Listen, I'm not a child. I know I'm paralyzed. But that doesn't mean that I can't do everything, well, just about everything, that any other guy my age can do. I'm not helpless. I just can't walk. That's it."

Blake focused his eyes on his brother's, nowhere else. "But you didn't have the arrangements. She was supposed to be there and take care of you. Get you off the plane, get your luggage, get you in the limo. She failed at that, and let us both down."

"So what? Boo hoo, I can't figure that out for myself? I'm a smart guy, Blake, whether you believe it or not." He threw his hands up in the air. "Change of plans. I need to find my own way to where you're playing your concert. Can't be too hard to figure out. Is that too much of a challenge for a grown man? No." Brent reached out and placed a soft hand on Blake's cheek, cupping it fondly. His voice lowered. "I'm not a kid anymore. I know you love to play the protector role, and I swear, I appreciate it. And the love behind it. But Blake, you need to let me grow up."

Ten seconds could have passed, or a full five minutes, Blake didn't know. But an overwhelming truth filled his head and wouldn't let him go until he shared it with his brother, for the very first time. "I have to protect you. It's my job to take care of you. Because it ... this," he motioned to Brent's legs, "was all my fault."

"What? No. Of course it wasn't."

Blake nodded, first slowly, then growing in pace. "Yes it was. This wouldn't have happened if it weren't for me."

Brent pulled back, rolled his chair backwards an inch or two. Joking, but not entirely, he said, "Are you telling me you were the one who set that fire, bro? Because uh, wow, that would be quite the confession."

"No, no. Of course not." He covered the short distance Brent had put between them by scooting forward on the couch and grabbing his brother's hands. "I should've been there. I never should've been safely across town in my friend's house. If I'd been there I could've helped you get out. Without hurting yourself."

Brent blinked, his face crushed with emotion.

"It's all my fault," Blake murmured. He closed his eyes and welcomed the tears shed. A waterfall of pent up tears over the mountain of guilt and regret he'd carried with him over the last dozen years. He hadn't been there for his family when they needed him the most, so he sure would be there for them now. He'd be the best protector and provider he could possibly be for Brent and Aunt Gloria. But it would never be enough to make up for his absence the night they needed him the most.

He'd move on with his own life, but he had to keep a clear sight of what was most important: his family. His responsibility to his family. And his efforts not to fail them again. Life hadn't been easy, but it had never been as hard for him as it was for Brent. Whatever he could do to make life a little easier for him, Blake would do.

The cushion on the couch next to him crumbled and he looked to see that Brent had maneuvered himself out of his chair and onto the couch. Brent put his arms around him and pulled Blake into a solid, warm hug. He was whispering softly, and Blake had to concentrate to hear what his muffled words were.

"Don't be a Superman. It's not your fault. Don't be a Superman."

Moments passed and Blake let his brother hold him, encourage him, make him feel better, his words swirling around the room and landing on Blake's conscience. He'd never allowed Brent to be the protector—had never needed him to be. But Brent was here for him now and he was glad.

Blake straightened and pulled away, using the palms of his hands to wipe away the remaining evidence of his emotional breakdown. "Sheesh," he joked. "What a crybaby."

Brent laughed, and Blake knew deep in his soul that Brent would never speak of this incident again. Never tease him, never remind him. But one thing was sure, it was healing. And Blake had a whole new perspective on how his own protectiveness, his obsession with protecting Brent, had outlived its usefulness. Brent was right. He wasn't a child, and Blake needed to allow his little brother to spread his wings without him constantly taking care of all challenges for him.

"So," Brent said, "where was Haley anyway? Did you ever find out?"

Blake shrugged. "She went to take care of an Ace in the Hole situation. Or at least, what she perceived as an Ace in the Hole situation."

"Well, that sounds like a very reasonable *and forgivable* offense."

Blake didn't want to analyze his feelings about Haley's betrayal. One major, life-changing revelation per night was plenty.

"Look, I know you don't want to talk about your relationship with me, bro, and I understand that. But let me just put a few things out there. Number one, she's awesome. She's the best thing that's ever happened to you, and I don't mean just professionally, although she's been awesome at that too. But personally. She's good for you, and you're lucky to have her."

Blake looked down at his lap.

Brent continued, "And number two, only you know what you can live with in a relationship and what is a showstopper. But I take *me* off the table." Blake looked up at him. "That's right. Don't use *me* as a reason you're mad at her or think you want to break up with her. This thing tonight ..." he gestured with both hands between the two of them, "has absolutely nothing to do with Haley. Her leaving me at the airport because she was off working for your business, that's no big deal. And unless you want to now load me up with unwarranted guilt, like you've been carrying around inside for way too long, then please. Don't break up with her because of me."

Blake dropped his head, suddenly exhausted. "How about we get back to the hotel?"

Brent nodded. "Sounds good to me. How about we trash the room like a real rock star?"

Blake shook his head and pushed out his amusement in a chuckle. They made their way to the door. "How'd you get so smart, anyway?"

Brent leaned forward and opened the door, gesturing for his brother to go ahead. "It happened while you were running yourself ragged, taking care of my every tiny need."

Chapter Twenty One

SOMETHING WAS TUGGING on her feet. What was tugging on her feet?

Haley drifted awake, and the first thing that permeated her consciousness was the muffled sound of Ace in the Hole music rising above the din of a massive crowd, a few rooms away. She was in the green room, she'd fallen asleep. She opened her eyes.

A shadow passed in front of her bleary vision, and she turned her head. A strong push from behind caused her body to flop forward at the waist, her face hitting her knees. She gasped and screamed.

"Shut up."

She wrenched at the waist, turning to see who was behind her, but caught sight of her own two feet bound together with, what? A rope? A zip tie? She used her full strength to pull her two feet apart, but it was no use. They were bound tight.

Now it was all becoming clear, her mind pulling out of its exhausted fog. Lindsay had entered the green room undetected while she was sleeping, tied her feet, and before she was fully awake, was now working on her hands.

"Stop it!" Haley shouted, then added in a "Help!" in case someone could hear her. But Lindsay'd had the benefit of timing, and wakefulness. Haley's hands were now bound together as tightly as her feet. Lindsay circled around to the front of the couch and stood over Haley, her facial features skewed with hatred, her arms bent and fists planted on her hips.

"Nice try, stupid," Lindsay smirked. "How do you expect anyone to hear your cries for help when the band is so loud?" She shook her head at Haley.

Haley's head was spinning. "Lindsay, we're onto you. I have the whole Bowery security team on the lookout for you. You think you're so smart? No. You left so many trails that you were going to cause trouble tonight, even I could follow it. You're not going to get away with it."

An angry crimson flush crept up Lindsay's neck and covered her face. Her hand became a striking serpent, slapping Haley forcefully with the back of her palm. Haley choked on the pain, unable to bring a hand up, determined not to give Lindsay the pleasure of seeing her react.

"Do you know what a useless wench you are? Just because you're a rich girl and you've had everything you've ever wanted handed to you on a silver platter, you think you can come in to our band and change everything. How self-centered you are. Let me tell you something, Ace in the Hole was just fine before you showed up."

Haley tugged at the ties binding her wrists behind her, gasping at the pain she was causing. They had to be either hard plastic or metal zip ties and they had no give whatsoever. Every bit of struggle on her part was ripping her tender skin. She looked up at Lindsay. "They were fine for a local cover band. Playing the same beach bars every weekend for crowds of about a hundred people. But look at them now. They're playing gigs they used to only dream about. The Bowery, Lindsay!"

Lindsay's face scrunched in disgust and she launched a ball of spit onto Haley's face.

"Eewww," Haley groaned when it hit its mark. How disgusting was that? A loogie of Lindsay's spit landing on her face that she had no way to wipe away. She worked on holding back the bout of nausea that had instantly formed in her stomach.

"Someone has to teach you rich people a lesson," Lindsay continued. "Someone has to show you that you can't just take some perfectly good thing and change it, just because you have the massive funds to do it. Daddy's money. You are worthless yourself, and have never done anything worthwhile on your own merit."

Haley opened her mouth to argue and then closed it. She let Lindsay's words simmer in her mind. She hadn't used any of Daddy's money to promote Ace in the Hole. In fact, because of her work with Ace in the Hole, Daddy had disowned her and made it clear that he wouldn't be supporting her at all. Everything she'd done for Ace in the Hole and Frontier Fire was because of her own hard work, innovation and can-do attitude. She hadn't had any experience with any of it. But that hadn't stopped her.

She wasn't one to toot her own horn, and she certainly wouldn't try to do it with such an unreceptive audience as Lindsay, but she was darn proud of her work. She'd accomplished a lot in a short period of time that no one else had.

Lindsay walked across the room to a backpack sitting on a table. She reached in. What did she have in there? Oh God, was it a gun? Was Lindsay crazy enough to execute her point-blank here in the back room of The Bowery tonight? Haley let loose the loudest scream she could emit from her mouth, no words, just a long, loud and terrified scream.

Lindsay pulled two long tubes out of the bag and turned, covering the space between her and Haley quickly. She reached out and slapped Haley again, trying to end the screaming. "Shut up, I said."

Haley stared, confused, at the items in Lindsay's hand. It wasn't a gun. "What are those things?"

"Wouldn't you like to know?" Lindsay said nastily, then she set one on the coffee table in front of the couch where Haley was bound. Haley studied the item closely. A tube about six inches long from end to end, the bottom was a black circular base. She couldn't tell if it was metal or a plastic material, but the base held in place a colorful tube, red with a cartoon rendering of a firecracker. A long fabric wick came out the top.

"A firecracker?" Haley said, alarmed. "What are you going to do with that?"

Lindsay left the first one on the table in front of Haley and moved to the far side of the room and set the second one up there. She turned to Haley and smirked. "Set it off, you idiot."

Haley's mouth dropped open. Lindsay was using two colossal fireworks as weapons. These weren't just the little sparklers you gave to children on the Fourth of July. These were the big mothers, part of an arsenal of fireworks used to entertain large crowds of Americans on their nation's birthday.

It was confirmed. Lindsay was a raving maniac.

She had to try to talk some sense into her. "Lindsay," she said, striving to make her voice come off as both authoritative and understanding. "Don't do that. That could hurt people. That's the last thing you want to do."

"Hey, if people get hurt, I can't really help that."

"So, what is your plan? Why are you setting off fireworks in the back room of a bar?" The question was so outrageous Haley couldn't believe she was actually asking it. She strove to keep all criticism out of her voice because she didn't want to incite Haley any further. The best she could do was hope that someone would wander by the room and help her before Lindsay's insane plan was set into motion.

Keep her talking. It could save your life.

Lindsay pulled a lighter out of her backpack and flipped it with her thumb until a small flame popped out. A harmless flame, no harm done until it was used to ignite the fireworks. Then, no telling what disaster would happen.

"Dear God, help me! Help us all! Stop this woman!" Haley didn't realize her prayer was shouted out loud until Lindsay looked over at her.

"He can't help you now. It's about to be over." She released the igniter of the lighter, and the flame disappeared. "This is my revenge. On you. On Jake, who dumped me. On the band, who abandoned me. I worked so hard for them, and never got a penny for it. We were a family. Until you came along." Spit flew from her mouth as she recited her monologue, her face twisted with jealousy and rage. "You came with your fancy clothes and your fancy sports car and turned Blake's head. You snap your fingers and all this stuff starts happening. And what about me?"

Haley gave up on struggling with the wrist ties and hoisted herself forward. Maybe she could get to her feet, hop over to Lindsay and hoist her body into her, throwing her off guard. It was worth a try. Time was of the essence.

On the first try, she lost her balance and fell backwards on the couch. She tried again. She managed to get to her two feet, but wobbled clumsily until she could balance herself. She bent her knees and hopped. She landed, stayed on her feet and hopped again. Four hops later, she'd reached Lindsay at the table with the second firecracker.

But Lindsay had seen her clumsy approach. She placed her hands on both of Haley's shoulders and pushed, hard. Haley fell backward, no way to help herself, and crashed to the floor.

"Maybe this will be a deterrent to places booking Ace in the Hole. Word will spread about what happened at an Ace in the Hole show at The Bowery, and the venues will no longer want them. Too much of a liability. Venues were warned, you know."

Haley wrenched her neck to look up at Lindsay. She was talking about the internet reviews. Lindsay's admission that she'd left them all, now claiming they were a warning to venues to stop booking the band before this maniacal disaster was launched.

"Ace in the Hole will fail. And hey, if it means their know-it-all manager has to die, oh well, right?"

Haley squirmed on the floor, struggling to get back to her feet. "No Lindsay, don't do it. It'll never work! You're going to get caught and spend the rest of your life in jail. It's not worth it! Put the lighter down. Walk out the door, and leave Ace in the Hole alone. Believe me. It's the only way."

Lindsay turned her head and came over to where Haley was shouting at her from the floor. She kneeled, heart-stoppingly close. "And let you win? Let you have everything you want? No way."

Haley shook her head. "I'm not winning! In fact, I'm losing. Everything." She had no intention of telling Lindsay her problems, but if it helped get through Lindsay's demented haze of a brain and alter her path of destruction, she would do it. "My parents have already disowned me. I don't have a penny of all that money that you seem to think I have unlimited use of. Nothing. Not one cent. And Blake? I did something to make him angry and I doubt he'll ever forgive me. Next time I see him, it wouldn't surprise me if he broke up with me. And I can't imagine he'd want me to be Ace's manager under those circumstances. So, you see? You think I have everything I want? No. I have nothing. I've lost everything." Tears welled in her eyes as she just now realized the truth in the words she was shouting at her worst enemy. "Don't make me lose my life, too."

Lindsay stared at Haley's face, her bottom lip trembling, her eyes tracking while her brain whirred. She was motionless for almost a solid minute, and Haley began to think she'd gotten through to her. Then Lindsay spit out, "You're lying. I can't believe a word a liar says. Because liars lie. And you're a liar."

Haley dropped her head back on the floor and heaved a sob. It was over. It was all over. She was going to be killed by a crazy woman in the back of a bar in a fiery firecracker explosion. She'd never have a chance to tell Blake she was sorry for abandoning Brent. Tell him one more time that she loved him. She closed her eyes and tried to remember the verses of the psalm about the shepherd. She'd memorized it in Sunday

School when she was a child, recited it in front of the church for some event. Every once in a while as an adult, when she was facing hardship, she pulled out her Bible and read it. The psalm had power, the ancient words that millions of people besides her had gained comfort from.

Our God was a strong God, an all-powerful God, and Haley knew it, in this moment, when her life was almost over. As much as she didn't want to leave the world this early, she trusted her Lord to be with her, to be in control, to take care of everything. She cleared her mind of everything except remembering those beautiful words. She spoke them out loud.

"The Lord is my shepherd, I shall not want."

Lindsay shook her head at Haley with a smirk, and got to her feet. She kicked the toe of her sneaker into Haley's face. Haley gasped at the pain, then continued her recitation, "He maketh me to lie down in green pastures. He leadeth me beside still waters."

Lindsay turned and retrieved the lighter that she'd placed on the table by the door. She removed the lid and flicked it, a flame appearing.

"He restoreth my soul. He leadeth me in the paths of righteousness for his name's sake."

Lindsay lowered the flame to the long wick of the firecracker sitting on the table, ignited it. She ran to a far corner of the room, throwing herself down to the floor.

Haley's eyes went wide and she raised her voice to a shout, "Yea, though I walk through the valley of the shadow of death, I will fear no evil, for thou art with me. Thy rod and thy staff, they comfort me."

From her vantage point, Haley watched the flame eat up the length of the wick, and then the firecracker detonated. The big tube exploded, the familiar whizzing sound of happy, celebratory Fourth of July fireworks contained in this small room. The tube flew into the air, and collided with the ceiling. But the power behind it didn't stop there. The ceiling gave way and the firecracker continued its powerful flight up, up through the drywall ceiling, up through the attic above, through the wooden structural boards, and all the way out through the roof of the building. Haley gasped, wide-eyed. She could see straight from her spot on the floor all the way through to the star-filled sky.

Her voice lowered and her recitation went into autodrive, "Thou preparest a table for me in the presence of mine enemies. Thou anointest my head with oil. My cup runneth over."

Through the walls of this room, in the open expanse of the bar, they knew something had happened. Ace in the Hole stopped playing, and in the absence of that amplified sound, Haley could hear the fire alarm chirping an urgent call. The crowd let out a cohesive scream as the sprinklers let loose with water, here in the back room, and Haley had to assume, in the big room too. Chaotic sounds reached her and she could imagine the clumps of people's feet making their frantic way to the door. She hoped Michael and Doug and their team were leading the people, restoring order, so that everyone escaped without harm.

Here in the room, though, Haley detected a shadow moving from the right side of her head. Lindsay had stood and gone to the firework directly in front of the couch, inches behind where Haley lay bound on the floor. "No! Don't!" she yelled but she caught the flicker of fire in Lindsay's hand.

Whispering now, Haley finished, "Surely goodness and mercy shall follow me all the days of my life. And I will dwell in the house of the Lord forever."

Building debris cascaded from the attic and Haley watched it approach her on the floor. It could've been remnant materials from the hole in the roof caused by the explosion. Or it could've been an object stored in the attic that no longer had a floor to rest on. But it was big and it looked heavy, and Haley watched it fall. She bent her legs, bringing her bound feet and arms to her chest in a fetal position, her best attempt to shield and protect herself in the seconds remaining.

Then, it landed on her head and shoulders. And all went black.

Chapter Twenty Two

THE BUZZING OF BLAKE's cell phone woke him from a restless sleep. He had no idea how long he'd actually been out, because since turning out the light hours ago his mind had whirred and whirred over Haley. Brent's words about not breaking up with her over him, had hit home. Since Brent had helped him see that Blake's attempts to make life easier for his dear brother were actually impeding his maturation into full adulthood, it all fell into place.

He was doing more harm than good caring for Brent. And he needed to cut it out and let the kid grow up.

In light of that realization, he now understood that he'd treated Haley unfairly. All she'd been trying to do was help and his anger at her was unwarranted. The next time he saw her, he'd apologize and pray to God she would give him a renewed chance to show her just how much he loved her.

He scrambled for the phone on the bedside table in the dark room. "Hello?" he said, keeping his voice quiet so he wouldn't wake Brent up.

"Blake, thank God we got you."

Blake shook his head and tried to focus his tired eyes on the digital clock. It was nearly four am. "Jake? What's going on? What's wrong?"

"There's been an explosion. At the Ace in the Hole gig."

Blake sat straight up in bed. Quietness forgotten, he barked into the phone, "What? What happened? Are you guys all right? Any of you hurt?"

Brent shifted in the bed next to his. He mumbled words, but Blake gave him a sharp, "Shhh."

"The three of us are okay."

"Thank God."

"But Blake ... Haley's injured."

Blake's brain shut down and he couldn't see or think of words. He was in a spiraling tunnel of black and he couldn't focus.

"It was Lindsay, man. She went crazy and blew up the place." Jake's voice caught and he sobbed and went on with a shaky tone. "She had Haley tied up and no one was there to help her."

Blake charged out of bed, throwing the blanket off and coming to his feet with one fluid motion. "Is she going to make it?" His voice croaked out the most important question. Nothing else mattered but the answer to that question.

"I don't know. She's unconscious."

"Where? Where are you?"

Jake gave him the name of the hospital and Blake wrote it down. "I'll be there as soon as I can." He ended the call, ran over to the main light switch and bathed the room in light. "Wake up. We're going to Myrtle Beach."

Brent pushed the blankets back and used his arms to swing his legs to the side of the bed. He leaned forward to pull his wheelchair close and lifted himself into it. "Haley?"

"Yes. She was right. And I was dead wrong."

With Randall and Haley both gone, he had no one to run logistics for getting them both from Pittsburgh to Myrtle Beach as quickly as possible. He had the number of the limousine driver in his Contacts and called him, cajoled him into driving them to the airport immediately. They grabbed the minimum items they needed and raced to the front lobby, where the driver dashed them to the airport. In early morning light traffic, they managed to complete the trip in twenty minutes. It was just after four thirty.

They checked the Departure board and saw that the next flight to Myrtle Beach was in two hours. They raced to the Ticketing agent.

"We need two seats on the six am flight to Myrtle."

The agent stared at them slowly, as if they'd woken her from a nap and she needed to reorient herself. She tapped into her keyboard, her eyes blinking in slow motion. Blake restrained his desire to reach out and wrap his hands around her neck and shake her. Anything to make her work faster.

"No, that flight is full." The ticket agent lifted eyes to his and popped her gum.

"When does the next one go?"

She returned her gaze to her monitor. "One o'clock this afternoon."

His heart wrenched. "That's too late. I have to get on that six am."

The big uniformed lady shrugged. "You and two hundred other passengers, who booked their flights way before now."

He let loose an anguished cry. "You don't understand. My girlfriend was injured tonight, and she's lying in a hospital, unconscious. We'd had a disagreement before she left and I now know she was right, and I was dead wrong. I need the chance to tell her. I need to get there and tell her that I love her, and ask her to forgive me for being such an idiot. I don't deserve her, but I need the chance. Please. Is there anything you can do to get us to Myrtle Beach?"

Her expression had transformed from bored and sleepy, to empathetic during the course of his speech. Now, he rested his hopeful eyes on her, praying that she would help.

"Well, boy, now why didn't you say so?" She patted his hand, put a big smile on her face, and went back to the computer. *Tap tap tap*. "Hmmm, no," she murmured. "Let's try this." *Tap tap tap*. She used her index finger to run down the monitor screen, then back to the keyboard. *Tap tap tap.* "Well, how about that?"

Her smile grew and Blake held his breath, hoping she'd found a way for the two of them to get on that six am plane. Brent wrapped his hand around Blake's forearm and Blake turned his head to meet his gaze. "If there's only room for one, then take it, bro."

"What? No! What about you? I wouldn't just desert you here."

Brent gave him an ironic eyes-wide-open expression. "If you have the chance to go, and there's no room for me, go. I'll find my way home."

Blake's mind ran with the implications. Frontier Fire was bussing to Philadelphia today and Brent was flying out from there tomorrow. How would he ever make it ...?

A calming force came over him. Time for a new approach, starting now. "Okay," he said to Brent. "My higher priority is being with Haley. You'll be fine on your own." *Even if it killed him.*

A happy smile formed on Brent's face. He held out a palm and Blake slapped it. "He is teachable," Brent said with a chuckle. Blake wanted to smack his brother's shoulder, but the ticket agent drew his attention back. She was printing some forms out of her printer. She ripped them off at the perforated edges and handed them to Blake.

"What's this?" Blake said breathlessly.

"It's two seats to Myrtle Beach at six o'clock, that's what that is."

Blake jumped into the air and whooped. He reached over the counter and pulled the ticket agent in for a kiss on her cheek. She looked pleasantly surprised, then she got back to business. "Okay, these are special tickets only available to family members of airline employees."

"But ..." Blake said.

"*But*, it was the only way to get you on that plane. You have priority over the other Stand By passengers, and I can see that there are most likely going to be stand bys pulled."

"Do we need to show ID?" Blake asked, terrified that they'd get this close, then be turned away for not having the proper identification. Since they really weren't family members after all.

"No. They will ask you if you are a family member of an airline employee, and you say yes." She shrugged. "It's the best I could do."

Blake shook off his nerves. Telling one little white lie if it meant getting to Haley's side was a decent payoff. "Thank you. I can't thank you enough."

She smiled warmly. "Now, don't you waste this chance. You get to your lady's side and you tell her you love her. For all you're worth!"

"I'll do that."

They turned and raced to the security checkpoint. On their way, Blake said a silent prayer. *Be with us, God.*

BUZZING FILLED HER ears, as if a swarm of bumblebees were crammed into her skull, all fighting for a way to get out.

Pounding at both her temples, as if a jackhammer was splitting into the bone.

At the slight turn of her head, a torturous ache attacked her neck where it connected with her spine.

Awareness continued to dawn, and with eyes still closed and moments ticking by, Haley came to one conclusion: she was alive!

She remembered reciting Psalm 23 as her entire world was exploding around her. She was bound and tied and unable to escape as a crazy woman who hated her blew the building up all around her. Haley had offered herself to God to rescue her and take her to his kingdom.

But here she was! Her body was wracked with pain. But bodily pain meant that she was still here.

The thought launched her out of the dark grip that had pulled her under and she opened her eyes with a gasp. She looked around the room. She was lying in a hospital bed and her hands and feet were no longer bound. She lifted her hands up and placed them on her head. It was wrapped in bandages.

"Hey," a male voice said, then another, "Haley!" Into her line of vision came two faces, both with happy smiles, Jake and Robbie.

"Hi," she tried to say, but her throat was dry and she coughed and tried again. "Hi, you guys."

They both laughed like it was the funniest thing she'd ever said. "Wow. Welcome back."

She cleared her aching throat again. "How long was I out?"

"Oh man, about seven hours?"

"Was I in a coma?"

Robbie shrugged. "We'll let the doctor give you the details but it sure seemed like it. We're just so glad you're safe." He leaned over her in the bed and covered her body gently with his own, attempting to embrace her.

"Do you remember what happened?" Jake ventured cautiously.

She nodded. "I remember everything. It was Lindsay."

They both stood looking down at her, their faces pained. "Yep."

"Did they get her? Is she in custody?"

"Yes. They got her, Haley."

Haley rested her eyes, exhausted after that little bit of interaction. Then the next question, the most important one, came to mind and she forced it out. "Was anyone hurt? Did everyone get out?"

"No one died," Robbie rushed to say.

"Thank God."

"But a lot of them are here. We made the doctors and nurses earn their keep last night."

"Lots of injuries?"

"Yeah."

Tears flooded her eyes and her voice cracked. "But nobody died."

"Right."

The knowledge of that good news made her body want to sink under its restful blanket again, and she said, whether out loud or silently, she didn't know, "Thank you, Lord."

BLAKE JUMPED OUT OF the taxi cab on the curb in front of the hospital. The cabbie popped the trunk and he pulled Brent's chair out and set it up near the car door so Brent could settle into it. All set, they raced into the hospital. Stopping at the Information Desk, they got Haley's room number and headed there.

The room was bathed in sunlight. The blinds were pulled and the early morning sun flowed through the windows. So appropriate for Haley, who was a source of light for all those around her.

He first noticed his two best friends. They were sitting in the corners of the tiny hospital room and they both came to their feet to join in a quiet group hug. No words were necessary between them, but they shared them anyway, "So sorry."

"Love you guys."

"Thank God."

Blake turned around to stare at Haley. Tears pricked the corners of his eyes and he struggled to push them back. Her entire skull was wrapped in white gauze bandages, like a mummy wrap. A crimson drip had soaked through over her right temple. The precious skin of her face, where not bandaged, was bruised and discolored. Purple and yellow and brown covered the beautiful features he loved so much, that gorgeous face that belonged to the woman he loved. Her right shoulder was held in a stabilizer device and both her hands were wrapped in ice packs.

But she was alive.

He turned to look at his friends. "Has she woken up?"

Robbie and Jake walked over. "Yes. She woke up about seven o'clock. She spoke to us and she said she remembered everything. That's good, because the police will want to question her. They're going to throw the book at Lindsay."

They all stood along the side of the bed and gazed down at her. Brent wheeled as close as he could. Robbie and Jake smiled when they saw him. "Hey, Brent. Just another dull weekend visit with your brother, huh?"

They all laughed, glad they could joke. Things were bad, but they were also so good. So much to be thankful for.

Haley's nurse walked into the room, took her vitals and entered all the figures into an electronic portable device. Waiting till she was done, so as not to interrupt her, Blake asked, "How's she doing?"

"Pretty well. We'll know more when she wakes up. The fact that she woke up once and spoke to her friends lucidly is promising."

The nurse left and the four men continued to watch Haley for any sign of movement. "So, what happened?" Blake asked resignedly.

Robbie and Jake answered his question by shifting the explanation back and forth between the two of them, both combining to the full story.

"Haley had an inkling that Lindsay was becoming unraveled because of the negative internet comments she was publishing constantly."

"When Lindsay showed up in the crowd at The Bowery on the first of our two-night gig, I let Haley know."

"She moved heaven and earth to get here in time for the second show. She met with the bouncers and the Bowery security team and had a good plan in place, what to do in case Lindsay showed up."

"But despite all that, Lindsay got into the back room undetected. She snuck up on Haley and bound her feet and hands together, then set off two majorly big firecrackers in the green room."

"What?" Blake exclaimed. "Fireworks? Like, the explosive kind you set off for Fourth of July?"

"Exactly. Lindsay must've swiped them somehow over the holiday and saved them for the attack. She must've been planning this for a while."

"When she set them off, they blew the roof clear off The Bowery. A fire started in the green room. The fire alarms sounded, the sprinklers started, everyone raced for the door. Since Haley was stuck in the back room right beneath one of the holes in the roof, debris rained down on her hard and knocked her out."

"Lindsay got injured too. We have no idea how bad. Policemen are guarding her hospital room door."

"And The Bowery?" Blake asked.

Robbie shrugged. "They'll have some rebuilding to do. They'll have to close down for a while, but they're insured. They'll be fine."

Blake staggered on his feet and left Haley's bedside. He stumbled to a chair in the corner and flung himself into it. "I can't believe I missed all this. I should've been here with you guys."

Again. It was like déjà vu. One more time in his life, the people he loved and cared about were placed in life-threatening danger, and he was safely tucked away, oblivious to the pain and destruction. He could've helped get people out. He could've made sure Haley was safe, and not captured by a lunatic intent on killing her.

He should've listened to her. She'd shared her concerns about Lindsay, and he'd dismissed her, time and time again. What right did he have to dismiss her fears so quickly?

A hand covered his and squeezed. He looked into his brother's face. Brent was shaking his head. "Don't go down that path again, bro. History repeating itself."

"What?"

"Blaming yourself for not being in the thick of the danger. You had no idea. It's not your fault."

Blake swallowed. Old habits die hard. For a dozen years, he'd held himself personally responsible for not being there when his family was torn apart by a house fire. But Brent was right. This was exactly the same thing. And he would not make the same mistake again. Last night, he had been exactly where he was supposed to be: in Pittsburgh, with Frontier Fire, singing a concert. This wasn't his fault. He couldn't have prevented this.

He had no way of preventing what was out of his control.

But he sure could address mistakes that were in his control.

He rose to his feet and returned to Haley's bed. He reached for her ice-packed hands and held them in his own. He leaned close to her face. "Haley, I love you," he whispered.

To his amazement, her eyes flickered back and forth beneath her eyelids, and then, she opened them. At the sight of her amazing emerald green eyes, he smiled. "Hi, beautiful. Welcome home."

"Blake," she said and his heart jumped into his throat.

"Thank God you're okay."

She nodded. "God was with me through the whole thing. I felt his presence. I thought it was my time to go. But God had different plans."

He leaned closer. "And I'm thankful for that. Because there's so much I want to tell you." He cleared his mind by staring at her damaged but beautiful face. "I'm sorry, Haley. I was wrong, and you were right. I never should've doubted you, and I'll remind myself of that for the rest of my life."

She stared at him, her brain almost visibly churning over his words. "But I let you down. I left Brent at the airport without anyone to help him. And I know how important he is to you."

Blake shook his head ferociously. "It doesn't matter. Brent's a big boy and I've been treating him like he needs my protection. He doesn't.

He's a capable adult. He's fine." Tears welled in his eyes as he struggled to put the immensity of his emotions into words. He'd learned so much over the last two days. "I love you, and I'm sorry I treated you that way. I was wrong." He sniffed and used the back of his hand, still holding hers, to wipe his eyes. "Can you ever forgive me, Haley?"

She watched him, and from her hesitation, he knew he wasn't out of hole yet. She had every right to hesitate after everything he'd put her through. His words rushed on. "I will never doubt you again, Haley. And if you let me, I promise I will put my priorities in the right order. You will be first, Haley. That's right. We're a team, and I want to be a part of that team forever. I'm sorry I screwed up. Please, don't give up on me. On us. What do you say, Haley?"

Her silence was killing him, tearing him apart. As much as he needed to hear her words of forgiveness, her decision to forget his thoughtlessness, he knew in his heart that he didn't deserve it. If she told him he'd blown it, and she'd never be able to get over it, it would destroy him. But it would be nothing less than he deserved.

She held the cards, and they both knew it.

"Maybe you need some time to think. Of course, you do. I don't mean to press you for an answer now. You heal and rest and think, and let me know when you're ready."

She opened her mouth and struggled with voicing her thoughts. She started with what could've been a chuckle, and it morphed into a cough, then a choke. He held tight to her hands, wondering what he could do to help. He shot a look of alarm to Brent, who pressed the red Call Nurse button.

Haley recovered and went silent for a moment.

"Don't talk. It's just enough right now that you're awake."

"No, listen, I ..."

The nurse swept into the room and looked at Haley's face. "Well, well, well, welcome to the world of the living!" she announced in a booming voice.

"I feel better," Haley said. "More awake. More with it, you know?"

"Great," said the nurse and launched into her vitals check all over again and Blake stepped away from the bed, giving her room. She tapped all the appropriate numbers into her device and smiled at Haley. "Doctor will be by later this morning. I think he's going to like what he sees."

The nurse bustled out, leaving a void in the room. The remaining occupants soon filled it, all gathered around Haley's bed.

Robbie was the first to speak. "Well, I guess I can leave now," he joked. "Looks like you've got this all under control, Haley." He winked at her. "Take your time to get completely healed. We've got work for you to do when Blake comes back."

He leaned over the bed railing and found a spot on her bruised cheek to drop a kiss.

"Thanks Robbie. Thanks for everything."

After he left, Jake took his spot. "I can't tell you how sorry I am that Lindsay turned into such a lunatic. I never thought in a million years that she was capable of hurting people like this. I was with her for almost two years and never saw this side of her."

"Oh Jake, it's not your fault. Not in the least."

"You're kind for saying that, but ..."

"No buts. She needs psychiatric therapy to deal with what she's done. But if I have my guess, she'll be doing it from behind bars."

Jake leaned over the bed just as Robbie had, and placed a kiss. "You take care. I'm so glad you're okay."

He left, leaving Blake and Brent in the room. Brent wheeled his chair to the door with an amused grin. "I'm suddenly hungry. Mind if I leave you two kids alone for a while? Don't miss me too much."

Blake stood quietly, staring into the eyes of the love of his life. It was enough right now that she had a solid health check with the nurse. She was awake. She had all her memories. That was a bountiful gift from God. Even if he was going to lose her.

"Blake," she said softly.

He came closer. "Yes?"

"My voice works better if I whisper. So listen closely, buster, because I'm only going to say this once."

He held his breath, her playful words causing a hopeful grin on his face.

"I love you. I forgive you. I never blamed you for being mad at me for dropping the ball with Brent because I know just how important he is to you. I find it a very attractive trait that your family is your first priority."

"But, ..."

She held up a hand. "Let me finish. You can tell me later about your epiphany about your brother and your family and your guilt. Let's just suffice it to say right now: I love you, Blake."

His blessings were complete. She loved him.

He yearned to jump and whoop and holler and hold her in his arms. But under the circumstances, he simply put a hand under her bruised chin and gazed into her eyes.

She closed her eyes, and as the seconds stretched into minutes, he wondered if she was going to nap. Suddenly, she jarred herself awake again and said, "Will you call my parents?"

"Of course I will."

And she drifted off to sleep.

Chapter Twenty Three

HALEY AWOKE TO THE sound of her mother's voice. Didn't the woman own an inside voice? Was her mother yelling, or was that Haley's imagination?

Keeping her eyes shut, she listened. Blake's voice, "Yes, Mrs. Witherspoon, she was in an explosion last night at The Bowery and got injured when a bunch of heavy debris fell on her."

"What? What is this? The Bowery? That's here in Myrtle Beach, isn't it?"

"Yes."

"I thought she was out of town. I thought she was on tour with you, young man. What is going on here?"

Her mother's volume was increasing and someone needed to calm her or who knew what would happen? She was about to wrench her eyes open and do it herself when she heard her dad's voice.

"Ruth, stop it. Don't interrogate him. Let's focus on Haley. We can work out the details later."

"Yes. Of course, you're right, dear. I am just so caught by surprise. I had no idea she was even in town, no idea she was in danger, and now I see she's unconscious in a hospital bed, all bruised and battered." Her mother let out a dramatic sob.

This isn't about you, Mom. Her silent thought must've come with a smile because her mother said, "Look! Oh, praise the Lord. She's coming out of her coma! She must've heard my voice and she pulled back from the light. I'm here, honey. Come this way."

Haley opened her eyes and connected gazes with her mother. "I wasn't in a coma, Mom. I was napping."

"Oh. Well. Thank the Lord anyway! I'm so glad you're okay."

Her father stepped closer to the bed and rested his warm hand on her forehead. "Looks like you've been through an ordeal, cupcake."

Her heart flooded with warmth at his term of endearment. She hadn't heard it in a while. "Yeah. Long story, which I'll tell you more later. But a crazed fan with a grudge plotted this attack."

"And," Blake interrupted her, "Haley was one step ahead of her the entire way. She's been investigating and knew exactly where to be to prevent disaster. If Haley hadn't been so on top of things, I shudder to think of the tragic loss of life at The Bowery."

She let her gaze linger on him for a moment and winked her appreciation. He was laying it on thick but it wouldn't hurt for her parents to believe it.

Her mother's mouth dropped. "Oh my. Sounds so dangerous. Why didn't you call in the professionals instead of trying to handle it yourself?"

Blake was quick with a response. "She did. She had a whole team of professionals there working. It's why the massive crowd filed out of the building with order and relatively few incidents. But unfortunately, Haley got the worst of it. Just shows how brave and loyal and dedicated she is." He sniffed. "We wouldn't be where we are today without her."

While her mother let that news sink in, her dad cleared his throat. "I never had a doubt that you had it in you, sugar-pie. You've got the heart of a lion, and the fierceness, too. We're proud of you, aren't we Ruth?"

Her mother blinked. "Yes. Yes, of course, we are."

"So, ..." Haley said, and let the syllable hang there. She didn't want to squash the praise her parents were giving her, or ruin a proud moment. But she had to be sure. "I'm back in the family?"

Her mother let out a scoff. "What are you talking about, dear? Of course you're in the family. You've always been a member of our family. Maybe that concussion is giving you crazy thoughts."

Her father leaned in close. "You are obviously a very savvy manager with a line of unprecedented success behind you. What's more, I foresee an endless future of more successes. You're dedicated and committed and brave and intelligent. You get results and you make the world around you better." He winked with a broad smile. "Sounds like a Witherspoon to me!"

Haley let loose a hearty laugh as relief flowed through her body. Coming from her dad, it was more of an apology than she could ever hope for.

The door opened and two men wearing suits came in. "Excuse me, folks. We're Detectives Hart and Salisbury of the Myrtle Beach Police Department. We need to speak to Ms. Witherspoon about her experiences with the perpetrator last night. Could you all clear out momentarily please?"

Her dad stood first. "We'll leave you be. But call us when you're getting released. You'll move into your old bedroom at our house and your mother can spoil you while you're recovering. No arguments!" He tapped her head gently with an index finger. "Gotta heal that ole noggin!" He dropped a kiss on her forehead.

Her mother was next. She brushed away a tear. "I'm so proud of you, sweetheart. I'm so glad you're okay. We'll have a good time. Swim at the pool, get pedicures. Mother-daughter time." She placed a short kiss on her lips, then waved as she left.

Blake stood. "I'll head to the cafeteria for some awful coffee. Text me when you're done and I'll come right back." He leaned in close and she hoped for a minute he'd lay a really good kiss on her, but he didn't.

Not in front of the police officers. But he did give her a heartfelt, "I love you, Haley" before he left the room.

Three Months Later

••••

THE NIGHT OF THE BOWERY Grand Re-opening had arrived, a highly anticipated Myrtle Beach event, advertised to the hilt on TV, radio and print. The popular bar and grill had financed an accelerated timeline for repairing the extensive damage from the "Firecracker Incident"—as the advertisements widely proclaimed. Crews worked around the clock for months, replacing the roof, building a completely modernized backstage series of green rooms for the comfort of their performers, and cosmetic touch-ups needed in the main room caused by damage from the explosion, the fire or the sprinklers.

Ace in the Hole was headlining tonight, a fact that was also highly touted in the ad campaign: "Can't keep a good band down!" with a graphic of a huge cartoon firecracker exploding.

Doug, the bar manager, had given them all a tour of the renovations, his pride at the finished design obvious. Now, they were all gathered in the green room, beautifully remodeled with new carpet, walls, furniture.

Haley hovered in the doorway, then entered the room cautiously. She took slow steps through it, her hand trailing over the gleaming surfaces. Blake noticed and came over to her, wrapping an arm around her shoulders. His strength exuded from him. "It's weird being here. Almost like it never happened."

He nodded. "All this new stuff could make you think it never happened. But we know what you went through. You doing okay?"

She sniffed and nodded. No way would she allow sad memories to alter this big night. When Doug had called her with the idea of Ace in the Hole appearing as their first headliner after their remodel, she'd loved the idea. She made room in their schedule and was glad they were making it happen. "It'll never happen again," she said softly and Blake squeezed her shoulder.

"That's right," he said. "Lindsay's in jail, awaiting her trial. But the prosecutor's case is strong. With you as the star witness, she'll be put away for a long time."

"And get the help she needs," Haley added softly. The time to mourn was over. Tonight was not a time to mourn. Tonight they would celebrate. She shook off her melancholy by shaking out her arms. "Big night!" she said to Blake with a smile.

The moment to take the stage was drawing near, and Haley moved to the middle of the room. She'd instituted a tradition since Blake had returned to Ace in the Hole, and she was managing them full-time again. They all gathered in a circle—Blake, Jake, Robbie and her—and took hands. They bowed their heads and took a moment for silent prayer. Then, Haley said aloud, "Lord, be with us tonight. Help us play our very best. Help our audience to be safe and have a great time. Watch over all of us. We thank you for all the blessings and we welcome you to be with us. Amen."

Haley checked the time. "Five minutes," she announced and they all walked into the hallway, where they could see the stage, hear their announcement but not be seen by the audience. Blake leaned close to her face and she inhaled his scent ... soap, mint and cotton ... before he placed his lips warmly on hers. Then her mind forgot everything except the sensation of his soft, warm lips working their magic on hers while adrenaline pumped through her body.

Doug climbed up onto the stage and took the microphone out of its stand, holding it comfortably in his hand. "Ladies and gentlemen."

That's all he had to say for the crowd, two thousand strong, to let loose a crescendo of sound in the big room, created by their whooping and hollering. He paused and seemed to soak in the moment. He laughed and finally lifted his hands. "Thank you. Thank you very much. Appreciate it." The noise subsided and he went on. "You are here on a significant night in The Bowery history. Three months ago, while Ace in the Hole was rocking the house, a little bit of evil did her best to destroy us here. To stop the music and send us all home. But guess what. It didn't work, now did it?"

Each and every fan in the house clapped and used their voices to show their support and approval of Doug's words.

"We don't do evil here at The Bowery! We have fun and we celebrate and laugh and dance and sing. We know some of you suffered injuries from the night of the Firecracker Incident. And we suffered with you and we grieved for your pain. But everybody recovered! Thank God for that!" Another explosion of sound from the receptive crowd.

"So, enjoy your night, make your way around to see all the interior renovations, and the bars are open!" He waited for the noise to dim. "And now, I have the honor of introducing Ace in the Hole, the legendary country band who was performing right here on the night of the Firecracker Incident, and lived to tell about it! You can't keep a good band down! Please welcome ... Ace in the Hole!"

The three band members ran onto the stage, waving to the masses of country music fans. Blake swung his acoustic guitar onto his chest, stood behind the microphone and waited, soaking in the wall of approval and support formed by thousands of yelling fans. He took a moment to absorb it, a happy smile on his face.

Then he turned and nodded at Jake and Robbie and yelled into the microphone, "We're Ace in the Hole. Let's let it roll!" And off they went with their set opener, a rowdy popular hit from a decade ago by Brook Garthson.

Haley's heart was happy. The Frontier Fire tour was over for them now, but the memories and the experience Blake had gained was invaluable. They were both back where they belonged, with Ace in the Hole, clawing up the ladder of success in country music. All the guys were writing their own music, and the band was dropping originals into their line up each night they performed. Gradually making the switch from cover band to original was Haley's strategy.

Meanwhile, she'd leveraged her partnership with Randall to make contacts with several recording studios in Nashville. Their goal was to get a recording contract and launch Ace into the country music stratosphere. Why couldn't it happen? Their path had been miraculously successful in a very short time.

Tonight, she'd just relax, sip on a Coke, listen to some great music, maybe dance a little, and talk to those around her who loved Ace in the Hole. What could be better?

As she made her way around the crowded, loud bar, she felt a tug on her arm. She whipped around and saw a most welcome sight. "Carly!" she yelled and pulled her best friend into her arms.

"Long time no see!" Carly yelled and then tugged her husband into Haley's line of sight too. "You remember Ryan?"

Haley gave his shoulder a pretend-punch and said, "Of course I remember Ryan. That tall hunk of a man. How's married life going?"

Carly swung her head, back and forth, her beaming smile giving Haley the answer she wanted. "So much to tell you. We need to have a girls catch up night. Can we schedule one?"

"Absolutely."

"I'll babysit," Ryan offered, "so you guys can have a Grace-free night."

Haley gave him a thumbs up. "So what are you guys doing here?"

Carly leaned close to her ear. "I wouldn't miss this night for you, sweetie. I've been keeping in touch with the whole saga through the papers. This is a huge night for celebration. But hey," Carly gestured to encompass the whole big room, "this is no place for talking. You enjoy yourself, and I'll call you tomorrow to set up our girls night."

"Deal. I love you, Carly." Traveling with the band left little free time at home, but Haley promised herself she'd make time for her best friend in the world.

Knowing their set list by heart like she did, she knew the first set was about to wrap up. She started moving toward the hallway that led to the green rooms backstage. Blake wrapped up the final song and instead of announcing their break, he said, "Thank you for being here for this special night, everyone. And now, I have an announcement. A very special and life-changing one. Well, for two particular people, at least."

Haley's forehead creased. What was he doing? This was off-script. What was his announcement about? She stood just in front of the stage for a better view.

"Ah, there she is," Blake said, holding his hand out to her. "Could you come up here please, Haley? Yes, you." He chuckled.

She stared up at him, eyes wide, heart pounding. She swallowed her nerves and reached for his hand so he could pull her up onto the stage. Everyone applauded politely.

"Everyone," Blake said, "this is our band manager, Haley."

Haley turned toward the audience and waved awkwardly. She leaned into the microphone and said, "Hi y'all. I never get on stage. Ever."

They all laughed. To get through this, whatever it was, she turned to face Blake and stared into his eyes.

"Haley is the best manager Ace in the Hole has ever had. But more than that, she's the best person I know. She's not only beautiful, *obviously*." He chuckled and the cheers from the crowd rose up. "But she's beautiful inside. She's smart and ambitious and innovative and creative. We love working with her, and she's brought us a long way." He let go of her hand to dig something out of his jeans pocket. "But I'm the lucky one. Because I'm the only one who can say, I'm in love with her."

Haley's eyes flew wide open. This had just transformed from an acknowledgement of her contributions to the band, to ... something else entirely.

"She's helped me to recognize how to be a better man, a better person. She has made me grow, in many ways. And the luckiest thing in my life is that she loves me too. So tonight, I want to show Haley how special I think she is, and how committed I am to taking this thing to the next level."

When he dropped down to one knee, Haley gasped. Now she knew what was coming next. And she had absolutely no doubt in her mind what her response would be. She concentrated on the handsome, loving face of the one she loved most in the world, determined to soak in every moment.

"Haley, I want us to be together for the rest of our lives. We've been through a lot in a short time. Success, failure, challenges, mountaintop highs, and some lows. But through it all I've come to realize. I don't want to do any of it without you by my side. Forever, baby."

He flattened his palm and revealed a little velvet box. He opened it and she caught the glow of a big, sparkly solitaire diamond inside. Her hand flew up to cover her mouth and her heart pounded a rhythm of her love and acceptance.

"Haley, will you agree to stay by my side for the rest of our lives? To lead me, to follow me, to be beside me for whatever comes next?"

"*Yes*!" She pulled him to his feet, and then into her arms for a tight hug. She kissed his neck, then his cheeks, then pulling his face into place, she gave him the happiest, most passionate, most communicative kiss she could manage when standing on a stage in front of thousands of people. "Yes, Blake Scott, I will marry you!"

He chuckled. "Ladies and gentlemen, I didn't even get to ask her that, but she knew exactly what I meant." He pulled the ring out of the box and guided it onto her finger. He beamed at her and they joined again for the first kiss of the rest of their lives.

THE END

••••
Leave a review!

DID YOU LOVE HALEY and Blake's story? If you did please go here[1], as well as the retailer where you bought it, and leave a review! Reviews help so much to guide readers to find good books to read! Thank you for supporting *Crescendo*, me, and Christian fiction!

---

1. https://www.goodreads.com/book/show/41043180-crescendo

Laurie's Letter to Readers

D ear Awesome Reader,

Hello! By now you've read CRESCENDO, Book 3 of my Murrells Inlet Miracles series and I hope you loved it as much as I did. I'm thrilled to bring you this book, that I call a rags-to-riches tale in the world of country music, because I was able to delve deeply into one of my favorite things in the world ... modern country music! I'm an avid fan. I attend at least a couple major concerts a year, and the headlining artists are always kind enough to include a couple opening acts, so that means I get to see about a half dozen live country performers each year. And I love it.

As I'm writing this (mid-August, 2018) life could not be any more exciting. I was able to retire from my day job earlier this year which was a blessing straight from God. Don't get me wrong. I was blessed to have such a long-lasting, successful, challenging and lucrative career with such a great company for such a long time! But for several years now, I was having trouble keeping up with the drain and the demand and the intense hours, while still maintaining what time I could on my writing career. I prayed and prayed for a way I could still support my family and our future while devoting full-time to my writing.

And God made it happen! An unexpected, but very welcome chance at an early retirement from my corporation with a pension; to leave the demanding world of Information Technology behind, and focus as much time on writing as I want. *My* timelines, *my* deadlines. While still having fun ... going to the beach, visiting friends and family. It's a dream come true.

And this book ... CRESCENDO ... is the first book I've written and published entirely while retired from the big day job. I hope you love it. I do have plans for a fourth and possibly fifth book in this series! I'm planning a rough publishing schedule of three books a year now,

Winter, Summer and Fall. And I'm also starting to muse on my next series after Murrells Inlet Miracles.

So, all is well in my world.

I'll also tell you that I've grown my newsletter subscriber list and if you haven't joined me already, I invite you to do so by clicking on this link right here[1]. We have so much fun! And this is the group that gets the FIRST notice of new preorders and releases, contests, giveaways and what's going on in my writing world. I'm also very active on Facebook, so if you want to take part in that, please join me here.[2]

I'd like to remind you that you met Haley and Blake in Book 2: Restoration[3]. Blake was the Uber driver that helped retrieve a certain little girl from a car accident late in the story. Here's a little excerpt to help you remember:

Haley and the Uber driver sat in the lobby of the ER, and came to their feet in unison when Ryan, Carly and Grace walked in. In a flurry of questions and answers, it was shared that Grace was absolutely fine, released to go home, and Ryan's mother was staying for observation, but also was expected to be fine.

Ryan shook hands with the Uber driver. "I can't thank you enough, man."

He shook his head. "I didn't do anything."

Ryan gestured to his blood-stained shirt. "Yes, you did. You pulled a deer out of a car, so my little girl could get out of there. And," he checked his watch, "you've lost out on an hour's worth of fares, just so you could sit with Haley and find out how everything turned out. In fact," he said and pulled some bills out of his pocket, "take this. This was the OT I made tonight. That's the whole reason my mom was on that dark road at that hour in the first place, because I agreed to work OT.

---

1.   https://www.authorlaurielarsen.com/reader-group

2.   https://www.facebook.com/authorlaurielarsen/

3.   https://www.authorlaurielarsen.com/restoration

Next time, I won't be quite so anxious for the money. Take it, please. It'll help."

The driver hesitated.

"Heck, you might need that much to dry clean your shirt," Haley joked.

He laughed and went ahead and accepted the small stack of bills. "Thank you."

"What's your name, by the way?" Ryan asked him.

"Blake," Haley answered for him. They all turned their heads toward her and stared. She blushed, a faint pink covering her cheeks. "What? His name is Blake."

Have a wonderful and blessed day!

Laurie

Excerpt to Book 4: Capsized[1]:

S adie Flynn breezed into the kitchen, her mind fixed on her To Do list for this sunny May day. No time to enjoy the beach or the sun, much to her dismay. She pulled open the cabinet, extracted her travel mug, and turned to the coffee pot. Half a pot of the elixir sat there already. She glanced around the room. Her dad sat at the kitchen table, enjoying a cup.

"Earth to Sadie," he said, then chuckled.

"Sorry. Did you say something to me?"

"Just 'good morning.' Your mind is obviously somewhere else. What's going on in there?"

She grinned and rolled her eyes. Being focused had served her well in her lifetime, in general, but sometimes it made her come off as ditzy. Or uncaring. And those traits were the furthest from the truth.

"Busy day today, Dad. I've got to swing by the college and enroll in my summer semester classes."

He stood and carried his empty plate to the sink. "One step closer to becoming a Registered Nurse." He leaned in and placed a kiss on her cheek. "I'm proud of you."

She took a moment to soak in his affection. She and her dad: a team, a twosome. The Dynamic Duo. It had been only her and him for so long, she could barely remember a time when there were three. Before her mom's health deteriorated, it was her dad who took care of her. Her mom had never shown interest in being a full-time mom, so it was lucky for Sadie that her dad filled in the gaps. But after her mother's car accident, and the resulting head injury that caused her to get worse and

---

1. https://www.authorlaurielarsen.com/capsized

worse for years, Sophie and her dad had become a tight, well-functioning team.

Burying her mother last summer was not as sad as it probably should have been. Her death was totally expected and represented the final chapter in a tragic life.

Dad pulled away from his daughter with a friendly wink. "What else?"

Sadie cleared her head of sad memories. "Then, to the gym. I've only got a week left before the marathon, so I've got some training to do."

"Good for you. Break a leg."

"That may be appropriate for an actor, but I believe it's a jinx for an athlete."

Shaw chuckled. "Okay, then how about, don't break a leg?"

"Better. And what about you? What are you up to today?"

"Annual shots for the Anderson cattle herd, and then heading over to the Myrtle Beach Zoo to care for a few animals that are under the weather."

Sadie smiled. Her dad didn't have a job like most fathers did. He never sat in a desk chair behind a computer, didn't even have an office. As a large breed veterinarian, his patients were out in the fields and barns all around the Grand Strand, South Carolina. He spent most of his time in his truck driving to where the animals were and caring for them. He loved treating all animals, but especially the big ones, wild or domestic.

"And are you seeing your lady love today?" Sadie turned her head and noticed the flush of pink that traveled up her dad's neck. After a long stretch of no love or affection in his life, he had met the right woman. Some things were worth waiting for. Shaw and Nora were distinct opposites, but proof of the old adage that opposites attract.

"Sure."

So that was all the answer she was going to get about her dad's love life. She laughed, not expecting any different.

"Well, have a great day. See you tonight." They both wrapped up their breakfasts and headed out.

About Laurie:

IF YOU HAD ASKED AN eight-year-old Laurie, "What do you want to be when you grow up?" she would've said, "Live at the beach and write novels." Such an enlightened girl for knowing at such a young age what her destiny would be. Now, almost five decades later (but not quite), that's still her dream.

And she's making it happen.

Being a goal- and results-oriented person, Laurie put into place a long-term plan. Twenty years ago, while she was building a successful career with a huge corporation that had absolutely nothing to do with living at the beach OR writing novels, she started writing her first book. That effort turned out to be her first published novel, *Whispers of the Heart* which released in early 2000. From then on, the act of writing took a fierce hold on her.

She has now written and published close to twenty novels, and for eighteen years, she split her time/effort/passion between the afore-mentioned big, draining, demanding dayjob and her writing career.

In 2016, Laurie and her husband bought their future dream home in coastal South Carolina. Currently they travel back and forth between both homes as the whim hits. And in early 2018, Laurie left the corporate world behind, retiring after 34 years and a ton of professional accomplishments.

That eight-year-old dream is almost a reality. Some dreams are worth waiting for.

Outside of her professional life, Laurie and her husband of 29 years have an empty nest, after raising two wonderful and talented sons. They are both educated and self-sufficient, working in their own careers and making Mom and Dad proud on a daily basis.

Laurie is a dog lover. Growing up alongside Laurie's two sons was Gracie the Wonder Dog, who sadly, they lost just last year. Both boys have their own dogs now, so Laurie enjoys spending time and lavishing kisses on her two grand-puppies, Izzy and Buster.

Laurie is a huge theater fan and goes to as much live theater as she can. And of course, her favorite place in the world is the beach.

Laurie writes life-changing, heartwarming inspirational Christian fiction that takes place at the beach. She's actively looking for fans who enjoys that type of book and looks forward to adding them into the fold of her supportive Reader Group. Visit her website for all the latest: www.authorlaurielarsen.com[1]

---

1.   http://www.authorlaurielarsen.com

Want to stay in touch with Laurie?

Her website/blog[1]
Her Facebook[2]
Her Twitter[3]
Her Bookbub[4]
Her Goodreads[5]

Sign up to be on her <u>newsletter mailing list</u>[6]! You'll get advance notice of all reviews, chances to win prizes and receive free books and other giveaways!

• • • •

Christian Fiction novels

by Laurie Larsen
The Murrells Inlet Miracles series:

---

1. http://authorlaurielarsen.com/

2. https://www.facebook.com/authorlaurielarsen

3. https://twitter.com/AuthorLaurie

4. https://www.bookbub.com/authors/laurie-larsen

5. https://www.goodreads.com/author/show/412692.Laurie_Larsen

6. https://www.authorlaurielarsen.com/reader-group

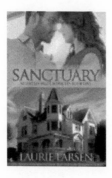

BOOK 1: Sanctuary[7]: Successful Philadelphia attorney Nora Ramsey never even knew there was another life for her before Aunt Edie left her with her ramshackle mansion and once-thriving horse business. Veterinarian Shaw Flynn seems a partner, then a love interest, before finding out his deepest and darkest secret.

BOOK 2: Restoration[8]: Young, single mom Carly Milner was making it on her own raising her toddler Grace and finishing her education so she could launch her professional career. When the love of her life, Ryan Melrose returns, wanting a place in Grace's life, can she ever trust him again?

---

7. https://www.authorlaurielarsen.com/sanctuary

8. https://www.authorlaurielarsen.com/restoration

BOOK 3: Crescendo:[9] A rags to riches story in the world of country music, with a twist! Black sheep in a wealthy family Haley Witherspoon has finally found the career that brings her passion, and it's with handsome aspiring country musician, Blake Scott. Can they overcome her family's disapproval, his own internal guilt, mounting danger from a fan to achieve success?

BOOK 4: Capsized:[10] God "overseas" everything. Two dedicated extreme athletes pair up to achieve victory in the world of competitive yacht sailing. With physical attraction tempting them, Sadie and Jet must keep their eyes on the prize. But God has other plans. As they face

---

9. https://www.authorlaurielarsen.com/crescendo

10. https://www.authorlaurielarsen.com/capsized

adversity and danger, will God's will have them racing toward one another instead of the glory of the win?

The Pawleys Island Paradise series:

BOOK 1: Roadtrip to Redemption[1]. *It started as a trip to lose old memories. It became a journey to find her heart.* A woman facing the most desolate summer of her life, follows God's direction and instead has the most rewarding and life-changing summer of all.

BOOK 2: Tide to Atonement[2]. *Life knocked him down. Faith raised him up.* A man has paid his debt to society and is released from prison. Determined to create a life to be proud of, he realizes his past isn't quite as willing to be done as he wants it to be.

---

1. https://www.authorlaurielarsen.com/roadtrip-to-redemption

2. https://www.authorlaurielarsen.com/tide-to-atonement

BOOK 3: Journey to Fulfillment[3]. *A traumatic family event. Distinctly opposite ways of dealing with it between husband and wife. Let no man put asunder.* A married couple deals with a family tragedy in different ways and works through the resulting collapse of their marriage to reconcile their love for each other.

BOOK 4: Bridge to Fruition[4]. *The old is gone. The new is come.* A young woman from an affluent family finds love with a man who grew up in the foster system. Can they let go of the trappings of their past and find love together in their present?

---

3. https://www.authorlaurielarsen.com/journey-to-fulfillment

4. https://www.authorlaurielarsen.com/bridge-to-fruition

BOOK 5: Path to Discovery[5]. A brokenhearted New York actress welcomes the escape from the hustle and bustle of the big city to take the lead in a beach-town dinner theater show. It's the solace and sanctuary that she's needed ever since her world came crumbling down. But then he walks in... back into her life and her memories of her worst nightmare.

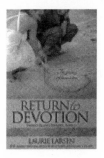

BOOK 6: Return to Devotion[6]. *Can men and women be "just friends?"* A military wife deals with unbearable loneliness on her husband's third overseas deployment, leading to an indiscretion with her new male friend. Will the truth destroy everything she and her husband have built as man and wife?

---

5. https://www.authorlaurielarsen.com/path-to-discovery

6. https://www.authorlaurielarsen.com/path-to-discovery

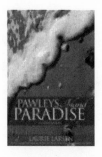

BOOK 7: <u>Pawleys Island Paradise: A Companion</u>[7]. Discover the stories and inspiration that led to the Pawleys Island Paradise series! A short, fully-illustrated non-fiction companion to the beloved Pawleys Island Paradise series of inspirational romance by award-winning author Laurie Larsen.

PAWLEYS ISLAND PARADISE boxset[8]: First three books in one easy download!

---

7. https://www.authorlaurielarsen.com/a-companion-nonfiction

8. https://www.authorlaurielarsen.com/boxset-books-1-3

PREACHER MAN[9]. *Laurie's EPIC Award winner for Best Spiritual Romance of 2010*: A beautiful, heartwarming Christian love story that will leave you feeling good.

---

9. https://www.authorlaurielarsen.com/preacher-man

Don't miss out!

Visit the website below and you can sign up to receive emails whenever Laurie Larsen publishes a new book. There's no charge and no obligation.

https://books2read.com/r/B-A-WTLE-CLFU

BOOKS 2 READ

Connecting independent readers to independent writers.

Made in the USA
Coppell, TX
28 November 2019

12045309R00141